NORTHERN NIGHTS

EDITED BY

MICHAEL KELLY

UNDERTOW
PUBLICATIONS

NORTHERN NIGHTS

Cover art copyright © 2024 by Serena Malyon

Cover design copyright © 2024 by Vince Haig

Interior design and layout by Michael Kelly

Proofreader: Carolyn Macdonell-Kelly

First edition

The publisher gratefully acknowledges the support of the Ontario Arts Council.

ONTARIO ARTS COUNCIL
CONSEIL DES ARTS DE L'ONTARIO

an Ontario government agency
un organisme du gouvernement de l'Ontario

Library and Archives Canada Cataloguing in Publication

ISBN: 978-1-988964-47-8

Undertow Publications, Pickering ON, Canada

Typeset in Hoefler

Printed in Canada by Rapido Books

Copyright information continues on last page.

For Ellen Datlow, Charles L. Grant, Paula Guran, David G. Hartwell, Don Hutchison, Stephen Jones, Douglas E. Winter, and all the others who helped pave the way.

LAND ACKNOWLEDGEMENT

I gratefully acknowledge that I am a settler residing on land within the Treaty and traditional territory of the Mississaugas of Scugog Island First Nation and Williams Treaties signatories of the Mississauga and Chippewa Nations.

CONTENTS

INTRODUCTION

MICHAEL KELLY

Oh, Canada!

I can thank David G. Hartwell and Glenn Grant for this volume. Don Hutchison, as well.

The late 80s and early 90s were a formative time for me, a nascent writer of short horror stories. Short fiction was my tonic, and there was an abundance of amazing anthologies published throughout that period to feed my passion: *The Dark Descent* (David G. Hartwell, ed.), *Cutting Edge* (Dennis Etchison, ed.), *Prime Evil* (Douglas E. Winter, ed.), *Silver Scream* (David J. Schow, ed.), *The Shadows* series (Charles L. Grant, ed.), *The Year's Best Fantasy & Horror* series (Ellen Datlow & Terri Windling, eds.), the *Best New Horror* series (Stephen Jones, ed.) and more.

I ravenously consumed these books and numerous other magazines publishing horror and dark, strange fiction. I wanted to be a writer. And I was. And still am, on occasion. Eventually, though, I figured out that what I really wanted to do was to gather and assemble the dark magic that made up those anthologies and magazines. I wanted to be an editor and anthologist like David G. Hartwell, and Ellen Datlow. They were as much my literary heroes as were my writing idols Shirley Jackson, Ray Bradbury, and Charles Beaumont.

Which brings us to Hartwell, Grant, and Hutchison.

In 1994 Tor published *Northern Stars: The Anthology of Canadian Science Fiction*, a reprint anthology gathering work from some of Canada's best-known writers of SF, like William Gibson, Peter Watts, and Charles de Lint, edited by the aforementioned David G. Hartwell and Glenn Grant. Then in 1999 Tor published a companion volume, *Northern Suns* (Hartwell & Grant, eds.), featuring Margaret Atwood, Cory Doctorow, and many more Canadian authors. Ostensibly SF, this volume veered into fantasy and horror. And from 1992 to 1999 a small Canadian publisher, Mosaic Press, published 5 volumes of the *Northern Frights* series, edited by the redoubtable Don Hutchison. Here then were anthologies that showed the breadth and collective talent of Canadian writers all across this vast country.

The seed was planted. One day I would edit an all-Canadian anthology of dark tales. And that day has arrived. Granted, it took some considerable time for that seed to germinate. Along the way I have edited numerous other projects. Always, though, that core notion lurked in the dim recesses of my mind, waiting to step into the light.

Northern Nights, then, is an homage to *Northern Stars; Northern Suns;* and *Northern Frights*. It's also a tribute to the editors and writers who shaped me—in turn shaping this very volume.

Herein you'll have discovered a selection of strange stories as varied as the Canadian landscape, their only shared commonalities, perhaps, being their sense of isolation, loneliness, and the adversarial nature of Canada's wilderness in the north at night.

I've always felt that Canadian fiction has a unique sensibility. The same is true of many other regions, of course, so Canada is no different. Some of our viewpoint is rooted in the literary traditions of Britain, France, and the United States. There is no denying that. But Canada's geography and culture—vast and increasingly diverse—is shaping new, very welcome, perspectives. To me, there is a candid earnestness to our literature. We're a young country with densely populated urban cities and great expanses of rural areas. It lends itself to honest and sincere writing. And that geographical and cultural expanse is the perfect backdrop for dark tidings.

Herein you'll find tales from both the west and east coasts; from the prairies and central regions. Stories in French settlements; and tales steeped in the history of Canada's conflicted past.

Our featured authors amply illustrate the talents of a varied cross-section of this vast land, showcasing a range and distinct spirit and sensibility exclusive to a night in the Canadian north.

I hope you enjoy your journey through these northern nights.

Michael Kelly
Ontario, Canada
March 2024

RESCUE STATION

NAYANI JENSEN

109 miles off the coast of Nova Scotia

IF ONLY THERE HAD BEEN A DOCTOR.

"We should never have come," his wife said. She sat perfectly still on the chair beside the small bed. "We shouldn't be here," she said. She whispered it over and over, until it lost all sense.

She didn't say it was his fault, but she also didn't look at him.

He stared down into the blankets, at his daughter's thin face pressed into the pillows. The room was too small; his bad leg twitched and slammed against the bed frame, and the bed rocked. Beneath the blankets, Anna twisted and moaned.

He took a deep breath.

"I'm going to the water," he said, but it was too loud in the small room.

He closed the door as gently as he could behind him.

He walked out of the small house, out through the garden they had dragged out of the sand and grass, out to where the water started. He allowed himself a moment of fantasy in which he sat in the room with the bed on his own, without anyone watching. Maybe he would play the piano (in his fantasy it was not out of tune and full of sand, as it was in life, as everything was). Anna had always loved the piano, but he had not played it enough for her, and when the steamer came last month bringing supplies, he had forgotten to ask about tuning it. It was a very small thing, but he had forgotten.

His wife could work on her garden and he could play the piano into the stillness of the house, the way it had been when they first arrived.

When they met half a lifetime ago, he had been a big, lumbering man, and she small and fierce. Not beautiful—she looked like the kind of girl who would cuss out a cab driver for taking too long. If he was being honest there was something attractive about that. It made his blood warm.

"She's too good for you," his brother had said.

His brother was right. Now he was greying, and she was thin and worn-down like the pale, stunted trees that fought with the gales.

He sat down in the sand with the water crashing nearby. It would be a rough night, the south-westerly wind already snarling. He thought about the two little crosses out by the ponds, and then tried not to think of them.

It felt like a very long time ago when he had first received the offer for this job.

"Turn it down, John," his wife had said. "There's nothing out there."

"I can't," he'd said. "It's a big promotion."

But three other people had already turned it down. He'd *wanted* to come. It was the idea of it—running this place, building things up on the sand, men who looked up to him, sons climbing around with the wild horses, a kingdom unto itself—

He would've died to grow up that way.

But their boys had not made it past a year, and then there had been only Anna. Even then he thought for certain Anna would be the one, that Anna would not leave them, and the older she got the more he had been relieved, confident. She was strong as a boy, a wild thing. Too wild.

If only there had been a doctor. He was quite certain the break in her arm could have been fixed, the infection avoided. There was a moment where she had looked up at him, from the floor of the unfinished barn that he had told her to stay away from—and he knew that she knew it was fixable, but that he, her father, did not know what to do.

Sand crunched against his fingers. Sand and sand and more sand. The water snarled.

He'd never thought much about sand before coming here.

I'll stop drinking, he thought. *I'll buy a whole new piano.*

I'll send another letter begging for the west light to be moved before the dune collapses. I'll rebuild it myself.

He wasn't much of a praying man. He felt awkward about it.

You can take me instead.

He'd read this somewhere and it had stuck with him, but it sounded idiotic and cowardly when he said it.

He stared towards the water.

I'll go back to the mainland. I'll give it up, leave it for someone else.

Or I'll stay here. I'll work harder.

The sky was deep purple overhead, but immediately in front the fog stretched out in a wall of grey over the water.

Out across the dunes the horn sounded, guttural, wailing.

It came so suddenly, so unexpected, that it had to sound twice before he registered it.

The relief was immediate. He scrambled to his feet.

Two quiet months, and now, at last, when he had asked for it—

It was a sign.

He was supposed to do his job.

The horn blared on, the peculiar, tinny sound of Station Two. A moment later the main station picked it up. He ran back to the house. The men were already moving, dragging out the cart, grabbing ropes and lamps.

His wife watched with her arms folded tight across her chest.

"Let the men do it," she said. "John—"

"It won't take long," he said. "An hour. I promise."

He couldn't explain to her about it being a sign; she wouldn't understand.

The horn paused and then started again. *Close enough for the ropes*, the signal said. *In-between stations*. He pulled on his long boots and ran, ahead of the cart. He was a fast runner. He couldn't feel his bad leg at all when he ran. The sand fell away; the grass fell back on either side.

He was faster than the horses.

Bob Morash was waiting at the edge of the water.

"Sorry, sir. Didn't want to call. We just spotted her. Might have been there a while, the fog was so thick."

The ship was visible only for moments as the fog shifted, up beyond the west light on the bank. Always that damn spot—there had been more wrecks there than he could count. He ran further along.

Small, three masts, fore-and-aft rigging—European, if he had to guess, a crew of eight or ten; probably merchant, nothing too valuable. They'd retrieve the goods once it was light. He couldn't see any lifeboats in the water: good, they were more likely to lose people than not in that fog.

"Tricky shot," Morash said.

Close enough for the ropes to reach, but already difficult in the falling darkness, and almost impossible with the fog.

They blew the air horn, and Morash handed him the megaphone.

"Barque crew," he shouted. "Barque crew, this is the Island rescue station. Help is coming."

His voice echoed out over the waves. He had the loudest voice on the island—they had tested it one afternoon. Foghorn John, the men said.

"Barque crew, we are looking for lights. We will send ropes."

Behind him the rest of the men and the horse came panting up with the cart, bouncing over the sand. In a few minutes the gun had been unloaded and secured in the sand, the ropes loaded in. They were so efficient; they had done this many times, rehearsed it many more. It pleased him.

Lights flickered in the fog, presumably bow and stern. Brighter than he'd expected: good.

"Where's Colly?"

"Here, sir."

"Your shot."

"Yes, sir."

They were unusually deferent, nervous; he knew they were thinking of Anna.

"Easy, boys," he said. "Focus. They'll be cold, if she's taking on water. They might have been out there for hours. Get the blankets and take them straight back to the house as they come in."

He lifted the megaphone again. "Stand back. Repeat. Stand back. We are sending ropes."

He helped the men line the gun up. It shone faintly in the lamplight, a beautiful thing.

There had been nothing nearly like this when he

arrived. Half the number of men, only three stations, fewer rescue shacks.

"Positions. Firing in three—in two—in one—"

The shot rang out over the water, and there was a faint splash.

"Too far to bow."

"Sorry, sir. The wind—"

"That's all right, Colly. Reel it in. Reset, everyone."

The fog was lifting slightly, the air bitter but not unbearable, the sea rough but not the worst he'd seen.

I'll build another rescue shack, he thought. *I'll inspect them myself; I'll double the drills.*

I'll report that hogshead of rum we recovered and stashed in main station.

"Firing in three—in two—in one—"

It landed. The line went taut as the crew on the vessel pulled it in.

He fixed the rig on the sand, slowly reeled the breeches buoy out over the water. Out it went: the life preserver ring swung back and forth, and the canvas leggings sewn inside it danced ridiculously into the fog.

The rope went taut under his fingers, straining.

"Pull!"

The first man came into view, limp against the ropes. He waded out to pull the man in. Waves crashed at his knees, louder than the voices of the men on the shore, louder than the creaking lines.

The man had a lumpen face, water-soaked hair. There was blood on his clothes. An accident on the ship, perhaps. Or injured in the effort to free the vessel.

"Nine," the man said. "Nine more."

Broken English: from somewhere northern, he thought.

"I'll get them," he said.

He lifted the man out of the canvas supports of the

buoy and deposited him on shore. The man hacked and coughed and dragged himself up the sand.

I'll be better, he thought, staring out into the water, watching the buoy vanishing again into the fog. *I'll do better.*

He thought of his wife when their first child was born, when everything was new and good.

He loved his wife. He did.

The buoy came back towards him.

Another man. Another. One man had a baby bundled to his chest.

He stared at the little bald head as the man carried it up the sand, gasping something. Perhaps thanking him. Like playing God, this life and death. How many men had he dragged from the water like this? Dead, alive, half-alive. Hundreds; eleven wrecks last year alone.

He thought of the two little crosses on the hill, of his wife screaming.

The waves slapped and heaved against him.

The next man was half-conscious. He had a soft, plain face, and his fingers were clutched around something—a pair of glasses. The man's eyes fluttered open, looked at him directly. There was blood coming from somewhere under his layers of clothing.

He felt like the man knew him, and was aware of a vague sort of shame.

The voices of the men on shore were faint, far away.

I'll trade him for Anna, he thought.

If he dies, Anna lives.

He didn't know where this thought came from, only that he was certain of it, the way he knew the distress signal had been a sign he was supposed to be here.

The man's fingers slipped, trembled, grasped the offered hand.

"Thank you," the man whispered. "Thank you."

He had seen many people die. He had seen even more

people who were already dead. They washed up like seaweed, or were uncovered like old wrecks by the shifting winds, and he would record them all in his logbook: *Young man. No uniform. Cross and flask. No other belongings.*

He held the man.

The water lapped at his waist, and the man floated in it, gasping quietly.

"Please," the man said.

He should pull the man onto the sand and wrap him in the blanket, should give him whisky from the flask.

He didn't.

It felt right, to stand like this in the ocean, to look down at the man's face. It was the face of a decent man, someone kind, patient. There was no use explaining how he knew this. He just did.

Maybe all men were good in the moment before they died.

Is this what you want? he thought, and the island moaned and shifted under his feet.

The man whispered something, no longer speaking English.

Time expanded and contracted. Breath for breath. He held the man's hand tightly. His palms were soft, but his grip was solid.

He thought of holding Anna's hands as he walked with her around the island.

The man's glasses slipped from his fingers and vanished into the water. There was a moment in which they were visible, the metal rim shining, and then they were gone into the darkness.

The man was still.

He closed the damp eyes, kissed the cold forehead, floated the man back to shore.

"Poor bugger," Morash said, and if he'd seen anything he said nothing about it.

He nodded. Inside his chest was a vague, hot sense of triumph.

"I should go back," he said.

He couldn't bear to be in the water for another moment. He wanted to clean the sand and clammy sensation of the man's hands away; he wanted to see Anna.

"There's only two more," Morash said. "We'll manage fine."

He could have kissed Morash, too.

He walked back—great, enormous strides with the sky deep blue overhead and the stars out.

His wife was waiting in the doorway. There was something in her face, something new and trembling. He put his arms around her and drew her close against him, kissed her full on the mouth. She put her hands in his hair. The other men came out behind her, blankets around their shoulders, all talking.

"There's a doctor," his wife whispered, into his cheek. "John, there's a doctor with them."

I knew it, he thought, and his heart was enormous. *I knew it.*

He strode into the bedroom and knelt next to the bed.

Anna's face was small and thin, pale like the man on the beach. He lifted her little hands onto his lap.

He wanted to tell her what he'd done.

The men were still talking behind him. He composed himself, took off his coat and long boots.

"Which is the doctor?"

The men tried to explain, translating amongst themselves.

"Surgeon," the first man said. "Going to Boston. Tall—"

He pointed to his eyes, gesturing.

Glasses.

"A good doctor," the first man said. "The Captain's friend."

"Where are the other men?" his wife said.

He sat back down next to the bed.

He watched Anna's breaths. She breathed like the man in the water had, little breaths, gasps.

His bad leg jammed up against the low frame. The bed rocked. In the distance, water pounded against the surf.

In and out. In and out.

THE NEEDLE SONG

SIMON STRANTZAS

WE ALL SANG THE NEEDLE SONG ON THE WAY TO Kearney. Or most of us did.

Our whole class gathered that cool Saturday in May around the school bus parked inside the Zellers lot. Everyone was there, along with our doting parents, for the annual Outdoor Education trip to which Mr. Parsons took each year's graduating eighth-graders. This was our year, and me, Eric, and Steig knew it would be something to remember.

I didn't expect Ned would join us. He never participated in class trips. Eric, Steig, and I assumed he preferred staying home with his mom. There was no particular reason why we didn't get along with him; sometimes kids just don't gel. The only time he crossed my mind that year was when Steig came up with calling him *Needle*, which led to the best song we'd ever written. It was so funny I breathlessly recounted the story for my dad that night when he got home. Instead of laughing he turned serious and made me promise to not make fun of Ned anymore. And asked me to look out for him instead. Maybe find something in common with him. My dad insisted it was important, though I wasn't sold. It sounded like a lesson, and I wasn't looking to learn anything I didn't have to.

Everyone else's parents were milling around the parking lot to see their sons off. I only had my dad there, and only because it was his weekend with me he was giving up. He said he and my mom had made arrangements to have me spend more time with him in the summer to make up for it, but I had a feeling my mom just wanted a way to extend her vacation guiltlessly. She had fought him for partial custody as a punishment. She knew being separated from me would be upsetting for him. She probably never considered what it would do to me.

And yet I was going away without him. It made me nervous, and I suspect it did the same to poor, frail Ned. He trembled as he waited behind the crowd of crying parents. Steig spotted him immediately. "We're only going for four days," he said incredulously. "We'll be back before anyone knows we've left."

That didn't seem likely. My dad was already looking lost and confused in the chaos. Even more so when Ned slid through the gauntlet of parents toward him. I saw my dad take a step back when Ned arrived, then the two of them spoke. It was a strange sight amid the harried departure; my two worlds—my private and my public—were colliding.

"You jealous?" Eric asked, pushing his elbow into my ribs. I jerked away.

"Screw off," I said. "Needle's just lost without his mommy to tell him what to do." Then I tried to shove Eric. I was the only one who moved.

Mr. Parsons then emerged from the idling bus and summoned us to board. Amid the rushed final kisses and goodbyes between the parents and my classmates I noticed Ned had already gone and my dad was now waiting for me a few steps from the bus's lowered platform. His eyes were full of tears.

"I'm going to miss you while you're gone, kid. Please be safe."

"I will Dad. What was Needle saying to you?"

"Please don't call him that. And promise me you'll look out for him. His mom says he doesn't have anybody else."

"You know his mom?"

"I know everybody's mom. I'm a dad," he said. "Now, promise me."

I rolled my eyes.

"I promise."

He wiped his eyes and gave me the longest, tightest hug I'd ever had. Then he handed me my overnight bag and I stepped aboard the bus. I was trepidatious at first, but by the time I reached my seat I felt excited. My first adventure away from home. Outside the window my dad stood among the parents waving, the joy on his face replaced by something else. Something that concerned me. Before I had a chance to question it the bus jerked to life and we were slowly pulling out of the Zellers lot and onto the busy street, heading toward the highway and adventure.

Four hours and one repeated song later we stepped off the school bus into a burning orange afternoon. Mr. Parsons had barely finished counting us before the driver swooped the doors closed and the bus pulled away, stranding us in the middle of nowhere. I watched taillights fade out and felt a knot form in my stomach. Before I could think about it too long Mr. Parsons hurriedly grouped us together, then marched us to the cabin.

I wasn't surprised to find it was made of logs, not as much as I was by the bunk beds. There was more than enough room for all of us in that small space, two boys to a bunk, and we ran when we saw them. Eric, Steig, and I clustered together in the furthest corner of the small room, the rest of the class radiating outward from us. All except Ned. He took a bunk at the front of the room instead. No one else wanted it, so he had both the top and bottom bunk to himself. Yet he still chose to be on the bottom. It made him harder to see and easier to exclude.

I don't know what prompted me—maybe it was the memory of my hurt dad's face as we drove away, reminding me of my promise; maybe I was stricken by an uncharacteristic sympathy; or, maybe I was already experiencing the nascent bonding the trip promised us—but I felt I had to do something about Ned's withdrawing before it was too late. If I could convince him to join us I was sure he'd be accepted. We weren't so terrible, after all. At least, I never thought we were.

As Ned unpacked his clothes I sat on his bunk beside him. Immediately he stopped unfolding and hung his head like a dog who'd done something wrong. He would not look at me.

"You should bunk closer," I said. When he didn't respond I fumbled for more words. "There's plenty of room. How can we talk to you when you're way over here?"

"I better not," he said into his chest.

"But you're alone."

He half-shrugged.

I didn't know what to do. I couldn't convince him to move, and Mr. Parsons would never force him. Then, surprisingly, Ned looked up at me; he stared me in the eyes as though he'd finally screwed up the courage to speak, and I thought maybe he was about to give in. And I got excited. That excitement curdled when I heard Steig's voice over my shoulder.

"Hey, Needle! Know any good songs?"

Everybody laughed. I took a step away.

I'm sorry, I mouthed as I retreated to my bunk while, around me, the air filled with singing.

$\sim$

THE NEXT MORNING Mr. Parsons took us hiking through the surrounding forest. We dragged our feet over fallen trees and across narrow streams along some invisible path only he seemed to know. All of us were nervous, and Eric made it worse when he suggested we were lost. Just as I started to believe him, Mr. Parsons turned and said, "Just past those rocks will be a pond," and my confidence in him was renewed. For a little while.

It was only after the sky grew cloudier that he stopped, checked his watch, then looked up. "Not much further now," he said to me, only because I was closest to him and he had to say it to someone. "We'll get there in time." I asked him where that was and he just smiled. I noticed tiny thistleheads caught in his dark beard.

When we crested a small hill a short time later, Mr. Parsons brought us to a stop. Ahead lay a field almost a kilometre wide, and as my classmates and I panted, glad for the break, Mr. Parsons did not look relieved.

"This shouldn't be here," he mumbled, before taking off his hat to scratch his head. "Not a field." He stared at the clearing as he thought, while I looked up at the dark gathering clouds. Already the forest had turned gloomy, and that gloom was affecting the others. They were getting restless. Even Eric, who never seemed to be afraid of anything, was anxious. A rumble from above told me what was imminent. It took a moment longer for Mr. Parsons to realize it too.

"Boys, we need to cross this field quickly. Does everyone have their partner? Good. Stay calm and let's hustle."

We strode single file through the long grass, Mr. Parsons in the lead. We had been chatty before, making jokes as we trudged between trees and through underbrush, yet in the open we were silent. Mr. Parsons's mood had unsettled us. When I felt a tug on my sleeve I looked

behind me and found Ned. His face was carved into anticipatory fear. He wanted to say something and I instinctively
knew I didn't want to know what.

A flash of lightning. Its suddenness startled us, though
it was the subsequent thunderous crack that made us
scream. Mr. Parsons glanced briefly at the sky, then turned
and yelled, "Faster, boys!"

Rain erupted immediately. Thick drops plummeted
from the sky, drenching us. We sprinted through the tall
whipping grass, Mr. Parsons and his long adult legs leading
us across the field.

He stopped unexpectedly ahead, and when I caught up
to him I found out why. Across the impossible width of the
field I saw stretched a long wire link fence, and it
prevented us from reaching the point a few hundred metres
away where the forest resumed. Mr. Parsons stood motionless in the pouring rain, trying to comprehend what was
happening. The sky had turned fully night under the thick
storm clouds, interrupted only by bright flashes and deaf-
ening thunder. I thought the world was falling apart. And I
wasn't alone.

"What are we going to do?" Eric screamed at Mr.
Parsons. Mr. Parsons looked at Eric. Then, at us. His eyes
worried me. They were either glassy or wet with rain. Then
he roused from his stupor and became himself.

"We have to find a way to the other side of this fence.
Everyone look!" He started running his hands along the
wire links while the rest of us exchanged drowned glances.
"Now!" he shouted, and we snapped into action, scanning
for an opening. All of us except Ned. Ned remained a few
feet removed in the grass, crouching as though to make his
body as small as possible. The rain continued to pour down
my back and into my shoes and I thought about my
promise and how little time there was.

"Goddamn it!" I cursed. Behind the sheets of rain Mr.

Parsons called to us. I saw Steig running. But I couldn't leave Ned alone.

"You have to get up!" I said, and yanked Ned to his feet.

He didn't resist. He simply looked at me full of trust. If only either of us knew how that trust would go on to haunt me.

When we reached Mr. Parsons he was on his knees, scooping mud out of a large puddle that crossed from one side of the fence to the other.

"Something big dug its way under," he shouted over his shoulder. "I think I've widened the hole enough for us to crawl through. Once you're across head for the trees and wait for us there. Everybody got it?"

He sent the biggest kid, Eric, under first to help pull us out on the other side. Then we lined up and were fed, one at a time, into the hole beneath the metal wire. I watched Steig shimmy his way through then leap up and slap Eric's hand in triumph. As I got closer to the fence I noticed Ned lagging further behind. I could have smacked him. Instead, begrudgingly, I shoved him forward, ahead of me in line. I needed to be sure he made it over. I'd promised my dad. Ned resisted, though, terrified. There wasn't time for hysterics.

So I shoved him again. Shoved him until he was pressed against the fence. Ned hesitated, looked back pleadingly at Mr. Parsons. He merely put his hand on Ned's shoulder and said: "You'll be fine. Quickly, now."

Ned nodded, swallowed, and crawled under the fence.

I suppose we should have expected it in hindsight. None of us, not even Mr. Parsons, really understood the danger. I watched Ned as he worked his way under the wire. Saw the wire catch on the belt loop of his pants. Saw Ned reach back to free himself. Saw Mr. Parsons step forward to help. All these moments are caught in my memory like photographs by the lightning flash. It was so bright I heard nothing. I found myself sitting on the ground, legs cold and numb, without knowing why. Ned was still under the fence, now face down in the puddle. And above him, Mr. Parsons was bloodlessly white, unable to speak. Eric and Steig gawked in terror on the other side of the fence. Then I saw them grab Ned's arms and yank him across. When he was clear they got their shoulders under him and carried him to the wooded spot where the rest of our class waited.

Mr. Parsons was shaken. I was, too, my body uncontrollable. I don't remember going under the fence right after. I must have because then I was on the other side and running. When I reached the forest I nearly fell over, unable to catch my breath. Mr. Parsons appeared immediately behind me, his hat lost, his hair plastered to his head. Too frantic to notice the cut along the width of his hand that bled down the front of his khakis.

"Is Ned awake?"

Eric, kneeling beside the unmoving boy, shook his head.

Mr. Parsons immediately started CPR. I'd only seen it before in the movies or on television where it was exciting. In real life it wasn't exciting. It was violent. Yet I stared. We all did. Watching Mr. Parsons huffing numbers as he counted compressions. Ned didn't move once while Mr. Parsons pushed down on his chest. He didn't even move to wipe the drop of water slipping down his face. I wanted to wipe it away but was too afraid to touch him.

Eventually Mr. Parsons slowed, exhausted, and then stopped altogether. He sat, legs folded under him, and watched nothing. His face, indescribably bereft and empty. And all I could think about was my dad, and how disappointed in me he was going to be. I was already so disappointed in myself.

We shivered and waited quietly for Mr. Parsons to come back to us. Ned meanwhile only grew more pale. It took Steig to muster up enough courage to break the silence.

"What are you going to tell Needle's mom?" he asked.

I'll never forget the way Mr. Parsons turned and looked at him.

∼

AND THINGS WERE WORSE when we got home. All of us, Mr. Parsons included, were traumatized by what we'd gone through in Kearney. Especially me, though I could never tell anyone why. The district school board allowed us a few days off and hired a grief counsellor to help, but we were back in class faster than anyone would have liked—a dazed horde of twelve-year-old zombies going through the motions, listening to Mr. Parsons teach and retaining nothing.

I'm not sure Mr. Parsons remembered the lessons either. His face sagged so much it seemed detached and his voice was drained of all verve. Ned's accident had transformed him into a dead-eyed creature, just as it had the rest of us. I kept hoping he'd snap out of it, though. We needed someone to guide us forward. And I needed ... well, I needed someone to talk to about what had happened in Kearney. I knew neither Steig nor Eric would understand, and I couldn't talk to my dad. I couldn't look him in the eye anymore. And who knew where my mom was. Mr. Parsons was all I had, and I couldn't reach him.

After Ned was struck it took us hours to find our way back to the cabin. The rain didn't help, so heavy it blinded us to anything further than a few feet ahead. The leaves above rattled furiously as though they were being beat with stones, which made it difficult to hear one another. Not that any of us were in the mood to talk. Mr. Parsons tried his compass repeatedly, muttering each time it didn't take us where we wanted to go. He was probably overwhelmed with everything that was happening, but it was worrying all the same. We'd implicitly trusted him to lead us, and seeing he had no better idea what to do than we did made things worse. Eric did his best to take over, though, and despite his own fear motivate us to keep going.

We took turns carrying Ned on the stretcher we'd jerry-rigged using a couple of fallen branches and our sweatshirts. I insisted on taking the lead when it was my turn, facing away from him as we marched through the forest muck. I couldn't stand to see how still he was. How lifeless. Steig had laid something over his face to protect him from the rain but it slid off at some point when no one was paying attention.

I don't know how we found the cabin. We were lost in the rain one minute, miserable, scared, numb from shock. And the next we were standing in front of it, as though it had risen under cover of the storm. Or maybe it had somehow been following us the entire time. It didn't matter which; as soon as I saw it I had to hide my tears.

As bad as it was coming home to my upset dad who wouldn't stop hugging me, seeing Ned's mom was worse. The sight of her weeping made me in turns both ashamed and distraught. I was so confused in those early days, so unsure, that I just wanted to be left alone, yet no one would let me. Even Mr. Parsons betrayed me, saying it would be a good idea for our class to go to Ned's funeral for closure. I didn't know how to talk him out of it, and when I realized not only Eric but even Steig agreed, I knew it was pointless to try. The following Saturday morning I let my dad dress me in a suit I'd already outgrown and drive us to the cemetery. It was the second-last place in the world I wanted to be. At least he didn't make us stand near Ned's understandably broken mom. He had enough sense to avoid that.

There was one moment, before Ned was lowered into

the ground, she turned to say something to me and my dad and her sticky voice caught in her throat. I think then she lost her nerve. My dad waited until Ned was buried before he, sniffling, still not himself, walked me over to offer my condolences. Her face was wet and swollen and reminded me of Ned's as he stared at me in the rain just before I pushed him forward. I wanted to say something, yet I didn't have any words. It didn't matter, though. She silenced me by taking my chin in her hand as my mom sometimes did and I really didn't like it—it felt unnatural. My dad refused to look her in the eye and she him. Instead, she focused all her attention on me. I could tell by her face she was a million miles away. And wherever she was, she wanted to be farther.

We all assumed it would be okay once we reached the cabin. As though everything would reset once we were safely indoors. Maybe Ned would be all right, revived by the comfort of familiarity. It didn't work like that, though. Mr. Parsons had us set Ned down on his bunk, then told us to get a fire going. He had an old rotary phone in his hand, the receiver against his chest, and was pulling the cord with him into the coat closet. When he closed the door we looked at one another, puzzled, then at the colourless Ned. Steig silently urged me to put my ear to the door and tell us what Mr. Parsons was saying though I refused. I didn't want to know. It felt wrong.

Mr. Parsons wasn't in there for long anyway. And when he emerged he looked as though he'd aged another ten years. He set the phone down where he found it and took a seat on the edge of Ned's bunk. We watched him delicately lift Ned's small damp hand and hold it. None of us spoke. We knew. Outside, the rain thrashed the windows harder. We never did build that fire.

After the funeral I shut down. I half-expected my dad to finally explain everything but he didn't bother. I guess he was too afraid. I wasn't the only kid in our class who couldn't talk about Ned afterward, of course—we were all stewing in our own strange concoctions of trauma, shock, and guilt—yet I was the only one who became disruptive and violent. Eric, to his credit, tried to reason with me even after Steig started distancing himself. I didn't want to be reasoned with. I didn't want to be calmed. Something inside me had decided it wanted out, and the only way to quell it was to destroy everything. First Eric left me and then school didn't want me, and when there was nothing else remaining I turned on myself.

I started fights and hung out with the burnouts loitering all day behind the school. Twelve-years-old is just old enough to get into trouble if your mind is set on it. My dad tried to sit me down after the police found me with half a bottle of his stolen whisky under my arm, but I had nothing to say. Nor did I have anything to tell the psychologist my mom sent me to—her one stab at helping before throwing up her arms and admitting defeat. "This is your fault," she screamed at my dad. "You both ruin everything!" Imagine their surprise when they discovered I heard them. They pretended they were sorry. Even if I believed it, it was too late. I already knew why they split and I didn't care. Not about that. Not about them. There was nothing inside me anymore that could. It had escaped, leaving behind a crushing vacuum that I spent the following decades trying to fill any way I could. Drinks, drugs, stealing, and whatever else there was to make me feel.

The irony was, the more I felt, the more I wished I didn't. The more numb I wanted to be. That's what got me admitted to Ranch Hill, got me my own private counsellor who says she wants to help me save my life. I don't think there's much worth saving even though she's adamant we try. Who am I to argue? I'm so sick of feeling empty that I'll try anything. Writing down this story is the first step, she says, though I know she won't believe any of it. She doesn't care. And she doesn't care that I've never told another soul about what happened to me. She says that's more reason to write it down. And she definitely doesn't care that I'm embarrassed about what she'll think. She says there's nothing to be embarrassed about. That we all have our own truths and no two people will ever share the same one. That's what makes admitting ours so important: it shows people who we really are. And when I tell her I'm afraid of failing she tells me no one ever fails if they're still trying.

So here's me trying.

I've been writing nearly forever and still I'm dancing around what really happened in Kearney. It's kind of funny: I've gone through the pain of withdrawal and the struggles of staying clean and yet telling this story is the hardest thing I've ever had to do.

We found out quickly that we'd have to spend the night in the cabin with Ned's body. There were no ambulances that far north, and the closest town was too busy dealing with all the accidents caused by the storm. No one considered Ned an emergency. He was dead, and it was not a suspicious death. Someone would be sent in the morning. Until the school bus arrived, we were stuck.

Eric was the one who suggested relocating Ned. If he was going to have to stay in Kearney, he didn't want to share the room with a dead person. Especially one he knew. No one else did, either. The question was where to put the body. Outside was obviously out of the question, so the compromise was moving him to the coat closet. If we couldn't see him, maybe it would be enough for us to get some sleep. Mr. Parsons and Eric did the work while the rest of us averted our eyes. We heard only the closet door close. I hated the sound; it reminded me of how I'd failed.

Unsurprisingly, we were all spooked when Mr. Parsons

turned out the light. All our energy and exhaustion and the pent-up anxieties went into overdrive. Whispers moved from bunk to bunk as we tried to work out what we witnessed and what was to come. Someone somewhere in the dark quietly cried. We couldn't tell who it was and no one needed to ask. We understood.

As the night progressed one by one the whispers fell away as the other boys gave into sleep. I tried, too, yet each time I closed my eyes I saw Ned's empty plastic face wet with rain and I jerked awake. Eventually I lost track of where or when I was. I might have already been at home with my dad or still sitting in the rain in the middle of nowhere. There was no difference in the starless night. The only sound that tethered me to reality was the miniature engine of a gently puttering snore. I suspected I might be the last person awake in the entire world.

And then I heard Ned's voice.

"Come here. I need to ask you something."

And I froze.

I don't know what a normal person would have done. It's so hard to be sure until you're in it. Sitting there in the black, I neither screamed nor ran out the door as though I were on fire. I didn't wake everyone in the cabin and beg them to confirm I wasn't crazy. I didn't shriek in terror or stammer in fear. I didn't really do much at all. Maybe I was stuck in some midnight daze. Maybe my brain was working so hard to parse the horrible events of the afternoon there was no room to process anything else. All I know is I whispered, "Okay," and flung my blankets aside.

No one else moved. No one else woke. When I reached the closet door I went to open it then stopped myself. Instead I sat in front of the closed door and pulled my legs up under me. Through the thin wood I heard him quietly shifting.

"What do you want?" I whispered.

"I can't see anything. Why is it so cold?"

I hesitated. There was no point in lying but I couldn't bring myself to tell the complete truth.

"When you crawled under the fence it got struck by lightning."

"Really? That's kind of cool. I bet everybody was scared."

"Yeah," I said. "Can I go back to bed now?"

"There's something else I need. It might sound weird, though."

I waited. Ned didn't say anything for the longest time. Long enough that I wondered if I was dreaming. When he spoke again his voice was quieter. More careful.

"So, I saw your dad. When you got on the bus."

"Okay?"

"Is he good? A good dad?"

A good dad? How was I supposed to answer that? What did Ned want to hear? That regardless of how my dad and mom fought, he never yelled at me? That whenever I did something wrong he would tell me I'd let him down, and that was worse than any punishment? That he helped me build tree forts and took me to buy hockey cards on his days off? Or was I supposed to tell Ned that when I was at my dad's house I was home in a way I never was at my mom's?

"He's okay," I said.

"I never had a dad. My mom was really young when she had me. He ... he wasn't part of our life. He had his own family. Another family."

I still didn't know what to say. "Oh," was the best I could manage.

"My mom made me promise I'd leave him alone. She said the reason he'd never met me was because I was a mistake and he didn't want to know me. She didn't want me to hurt more than I already do. The truth is I've already met him. And I think he wants to get to know me. I think he wants to be my dad. Can you imagine how that feels?"

The excitement in his voice. The hope ... I had to tell him.

"Ned, there's something you need to know."

"I think I already do."

"When you were crawling under that fence .... You died, Ned. You were struck by lightning and it killed you." I don't think I really believed it until the words fell out of my mouth. I could hear my voice breaking. "I promised ... I promised my dad I'd take care of you. I promised I'd make sure you were all right and I couldn't. I couldn't save you, Ned. I couldn't."

There was no stopping myself; I started crying. At first I hoped it would only be a few tears, but as they came there were plenty more behind them. I fought the best I could and they pushed through all the same.

"I'm ... I'm dead?" Ned said. And, stupidly, I could only nod. When my dad found out I knew nothing would ever be the same.

I'd let Ned die.

Outside the storm raged, and the rain pelting the roof made a staccato sound that thankfully drowned out most of my sobbing. I prayed I wouldn't wake the others; I didn't want them to know. I was ashamed of so many things that they layered on one another, multiplying their intensity. All I wanted was to see my dad, hear him tell me things would be all right. That we all make mistakes. I knew it wasn't true. He would never have made such a huge mistake, I told myself. He couldn't. Not ever.

"I'm sorry," was all I could muster when I finally got control of myself. I laid my hand on the closet door as I said it, hoping my sincerity would somehow cross to the other side. Hoping Ned would know how much I regretted everything I'd ever done wrong. And I think he did know, ultimately. I just don't think he forgave me.

"Do you remember the Needle song?" he asked. His voice had turned and it startled me out of my blubber. "I don't remember which of you made it up. Maybe Steig. Maybe you. I do remember how you all sang it every day for weeks. And I remember how first I tried laughing with you, and when that didn't work I tried getting mad at you. Nothing stopped it."

"We didn't mean anything by it. We—"

"Don't lie to me. I'm dead, remember? Nothing you say can hurt me anymore. Not like it hurt me then. You know, I even went to Mr. Parsons to ask him for help. I thought he was always helping you with homework or having Eric act as his assistant. He'd help me, too. You know what Mr. Parsons said? He said 'the boys are just being boys, Needle. You need to toughen up.' He might have said more but I didn't hear it. He called me *Needle*. Like in your song. And he had a smirk on his face the whole time. As though I deserved what happened. As though I *encouraged* it."

"Ned, I .... If I'd known—"

"And you want to hear the really messed up thing? Part of me liked it. When you sang that awful song at least you saw me. For a moment I wasn't a nobody, ignored until you thought up some new way of torturing me. But I knew you'd eventually forget. You always did. You always will. It's funny; sometimes I used to think all of you would regret how you treated me if I died. I thought you'd all be sorry, and I got some satisfaction out of that. God, how stupid could I have been? Dying doesn't teach anybody anything. I died as happy as I was ever going to be. And it wasn't nearly enough."

Rain intensified against the windows. It was harder to hear Ned speak. I put my ear closer while the storm pulled his words back, made them sound further away.

"Let me ask you one more thing," he said.

"Anything," I said. And I meant it.

"Were we friends?"

I wiped the tears off my face. My entire body jittered from exhaustion. I wasn't going to lie to him. Not again.

"No. We never were."

"Yeah, I guess you're right," he said. "But if we weren't friends, why are you talking to me?"

I shrugged.

"Because my dad told me to."

"Yeah. Mine, too."

And then he laughed. I'd never heard a sound like it before. It was dry and weird, and it scared me. Because I didn't know what it meant. Or maybe I just hoped I didn't.

"Ned?" I said, and this time he didn't answer. Instead, as the heavy rain rattled across the cabin's roof I heard something else. I heard him singing. It was the Needle Song. And I knew it because I'd helped make it up, one way or another. And yet it was Ned who knew all the words by heart. He sang them over and over as the storm dismantled the sound. Broke it down into pieces until it was something near nothing. The sound of everything coming undone.

And yet, for me, sitting there alone in the dark, all the pieces were only starting to come together.

SANDSTONE

SILVIA MORENO-GARCIA

THE BOOK SHE'D BOUGHT FROM THE TINY VISITOR'S centre explained that the puckered rocks blanketing the beach were sandstone eroded by salt, a common sight in the Canadian Gulf Islands. But the bizarre geometry on display seemed like patterns traced by an alien hand rather than the elements. One could imagine this was a lonesome seashore on a distant planet lit by a dying sun.

The honeycombed patterns unsettled her. She sat uneasily upon the rocks, her feet resting by a shallow pool of water. Crabs scuttled by her toes. In the distance, she heard Joseph laughing. He was talking to a trio of young tourists.

The hotel was stifling. Online, it advertised itself as a "quaint, magical experience with all the comforts of home" but the rickety fan spinning in a corner was unable to cool the room, the TV was busted, and the wi-fi remained, at best, unreliable. They'd come for a romantic vacation, but she couldn't sleep at night, her skin covered with a thin film of sweat, and the noise from the other rooms waking her up at random intervals.

The walls of the rooms felt paper thin, she thought

she might be able to slide a hand through them. The creaking and croaking of wood, the whisper of water travelling up ancient pipes, mingled with bizarre noises she couldn't always identify. She recognized the shuffling and dragging of feet, but the rhythm of this shuffling seemed odd. As if a large animal, perhaps a horse, was walking above their heads. Or there were voices that seemed to bubble and gurgle as she stared at the ceiling, moonlight filtering through a gap in the curtains.

Joseph didn't care. He slept like a log and rose early, chiding her for her tiredness during the day.

"If you weren't up until three a.m. on your phone you wouldn't be so sleepy," he'd told her earlier.

"I wasn't on my phone. Someone was dragging furniture into the room next door. And then there was a slithering noise ...."

She paused, unable to describe what she'd heard. It had been a wet, fleshy sound. Unnerving.

Thin places, she thought. There are places as thin as the skin of a soap bubble. Through their permeable membranes things slip in and out, both errant dreams and indescribable nightmares. She'd had a roommate from Cork who'd told her as much, back when she was a student, analyzing the musculoskeletal systems of invertebrates and pondering the morphology of starfish. Before Joseph whisked her off her feet and she put away her textbooks and lab specimens.

She licked her lips. "There's something wrong with our door. It doesn't close correctly. The angle of it ... it's crooked. Several of the walls are crooked."

"It's a small island and it's the only hotel. You wouldn't stay at a bed and breakfast."

"It's wrong. Why don't we head back to Vancouver?"

She'd pleaded with him as soon as they'd reached the

hotel, the sight of the beach had turned her stomach. He had not taken it well. Now, his eyes narrowed at her.

"Everything is wrong with you," he muttered.

"The land is hungry here," she said. She had no idea why she'd spoken those words. It was the sort of cryptic line of poetry Joseph might have written in a tiny notebook when younger, toying with the idea of art, penning haikus. He'd tired of that, and of her.

His eyes changed, filling with suspicion rather than simple dissatisfaction. "Are you off your meds again?"

"No. I swear."

He nodded, not entirely convinced. Then he stood up and walked away from her and towards the trio of tourists. They were American university students on summer break intent on exploring Western Canada. Their next stop was Vancouver. She'd learned as much the previous night when Joseph had introduced himself and dragged her to their table. Mr. Sociability.

The rocks around her looked like giant sponges. Tafoni. That was the proper name for them. The book she'd bought said tafoni could also be found on Mars.

She'd been studying biology when she met Joseph, over 20 years before. She remembered staring with awe at Haeckel's lithographs: the delicate tendrils, meticulous silica shells, and elegant axopodia. The radiolarians he drew did not seem like organisms that could exist in nature, the plasticity of forms rendered with his brush emanated from a different universe. Protean biology, showcasing the unexpected potentiality of life.

Thousands and thousands of years before, things that looked like crabs might have scuttled on ancient beaches in distant planets, tracing a path around heavily pitted rocks. After all, life tends to evolve into crab-like forms. Carcinization.

Shielded behind the darkness of her sunglasses and her

41

wide brim hat, she pretended to read her book and instead looked in her husband's direction.

She couldn't hear what he was saying, but knew he was delivering the right combination of careless bragging and self-effacing charm. When she'd first met Joseph, he'd impressed her with his adventurous hobbies—surfing, sailing—mixed with his faux-bohemian charisma. He'd long stopped surfing, and nowadays he dangled his high-tech job and expensive car in front of people's eyes rather than pretending he was a poet in a garret, but the basics of his method remained the same. He'd mention his interest in fine wines and juxtapose it with a story about the time he'd hitchhiked from Seattle to Los Angeles after he lost his wallet.

He'd get the young woman's number and there would no doubt be a quick rendezvous in Vancouver for them. He'd make it up to his wife with another cozy vacation. Maybe to Whistler, this time. She'd stopped counting his affairs. Joseph had wanted a wife, not a scientist, so she'd long stored away her degree and smothered her misgivings. Like a fish swimming in the oxygen depleted waters of a shallow tide-pool, she'd developed adaptations to survive her threatening environment.

It was growing dark, the twilight hour giving way to night and the tourists picked up their towels and coolers and headed back to the hotel. She looked at the book between her hands and waited for Joseph to return to her side, but he was taking his time. Even after the last of the tourists stepped away, he remained in the distance, surveying the water.

She didn't want to be out there after nightfall. The stars seemed faintly wrong when she looked at them from the window in their room, as if they'd changed course, all the constellations were askew.

The shadows that crept upon the hollowed rocks made her shiver.

"Joseph! It's time!" she yelled, though he didn't like it when she spoke like this. They rose when he said so and went to bed when he declared he was tired. She was not supposed to issue reminders or commands.

But it was becoming dreadfully dark, and the stench of seaweed left to dry on the rocks drenched her nostrils, growing more pungent. The crabs that had scuttled around her feet had vanished, but the rising tide would bring other creatures to the shore. The ocean teems with life, quiet, beneath the waves.

He walked towards her, hands in the pockets of his shorts, and gave her a dismissive look. "I think I'll go night swimming."

"The restaurant won't be open for long."

"I'm not hungry."

"It's getting late," she muttered. "It might be dangerous."

"Nonsense."

"Please, Joseph. Don't!"

She clutched his arm. Her eyes were wide with fear. Once upon a time, he might have taken this fear seriously. He might have embraced her and smoothed her hair, like he did when she awoke from an awful nightmare. She'd been afraid of the dark as a child, distressed by things that might creep out from under the bed and climb the walls. This dread followed her into her early adulthood, his embrace keeping it at bay. But he'd long learnt to ignore her frailness, as she ignored his lapses.

"You go back if you want," he said curtly.

She knew he expected her to remain there, no matter what he said, and she stayed perched upon the rock, waiting, as he slipped into the water. Joseph swam away and she turned the pages mechanically. Reality was as porous in this place as the rocks beneath her feet. She quickly wrapped herself in her thin sweater, clutching it closed with one hand and holding the book in the other.

The minutes dragged on. Like Andromeda, she remained chained to the rocks, and like Andromeda she looked towards the foreboding sea.

The evening was chill and the water black as ink with bursts of silver, the waves licking the shore to a discordant rhythm. The beach felt protean, awake and drenched with a horrific vastness, as if she really was standing at the edge of a distant planet. The last remnants of daylight vanished from the horizon. She could no longer see the words in her book and clapped it shut.

Quickly she gathered their things and walked back to the hotel, where the windows glowed golden with electric lights, like a beacon, or distant suns. She almost slipped upon a rock and shut her mouth, stifling a scream, so that it became a sob. She hurried up to their room, her heart hammering.

She should have stayed and waited for him to come out of the water, but her aversion to that beach was more powerful than her fear of her husband's exasperation. She lay on the bed, the useless book still clasped between her hands.

He'd give her the cold shoulder when they boarded the ferry back. He'd say she always managed to ruin their vacations with her nit-picking and her fretting.

The tired clock on the wall ticked away. She dozed off. When she woke, he still hadn't returned to their room. Perhaps he'd gone directly to the restaurant, to flirt with that American tourist. Or perhaps he'd slipped inside and changed while she napped. But his clothes were hanging in the closet.

She headed to the restaurant. The three Americans

were eating together, but Joseph did not sit with them. Unmoored, she drifted by their table, and sat in a corner of the dining room, thinking he would come in and join her. Even though she ordered a drink and then a soup and then a main course, he did not come.

Where could he be? Swimming still? Yes, why not? He'd stay out as long as he could, stoking her anxiety. She remained at the table, looking at the squat candle resting at the centre of it, her hands clasped together in her lap.

Eventually, she retreated to her room and stood by the window, carefully pulling aside the curtain, and peering outside.

Night now blanketed the land. Devoid of the glow and light of the city, the beach was an infinite empire of shadows. Here and there one could perceive the smudged forms of rocks, the swell of the sea, the pinpricked night sky. But the view was of an amorphous, unknowable collage.

The beach at night bore a faint resemblance to the beach in the daytime, but underneath the shallow membrane of mundanity there pulsed darker, noxious elements.

Outside, the paper-thin walls of reality melted and the stars rearranged themselves, tracing shapes she'd never seen before. It was a hungry land, just as she'd told Joseph. She could feel it now, shivering and opening and breathing; a land, which called to mind the Earth in days past, when the bubbling cauldron of its waters spewed forth the first fish and reptile. Between those denuded rocks, there drifted crab-things and slippery, slithering aquatic beasts and shapeless beings of coral and muscle. In the depths of the tidepools there squirmed boneworms awaiting to feast on carcasses, and gelatinous blobs drifted on tube feet, showing their teeth. Primal and eager, the creatures of the dark sea unhinged their jaws.

She let the curtain fall, locked the door, and flicked on

every light in the hotel room knowing that if anything ever slipped out of the water and crept upon the rocks, it would not be Joseph.

PRAIRIE TEETH

EC DORGAN

She looks out the window and wants so badly to see a picture-perfect town in New England. Like in her paperbacks. When the leaves on the trees are golden and red and it's the week before Halloween. She imagines she's a heroine in one of the stories; they're all the same: a young woman on the verge of discovering her powers. On the cusp of something.

But outside is reality. A Canadian prairie blight: scrubby grass, long weeds, dried out wild rose stems. The horizon is all refineries, obscured by wildfire smoke. And beside her window, a farmer's field in fallow, a wooden fence, and a rotting cross in its centre. Barbed wire all around, and a sign reading, "No Trespassing."

The truth—she hates it. There are no would-be heroines coming of age on this barren prairie. She's a spinster. She went grey in her twenties, hit menopause in her forties. Lived too fast and too hard. She's no one's fated love.

And this isn't New England. Here trains scream into the night and vomit black crude into not-so-pristine earth. The farmers carry long guns.

Still, she tries. She stands at the mirror and pretends she used to be pretty. She lives vicariously through her paperbacks. Some nights, when she's lying in bed, she imagines a future that's different.

The week before Halloween, she opens her door and stands at the threshold, taking in the morning-dark sky and the frost-burned grass. She watches her breath and cold burrows into her spine.

She tries to work. Her job is with the county. She sits at her kitchen table and answers questions by email about building permits. No one talks to her. Her mind wanders.

Every week, she reads a new paperback about a young woman in New England who comes into her power. Usually a latent witch. She orders new books every week. The plot's never different. They'll never stop printing them.

She doesn't think about how the book heroines are so much younger than her. She imagines her skin is soft like theirs, and that her eyes aren't so shadowed. That she doesn't have an alcoholic's nose.

She doesn't know how she ended up alone. Why she never found her soulmate. In high school, she had friends. She doesn't understand what happened. It's like she missed some essential guide to life.

The day before Halloween, the temperature drops. She goes for a walk and her feet crunch through thin, dry snow. She stares at the field. It will all be canola in summer.

Her grandma told her it used to be different. She said this place was a home. She said she used to hoe potatoes. She pointed her lips at the grave and said there was their family.

Family. She can't imagine it. She misses her grandma. Her parents and cousins used to live here. They moved to the city, and the coast. They gave up on this prairie. Got sick of that strutting farmer, and renting. She still doesn't understand how the farmer owns everything.

She walks along the field. It's surrounded by wild rose. The dried stems and the leaves are crimson. She takes off her gloves and brushes her fingers. The thorns prick, but not enough, so she stops and grips the stems. She still doesn't feel anything.

She eats pumpkin pie in the dark. Looks up her old high-school friends and lurks on their social media. They stayed in touch until their mid-thirties. After that, it got awkward. Her friends have kids and perfect partners. They're renovating their kitchens for the third time.

Outside, coyotes yip and she envies that they have each other.

~

ON HALLOWEEN, she wears a sweater she bought online from Etsy. There's a ghost on the front and a pumpkin on the back. It itches. She puts on music and waits for visitors.

She does this every year. She still has hope. Though she knows by now not to buy candy.

It's after nine, and she's about to start her latest paperback when something outside rustles. She pauses her music. Nothing. And then—something she's never heard in all her Halloweens. A thud on the door—once, twice. A voice calls out, "Trick or Treat."

Her heart races. Could it be? She almost doesn't dare think it. She knows this moment from her books—the bated breath before everything changes. Something in her gut surges—hunger, fear, and hope.

All of her hairs are standing. The nape of her neck is cold. She pushes down her screaming instincts and walks to the door.

The world tilts when she opens it. At first she thinks, *a vampire.*

He says, "Can I come in?"

She can't speak.

He tips his hat. He's wearing jeans and a lumberjack jacket. Gloves and a belt buckle to go with his cowboy hat. Boots with spurs.

She steps backward. When he raises his eyes, the room shifts a second time. She reaches to the wall for balance.

Those eyes. For a moment, she can't place it. But her gut knows. There's a funny taste on her tongue. An old memory, in her bones and her teeth.

She grew up hearing stories about this one. Winter stories, told on cold, clear nights. This is no vampire. This is something worse. There are no mail-order paperbacks written about this handsome stranger.

She holds her breath.

He walks over to the kitchen table and plonks into a chair. Puts his boots on the table like he owns it. The house shudders.

Her pulse jitters. The thorns in her hands are prickling. She doesn't know what to do. She's not used to feeling alive like this.

He looks at her. His eyes shimmer. She breaks out in a sweat.

He half-smiles and pulls out a pipe.

"Coffee?" She feels like a fool but can't help it—it's her upbringing.

He smiles like he knows it.

"I'll take a light." His voice is like a cat.

She fumbles looking for matches. Sweat runs down her cheeks.

He lights the pipe like a showman. She watches him smoke.

On the surface, he's handsome. Not so young as those actors on TV. He could be her age, or older. He has a dimple in his chin. His hair is pitch.

But those eyes—they're black-iridescent. When the

light hits them, they shine oily-green, like crude or spoiled meat.

She keeps her voice steady. "What brings you to the prairie?"

He grins. Even the pipe-smoke has a sheen.

"I never left."

He takes his boots down from the table. The heel spurs leave a dent. She watches, rapt, while he rises. He walks to the door and his Stetson brushes the ceiling. He didn't seem so tall when he entered.

"Thanks for the light."

She doubles over coughing when he leaves. She's used to wildfires and smelling the refinery, but this oily smoke is something different.

She stands in the doorway, catching her breath, and the night's cold climbs up her back.

SHE SPENDS the winter making ketchup and beet pickles. Working remotely from her kitchen, answering emails about building permits. It bores her. She reads her books. She stares out the window. Some days, the sun is so bright on the snow she can't look at it.

When spring comes, she cleans out her cupboards and plants potatoes. She barely sleeps the whole month of June; the nights are short. The coyotes barely sleep either.

Before she knows it, it's summer and the land is bursting with wild rose blooms. It's blooming with wildfire too. Some days, the smoke is so thick she can't see the cross in the field. She keeps her air purifier on all the time. The canola crops are eye-breaking yellow. They're almost as tall as she is.

One July day, the smoke is thinner. She stands in her doorway and slips off her shoes. She walks to a rose bush and lingers. She plucks a bloom and the thorns prick her fingers, but they only bleed a little bit.

She walks to the barbed wire. Pushes down her rising fear, and wishes she were brave like her book characters. She steps one foot over the fence, then the other. The earth is dry and compact. She skulks through canola like a spectre.

She cowers when she reaches the wooden fence. She's never felt so exposed. She imagines the farmer with his long gun, watching her. She doesn't have the courage to go closer. She bends an arm over the fence to leave a rose, but flinches when she hears something rustling. She looks over her shoulder for the farmer. The fear's too much. She tucks the rose into her pocket and scuttles away.

∾

COME HALLOWEEN, she waits in her kitchen for the Devil. She keeps her music low so she'll hear his heavy knock. She's bought a special sweater from Etsy. It says, "Ready for the Devil."

She grinds coffee. Puts her air purifier on high. Tries to read, but her heart races. She puts her book down—she can't concentrate.

At ten to nine, she gets water for the kettle. She chooses a mug. Pulls a chair to the front door and sits, unbreathing. Trains scream and coyotes yip, but she doesn't hear any rustling.

She's still waiting when the sun rises. Her eyes have more bags, and her cheeks are all shadow. She opens the door and stands at the threshold. The field is a frozen blight. There's another layer of barbed wire, and a new sign reading, "I shoot."

She reads paperbacks until evening. She doesn't eat, yet

something foul and acid rises inside her. She forces it down and gags. The vilest taste is truth.

She puts down her book. The Devil didn't come. No one did, all year. And apart from those moments as a ghost in the field, she never left this house.

∼

TWO YEARS PASS. She reads dozens more paperbacks. She confuses the characters and titles, but it doesn't matter since they have the same plot. There's no limit to the demand for them. Not like her story. No one wants that.

When Halloween comes, she doesn't bother with an Etsy sweater. She keeps the air purifier off. She walks to the window and looks outside. The moon shines bright and the field is cold and barren.

She almost misses the knock.

Her heart skips. She almost trips in her rush to the door. She opens it wide.

He's still dressed like a lumberjack. He takes off his Stetson.

"About that coffee?"

It's only French press but he takes it.

He smokes his pipe and cracks his knuckles.

"Playing cards, fiddle?"

She threw her cards out years ago—tired of playing alone. And she flunked out of violin in grade three for playing crooked.

"I have potatoes." Her cheeks burn when she says it. Two years to think of something—and this?

"Dice then."

He puffs an "O." Takes off a leather glove and smiles at her. He reaches into his maw while she watches. Pulls out his hand and opens his palm.

Two dice. She thinks.

She's never played dice, but it can't be that different from cards or bingo. She knows those. Her grandma taught her.

She sits down. The thorns in her hand are killing her. She reaches for the dice but he closes his fist.

"We play with four."

He opens his palm. She jumps backwards.

Teeth.

Her gums throb at the sight of them. She looks up.

He puffs his pipe, grinning.

She should say, "Enough." Shoo the Devil out into the cold, where he came from. She breaks out in a sweat. The paperback heroines are never this desperate.

But she's tired of hoeing potatoes. Living vicariously through books. Tiptoeing like a ghost. Holding onto thorns just to feel something.

She nods and the room shifts.

He holds out pliers and she takes them. The metal is heavy. She fits them into her mouth and winces when they brush a filling.

She must have been six when a dentist pulled out two of her teeth. He said it would feel like nothing and sound like ice. It didn't. Fifty years later she remembers the pain.

She closes her eyes and grips.

This is worse than those two teeth at the dentist.

Her eyes are tearing. She's choking on blood. Her skull throbs. She wipes the teeth on her jeans and throws them at the Devil.

He doesn't move, he only smiles wider. She dries her eyes. For a moment, he doesn't look like the Devil. He wiggles like a toddler, giddy.

∾

THE DEVIL COUNTS by the tooth cusps—molars have three or five, those with fillings are flatter. Upside-down teeth with four roots count for four when the Devil gets them, but when she rolls them, they count zero.

When she questions the logic, he mansplains her. The ache in her jaw makes her eyes water. When she throws, the Devil blows oil-puffs and her hand goes sideways.

She's losing badly. The Devil is downright gleeful. He claps when her molars go crooked and his land cusps-up. His cheeks puff, and he preens.

She clenches her jaw. Can't stand to look. This is where in the paperbacks the heroines come into their power. Realize they're stronger than they thought. But she's no heroine. And she doesn't want him to leave.

The room shifts and she grabs the table. He takes off his gloves and reaches into his mouth. Slams his palm down hard on the table.

"I'll raise you two."

She leans forward. Two incisors.

The thorns in her fingers are tingling. Her face drips with sweat. She stands so fast the teeth fall to the ground. She rushes to the window to think.

She feels him grinning behind her.

"Take your time."

Time. That bastard. He knows she doesn't have it. She's not some twenty-something beauty like in her books. She's past her youth. Menopause was years ago. There will be no renovating this kitchen. The time she has left on this prairie will be alone and scared.

It's futile, the Devil's fixed the game and she knows it. But she can't let him leave. She hates herself for it.

She walks back to the table. She *has* to win.

He holds out pliers. She shakes her head. Puts her thorny fingers in her mouth and rips out two incisors.

The room shakes. He grins.

Sparks fly when he throws his teeth.

She spits blood onto her palm.

He lifts an eyebrow.

She says, "For luck."

His eyes shine.

They keep playing. Upping their bets. Adding teeth. She catches up to her earlier losses. For a moment, she's almost beating him. But he has bigger hands. Her palms can't hold all their teeth. The table is crimson.

He collects the 16 teeth from the table. Then his oil-eyes flash, rotten, eager. He rips out all four canines.

She tastes bile. Feels a chill at the base of her neck. Runs her tongue along her few teeth remaining. His eyes flash and the room goes sideways. His mouth is so swollen, she can't tell if he's smiling or frowning.

The heroines in her books have perfect smiles. Perfect teeth. She forces down blood but it rises up her gullet. She should stop. Keep the few teeth she has left. Give up on that dream of change. Of not being so lonely.

Her eyes tear. She sees herself in twenty years, shivering in the kitchen, hiding from that farmer. Surrounded by piles of paperbacks that won't stop being printed. Some things are worse than being toothless.

She grabs the pliers out of his hand. Her canines pop when she pulls them. Blood splatters on the floor and on the ceiling.

The Devil claps. "Let's play!"

He throws the teeth and they land cusp up.

When she takes the dice, she can barely hold them. She throws, and half the teeth fall on the floor, counting as zero. The rest land cusp down.

The Devil *tsks*. "You know, we're not just playing for teeth."

The pain in her mouth is inconsolable. She bends under the table to collect the teeth. Her fingers are so bloody she can't get a grip. She can't see through the tears. Her mouth is a swollen mess. Her cheeks are all blood.

The Devil pushes his chair back from the table. Holds his chest puffed and prances around her kitchen like a rooster. When he catches her eye, he claps and clicks his spurs.

He reminds her of the farmer. So certain of his space. Moving like he owns it, like he's entitled to everything.

Her fist tightens around her fallen teeth. She grits her few remaining ones. Years of bottled-up bile bubble up her esophagus.

He dances around the kitchen, oblivious.

She's spent. Done with this solitude, this silence. Living like a ghost. Too scared to leave a rose for her own blood and kin.

She's no paperback heroine—she doesn't even have teeth. All she has is her bitterness, honed sharp from years alone in the dark. Fortified by hoeing potatoes.

She turns to the Devil. Stares down those oil wells to the bottom. "You want to play more?"

He's in his seat before she stands. She reaches both hands into her mouth and rips out every last tooth.

His eyes widen. She waits.

He licks his lips. She doesn't blink. The room shifts.

She claps when he puts his teeth down on the table, though if she's being honest, she doesn't give a damn about the game—she's sick of being cowed by men with hats who walk on this prairie like they own it.

She throws the dice crooked, and the Devil flinches.

In the morning, her paperback can't hold her interest. She puts the book down and opens her front door. Stands at the threshold and takes in the scene: the rose-killed field, the cross surrounded by signs, and on the horizon, refineries.

Somewhere in the distance, a train screams. Coyotes are yipping, but they stop when they hear her. She walks out in bare feet.

She feels the cold, but it's nothing. The icy field reflects sun. It's early morning, but the sky is bright.

Her feet are frozen by the time she reaches the farmer's field. She holds up her palms to the two wooden signs. There's still blood on her fingers from last night's tooth-pulling. She runs her hands along the cold wood, then curls her fingers around the sides and tears the signs down. Splinters dig into her skin and under her fingernails. Blood bursts from a grazed nail. She doesn't mind the pain, it feels liberating.

She stomps down the barbed wire with her bare feet until it's only twisted metal. She walks to the grave. She'll take better care of it now; she won't be so scared. She touches the wooden cross. Family. Now that she's close to it, she doesn't feel so alone.

She walks back to her house with a straight back and bleeding feet. The farmer, if he sees her, is too cowed to do anything. She doesn't know if the Devil is out there somewhere on the horizon, watching. Last night she only saw the back of him, running toothless into the dark.

It wasn't just his teeth. He was skunked, plain and simple. And a bad loser, to boot. Her grandma hated a bad loser. She would have chased him out herself. The Devil left his teeth and his Stetson. He was so much shorter, on the way out.

Her eyes still have bags, and her hair isn't any darker. But still, she feels something in her that's new. Not younger. She's not one of those paperback heroines. She's something more solid, substantial.

Substantial. Like her plans. She'll be coming here more

often now. In the spring, she'll plant potatoes. Come summer, she'll bring a rose. She likes the field without those signs. Without the barbed wire. It could be a picture.

She walks back to her house and stands in the doorway. The Devil and the farmer can come for her. She'll be waiting with her thorns, her grin, and maybe her Stetson. She takes in the morning. Her smile is perfect.

LIGHTBRINGERS

K.L. SCHROEDER

THAT WINTER, THE DARK CONSUMED ME. IT WAS WAITING in the dead ptarmigans that dotted the shores of Yellowknife, in the woman shivering in the doorway of the KFC, and the pale sun sliding along the snow-covered horizon wasn't strong enough to burn it away.

I don't know how I didn't see it coming. By late October I already had a pile of cheap rye bottles collecting at my back door. Work was hell. I just wanted to switch off from the exhausting hours of tagging diseased geese out at the research station. Little point in tracking corpses. Halfway through November, when the sun barely made it over the trees, I was driving past Gary's house every week for whatever he'd sell me. The dark was there too, in the stale smell of the green carpet and the quiet girl with heavy eyeliner who sat on the bed. I didn't stay long, tried to put it out of my mind with the rest of it. But her dark eyes began following me, swimming through the blurred nicotine spots I stared at on my bedroom ceiling. Accusing. Everyone had their own shit to deal with, I told her, told myself, told everyone. Winters were always rough up north.

At the end of November, when the sun had all but

turned its back on us, I figured I'd found the bottom. Nowhere to go but up, right? My supervisor Rod woke me with a bang on the table I was sleeping under, too spaced from some pills I got off Gary to get myself home the night before. He muttered to himself in Wıılıideh yatı, rubbing his face.

"Go get yourself together, Alexander," he said. "Everyone's saying the dark's bad this year, but keep your head on straight. You're not helping any wildlife like this."

I shrugged him off and walked out into the dusk of midday, red-eyed and sweaty. The world was going to hell whether I was lucid or not. I drove downtown, wandering through the Centre Square mall into the Independent to get something for my seething stomach. Sparrows flitted overhead, protected inside from whatever flu was killing the wild ones, unbothered by the smell of mouldering food and exhaust in the old grocery store. It turned my stomach. I leaned against the door of a buzzing freezer, the glass cool on my forehead, and that was the first time one of those women talked to me.

She was wearing one of those pioneer dresses, a somber child in one hand and discount chicken in the other. Gary said he heard one of the older ones stole a microwave once, held between her knees under her skirt. Just waddled right out, held up by the others, and no one dared to call any of them on it. This one walked down the frozen food aisle though, passed behind me close enough that I could smell the herbs of the homemade soap they all used. I watched her out of the corner of my eye. She had a kid hanging off her, its hand wound into a white scarf covered in stars that was draped across her shoulders. She paused, studying the bags of freezer burnt peas, and I heard her, in a whisper thick with their accent.

"The dark will consume you."

I flinched back into the freezer door, elbow banging the

glass. She didn't react though, just lifted out some peas and continued walking. The kid looked at me for a second before being pulled down the aisle, staring, like kids do. Rod was right. I had to get it together if I was hallucinating in the Independent.

I called Gary from my truck, shivering while I scraped at the ice that had crept back across the inside of the windshield. There was a clear spot the size of my fist when he finally picked up.

"What the hell did you give me man?"

"Hey relax, it was just benzos from a buddy's script. Nothing crazy. Why, you all right?"

"Yeah." I ground my teeth. "No, it's fine, just thought I was hearing shit for a minute."

"Nah, they were nothing that'd make you trip like that. Don't worry. Maybe it's all those sick birds you've been dealing with."

"Yeah, maybe."

As Gary talked me down the woman came out of the mall, child and bag in hand, and joined a group of other women dressed like her. Black dresses, thick plain coats. The frost had receded enough to be able to see them as a van pulled up and they climbed in. I swore she looked straight at me before closing the door.

It could just be the birds. I shook it off easily enough, promising myself to cut down on buying off Gary for a while. That didn't last long. A week later I was at the bar with Rod and Natasha after work, sucking back rye and cokes in weary silence after a day of hauling dead birds off Jolliffe Island.

Rod took a deep breath, greying eyebrows rising on his tan face as he tucked cash into the bill folder and stood to leave. "See you back at it tomorrow. You better be leaving your truck here tonight, Alex."

I didn't think Natasha would hear my grumbled

response, but she frowned, eyes glassy, hands worrying blue felt mittens covered in stars. "If you spray your brains across the snow, it will be months before they can convince another biologist to come up here. It's like the plagues of Egypt. I have a flight back in January, and that's really pushing how long I can keep up the fight."

I snorted. "Yeah, wouldn't want my death to keep you up here."

She shook her head. "I am counting the days. The geese are in rough shape, and then all the other shit. That guy from the mine cornered me on my way out of the station yesterday. Wouldn't stop asking why I haven't answered his texts."

"Yeah yeah, the guy from the mine." I drowned her voice out. She went home with this guy months ago, wasted, and I was sick of hearing her freak out about him.

"You're being an asshole."

"Well what do you want me to do, Tash? Report it to the cops if he's bothering you."

"His brother works—no, forget it." Her mouth trembled, then flattened. She didn't look me in the face the rest of the time we were there.

Not wanting to piss Rod off more, I left my truck and stumbled home through soft, thick snowfall, footprints tracing a drunken line quickly erased. It was warm for December, the low clouds yellowing where they passed over the city lights. I took Frame Lake trail, staring up at them until I tripped over a snow-covered shopping cart on the edge of the children's park. Four dark eyes stared out from a heap on the bench, and a laugh that morphed into a slow bubbling cough. They watched as I blundered to my feet, laughing, snow sliding off a star-covered blanket wound around their lumpy forms. It was unnerving. It was disgusting.

"What are you looking at," I mumbled.

"Your silence makes you complicit." One voice rasped in the snowfall.

"Fight the dark, or it will consume you." The other woman called.

"What the hell, are you following me? Leave me alone." I barked, kicking their cart over and stumbling away.

They were crazy, I wasn't complicit in anything. But this time the words rang inside my head as I walked the rest of the way to my place and lay staring at the stained ceiling. I dreamt the girl from Gary's place was burying me in the snow, packing it around my face, into my throat, docile and passive while a blinding sun burned furiously over her head.

After that, I flushed the pills, trying not to think of what they'd do out in the lake. I took the empty rye bottles to the recycling, poured out the ones sitting on my counter. The next week I took vitamin D religiously, paid $17 for a pithy orange every other day to stave it off, but still couldn't shake the women or the words from my head, and now I could feel the threat. The dim twilight of day was no reprieve from the gasping black herons that chased my dreams, their eyes followed me from the shadows of the street, the research station, the Independent.

A day later a thaw came through and melted all the snow. Yellowknife grew darker, the meagre light swallowed in the black ground. Warmest December on record, the news said. The rocky soil began collapsing under the weight of the water, deep sinkholes appearing in town, dragging trees into stagnant pools. With the thaw, piles of birds showed up, skeletal, their moulting feathers dark with grime. The smell followed me around. It was in the air outside the bar after work, the taste of it was in the fish I ate, in the dull look the girl's bruised eyes gave me from under her hair when I ended up back at Gary's, pacing across the filthy carpet.

"It's the birds, Gary, it's gotta be. I can't cope man, I'm

a fucking conservation biologist, but there's nothing to conserve, just piles of dead birds waiting for incineration at the station and they ...." *And they're watching me, Gary.* I swallowed hard. "They just keep getting bigger."

"Take it easy Alex." He took a hit off his joint. "When's the last time you took a break. Go south for a while. Relax. Meet some ladies or something. Take the edge off. The darkness up here gets to you."

Gary patted the girl's head at the last and her eyes flicked to me, massive pupils pinning me for a second before lolling back. I raked a hand through my hair. I wanted nothing more than to get out, away from the dead birds and Natasha's fragility and this drugged up girl haunting Gary's apartment.

"Rod said runway's too flooded to fly out now."

"Take highway 3."

It was the first time I heard her say anything. Her inky pupils fixed on me again, two points of impenetrable and absolute dark.

"If the runway's washed out, the highway will be too."

"Drive slow," she murmured.

"Lucy, baby." Her eyes bored into mine as Gary rubbed her shoulder, crooning to her. "You don't need to worry about this."

My skin crawled as he pushed her against the wall and laughed, taking another hit. I left Gary, heart racing as I slammed the house door behind me. The yard and the street were empty, the air was thick with wet rot and death, and the black of Lucy's stare.

Highway 3 it was. I peeled out and drove to the Petro-Can for gas and food, stepping over a dead goose that lay on the threshold, teeming with insects revived by the thaw. I bought a map, tracing the highway circling Great Slave Lake, connecting Yellowknife to Edmonton. Safe haven in about eighteen hours—without any detours. A long drive. I was so preoccupied with the map I nearly ran into him. Or her. I honestly don't know. It was a kid, maybe fourteen, standing behind my truck with their hands in a coat that hung off them, a broken nose and split lip. Unbothered as the sparrows in the Independent by the hell around them, a chain of tiny silver stars dangling from one ear. Under the bright lights swarming with awakened beetles, the fever of righteousness burned in their dark eyes.

"You can't run. All must fight."

I fumbled with the truck door and fishtailed out of the parking lot, making for the highway. The road was slippery with frost, eye glare glinting from the abyss outside my headlights, but I drove as fast as I could without losing control.

Less than two hours in, the dark lunged up, swallowing the road and the truck, my arms and head and knees battered on the way down its jagged throat, voices of the hoarse birds battering the inside of my skull, until it stopped in an aching quiet. It was hard to breathe through the stench of decay, to focus on the dash lights dimming in front of me. Glass tinkling off my arm as I moved a scraped hand to the broken window.

Sodden earth.

I laughed, releasing the seatbelt and slumping against the wet door. Not some monstrous stomach. I had rolled the truck.

Climbing out of the passenger window I stood in a black crater under a star-filled sky, the road crumbled into wet earth that sucked at my boots, twisting my legs as I staggered away. The field guides all said to stay in the vehicle but the smell was overpowering, so I climbed up to the highway and kept going, nose buried in my jacket. Yellowknife was probably closer than Fort Providence, but being alone in empty territory was already a dead man's game.

Up the first hill I caught sight of smoke, the thin column of a campfire rising against the stars, and the relief was overpowering. Enough to ignore the clusters of writhing moths on the thin trees as I stumbled through them, enough to push out the smell of death in the air. I chased the smoke curling from the tops of the black trees to a clearing, and didn't slow at the voices, or the number of shadowed figures, or the bonfire. Only when the dark mounds I thought were boulders resolved into great piles of dead birds. And by then it was too late.

Bony fingers dug into my bruised arm.

"You left them all to suffer." The voice of the herons spat at me from the mouth of a white-haired woman with broad shoulders, holding me in place. "You saw them be consumed, and were silent."

"Get off me!" I shoved at her, and another pair of hands closed over my shoulders. It was the woman from the Independent who gripped my forearm, eyes red, expression blank. None responded to my shouts as I was dragged forward, pushed inside the circle of murmuring and weeping women. The limp webbed feet of a snow goose dangled as one of them placed its body into the fire to burn. Others sat resolute, wrapping the bodies of dead ptarmigans and sparrows with star-covered ribbons. The more I struggled, the more hands gripped me, thrusting me down at the edge of the pile, beaks and wings under my knees and hands, decomposing and stinking. I vomited into the mess.

"You're all fucking crazy," I gasped. "It's just a bird flu."

"It's bigger than that. You have seen the darkness that led to the destruction of these birds." The light of the fire glinted off her teeth as she spoke, holding a ribbon out to me. "All must fight to bind it, free the lightbringers."

I sat retching, pinned. A heavy woman with matted hair lay a murre into the fire, a thick bubbling cough hugging around her sobs. Snot flooded from my burning sinuses as the murre contorted and charred, and the flames lapped a swollen human face, dark hair burning in a spray of embers. I knew that face. Feathers crisped to ash, eyeliner to soot, her eyes staring naked from the fire. Anger threaded through fear. It wasn't my fault, I had nothing to do with her. Nothing to do with any of these women. None of their problems were my fault. I wrenched out of the woman's grasp and aimed for the smallest girl in the circle, her body bouncing off mine with a crack as I broke through, escaping their fetid pile.

Cries pealed over my thundering feet, but quickly drowned in a deep groan that rumbled in the earth and echoed in the sky. I should never have looked back. Two points of light peered out of the night, so bright I could hear the pain. Tendrils crept from the ground, full of disease and violence and greed and collapsing earth, swimming through the frighteningly warm air, choking the stars from the night, and it was only then, in the fear of my own death that I understood that they were right. They couldn't fight it alone.

The last thing I saw was a flash of Lucy's eyes, grey as a heron, and then the dark consumed me.

IN THE GULF, THE NIGHT COMES DOWN

SIOBHAN CARROLL

THE INVITATION CAME IN THE PARKING LOT, AS THE parents picked up their kids from Quiz Team practice.

"We're going sailing next week," Mrs. Gotter pronounced. She was a big woman who moved in a cloud of perfume and spoke like a wine glass being struck with a spoon. "Alan would love it if Sam could come."

Sami stared at the strange gash Mrs. Gotter's lipstick made around her mouth and tried to figure out why a cloud seemed to have descended over the day. Beside them, they could feel their mother leaning forward, straining like a dog on a leash.

No, Sami thought, *please, say no,* but Mom smiled and said, "Sami would love that."

Afterward, Mom listened to Sami's objections with a grim set to her face. "We can't turn them down now," she said in her Most Reasonable Voice. "I already said you could go." Outside the car window, the Vancouver streets smeared by, grey and wet and green.

Finally, Sami said, "You could have *asked* me."

"You just complained that you didn't have many friends at Carnarvon," Mom said, still being Reasonable. "This is a chance to get to know people better." She peered at the traffic lights and muttered a curse at a cyclist skidding around the corner. Then her brow furrowed. "Why don't you want to go? You like Alan, don't you?"

Sami did like Alan. Alan liked anime and WotC books and had shown Sami a spot to hide under the stairs where the mean kids never looked. He'd taught Sami how to play *Magic the Gathering* and didn't mind that they didn't have money to buy expansion packs. Alan was the only person at Carnarvon Prep Sami had thought about talking to about Everything, though of course they hadn't. Sami had made the mistake of saying too much in the past, and here the stakes were higher.

Carnarvon Preparatory was an all-boy's school, first, foremost, and always. Some of Sami's relatives had gone to Carnarvon, back in a misty past that didn't matter to Sami but did to mom's Aunt Magrid, who had agreed to pay their fees. 'It's the best school in the province,' Mom had told Sami when they received the acceptance call, her face alive with delight for the first time in many years. They needed something good in their lives and this was it: a chance at a new school, a university scholarship, and somewhere beyond that, a future where Sami's stomach wouldn't tighten every time the recess bell rang or the rent came due.

"Why don't you want to go? Is it Alan?" A panicked gleam had entered Mom's eyes. In another second, Warrior Mom would arrive, and Sami would have to try to head her off before she made a high-pitched call to the principal. And if the principal did nothing, what then? If Sami withdrew from Carnarvon, Aunt Magrid might stick Mom with the tuition bill, and that would be Not Good.

"I like Alan," Sami said hastily. "He's fine. I just don't like ...." What could they say? They knew Alan's family had a boat they sailed through the Gulf Islands every year, in one of the weeks when Alan's father was back in town. Alan said he looked forward to it every year, his voice sounding cheerful but unreal, like the chorus in an advertising jingle.

"Boats," they said, weakly.

"Is that all?" Mom turned the steering wheel vigorously, swerving the car into an empty lane. "You'll get used to it. And," she said, Being Positive, "you'll have a great time."

Mom talked about what Sami should pack for the trip, what they should wear, how they should act, until Sami reached over and turned the radio back up. "I like this song," they explained, even though it was some Taylor Swift thing they detested. Sami turned back to staring through the rain-lashed window.

You can't make things okay just by pretending they are, Sami thought at their mom. *You can't.* Like most of Sami's thoughts, the words lodged in their throat like a ball of spiked glass, neither to be swallowed nor spoken aloud.

Why didn't Sami want to go? The dread rising within them was formless, a cloud over water. They put their hand over their stomach, trying to let the words well up from wherever they were hidden. *Because it will be bad,* they thought. *The sailing trip will be bad.*

As usual, they were right.

～

THEY MET Alan's family in the dockside parking lot, on a crisp morning that smelled of sea. Alan's father was a big, bronzed man with a hearty smile. Beside him, Alan was eager and happy, and Mrs. Gotter ("Call me Aurora!") was a cloud of smiles. They looked like a photograph of a family.

As the grownups talked to each other, Alan helped Sami put their lifejacket on. "Dock rules," he said. "They won't let you walk to the boat without it."

The jacket made it awkward for Sami to hug Mom

goodbye. It felt strange to do this in front of Alan, even though they knew Alan had parents too. Mom said, "If anything goes wrong, call me." Lines of tension had formed around her eyes. It was as if all Sami's worries from the previous day had passed to her, leaving Sami excited.

Mom didn't have a lifejacket so she waved goodbye from the gate, one hand clamped over her hair to keep the wind from blowing it into her eyes.

"Call me Tom," said Alan's father, pulling Sami aboard with a hard tug. "Ever been on a boat before?"

Sami had, but Tom seemed like a man who liked to explain things. They watched, patiently, as Tom pointed out the starboard and the port side, the bow, and the stern.

There wasn't much to see on the boat, but Sami admired it all anyway. The GPS locator and radio, the cramped wood-panelled cabin area with its shut-away beds and tiny galley kitchen, the deck seating area with its blue cushions and coils of rope, and finally, the bow, which you could only get to by stepping gingerly between the guard wires and the cabin.

Sami knew Alan's family didn't have money the way other Carnarvon families did, though they had more than Sami's family, and looking around the boat they could see evidence of this: the stains on the seat cushions, the generic brand of cereal in the cupboard. It made Sami feel guilty to notice these things. It made them wonder what people noticed about Sami.

Sami and Alan sat on the bow as they sailed out, feeling the spray dash against their faces, talking anime over the rumble of the engine as Tom steered them out of the dock and toward the islands.

Over dinner, Sami helped Alan's mom serve hard, salty pasta onto tin galley plates. Dinner conversation consisted of Tom talking while Alan and Alan's mom nodded. Tom listed the names of the countries he'd visited since he'd last seen them; the hotels he'd eaten at; and the money he'd spent at this or that restaurant.

Listening to Tom talk, Sami felt a weight settle in their chest. In Sami's luggage was their mother's envelope with $300 to cover dinner for Alan's family on the last day; that was a third of the rent on their East Van apartment. The white envelope was not worth the hope their mother had invested in it. It would not be enough.

Night was different on the water. In the gulf, the night comes down like a curtain. The West Coast's familiar purple and pink sunset was masked by clouds that screened the moon from view. Darkness rolled over the waves like an answer to a terrible question.

In the cabin, Sami lay limply on the thin mattress, a piece of driftwood carried by the waves, and tried not to think about the envelope, or about the way their face already hurt from smiling. From time to time, the wooden shutter sealing them into the bunk pressed against their arm as the sea rolled them one way, then the other.

This will all be over soon, Sami told themself. This was the mantra that got them through their last year at Grayson Secondary, and through Lord Selkirk Elementary before that. The sailing trip would only last seven days; and school would only last another four and a half years. If they got a scholarship, Sami could move somewhere else, and pay for themself, and Mom wouldn't need to worry so much about bills. They could all finally be whatever they wanted to be.

They repeated their mantra as the boat swung back and forth, until night smothered Sami in darkness and pressed its thumbs into their eyes.

∼

GANGES HARBOUR WAS TOURISTY, Tom said, so they weren't going to spend much time there. Sami looked longingly at the souvenir shop with bins of polished stones gleaming in the sunlight, but Alan was following his father toward the fishing shop, so Sami had to go too.

"You boys should go look at the market," Alan's mom said after they'd spent a while looking at fishing tackle. Sami tried not to wince at the 'boys' part of the sentence.

"Sorry about my mom," Alan said as they walked toward a row of market tents. "She's just like that."

Alan had been with Sami when they ran into their kinda-friends from Grayson. He knew what pronouns Sami used outside of school, but he'd never followed up, never asked questions, and Sami had never said anything either. Sami knew how to play by these rules; they were familiar, if sad. But now this comment: was Alan saying he was okay with Sami being how they were? Had he told his mom? What should Sami say back?

"What do you mean?" Forcing the words out made Sami feel cold. Once words were out there, you couldn't call them back.

Alan shrugged and looked at the horizon. "Aw, nothing," he said. "You know how parents are."

"Yeah," Sami said. A mixture of relief and disappointment settled over them like a blanket. "I know."

ON THE THIRD DAY, the weather turned. The sea became choppier; the bow slammed against the waves. Tom had wanted to sail but the winds were too high, which put him in a bad mood; their progress was slow, which made things worse. At the breakfast table, he snapped at Alan's mother for making too much noise cleaning dishes. He told Alan he needed to help more. Sami leaned back against the hard, barely-cushioned bench and tried to disappear.

They were in what Tom called the 'real' Gulf Islands

now: wind-scraped boulders of rock and twisted arbutus trees hunching above the waves. There were no harbours here, no touristy places. Sami's phone had long since lost any signal. When night swept in, they tried to use the phone as a light to read by in their tiny-bed coffin, but the swell and plunge of the ocean was too much for their stomach. The ocean didn't care that Sami wanted to sleep, or Tom wanted to sail, or that Alan had become quiet and sick-looking, or Alan's mother had stopped singing as she did the dishes and barely spoke at all. The trip still had four days left.

Day four brought better weather, but the boat had to wait for the tides to slacken to sail between islands. Perched on the edge of the boat, Sami watched small black whirlpools form around the hull as the boat slipped between rocky crags. Under the boat's shadow, purple starfish clung to beds of mussels, oblivious to their passage.

"This was one of Brother Twelve's islands," Tom told Sami. He'd told Sami to take the rudder, and so Sami had, eyeing the rocky coastline nervously. Alan watched them awkwardly from his seat on the leeboard side, half-hidden behind Tom's shoulder. After a few minutes he got up and darted under the boom to flop on the cushions beside Sami, in the direction Tom was looking in when he wasn't studying the waves.

"Brother Twelve was a pirate," Alan said. "It's in the book." He'd been reading a Gulf Island history book Tom had picked up at Ganges, though his father no longer seemed interested in it.

"A cultist," Tom corrected. "A sex cultist, they say," he laughed to himself. Sami smiled tightly.

"Well," Alan said doggedly, "he stole gold anyway, and hid it. They say he buried it somewhere around here."

"Like an Oak Island thing?" For a moment Sami's attention was snatched away from the smooth wood of the rudder. They'd loved the Oak Island story since reading *The Hand of Robin Squires* in Grade Six. Imagine stumbling across a buried treasure. Imagine accidentally triggering a trap when you tried to dig it out. Imagine a mine shaft filling with water, the water filling with silt, leaving only glimpses of the mysteries below. There were things like that in the world, somewhere. Maybe even in places like this.

"Totally." Alan's face reflected back the gleam of Sami's excitement. "And not just him, either. There were a bunch of cults around here, crazy witch stuff—"

"Brother Twelve had a mistress called Madam Z," Tom said loudly, taking over the story. "She got up to all kinds of crazy things." He paused, waiting for some kind of sign that Sami and Alan didn't give. His mouth twisted as he went on. "Real crazy lady, that one."

"Dad," Alan said warily.

Tom laughed, and Sami had the sense they'd just steered past a rock of a different kind. "Ah, no worries kid," he said to Alan. His voice had a contemptuous ring to it. "You guys are too young for that kind of thing." Deflated, Alan turned to look at the shoreline, the excitement over buried treasure gone from his face.

Was Sami's father like this? Sami didn't often think about their own father, who'd left when they were still a baby. He'd gone to make money in Asia and stopped communicating with Sami's mom soon afterward. He'd had other kids since then, but he'd never wanted to know Sami and Sami didn't want to know him. Is this what it would have been like, if he'd stayed?

"Alan? Do you want to take the rudder?" Sami said, but Alan didn't look around.

"Nah," Tom said. "You're good at this. Best if you keep your hand on it, kid." He pointed ahead at a blazingly white strip of beach that interrupted the cliffs. "We'll drop anchor there."

~

THE GULF ISLANDS were famous for their white beaches, made up from broken shards of seashells. From a distance, it looked like a beach that might show up in a Black Panther movie, CGI-beautiful; someplace you'd never get to go. But Sami was here, crunching across the beach in Alan's wake. They'd tried taking off their shoes and walking on the impossible whiteness, but the shell-sand pricked and sliced at their feet, forcing them to put their runners back on.

A beautiful white beach you can't walk on, Sami thought. And then they felt guilty, because they knew they should appreciate this opportunity. They should appreciate everything. It's just that sometimes, they didn't.

"Come over here," Tom said. "Sam, I'll show you how to put up the tent." So Sami had to follow Tom up the beach into the woods, while Alan stayed behind, kicking shell-bits in waves of rattling spray.

"Alan tells me you're good at math," Tom said as Sami waited, holding the tent poles. Sami's job was to hand the poles to Tom one by one and watch how Tom put them up.

"I guess," Sami said. They knew they were good at math. And English, and Social Studies. They didn't have a choice not to be.

"I wish Alan would take a leaf from your playbook," Tom said, connecting the poles together. "He just doesn't work hard enough. I tell him: you've got to study more. Like this Sami kid: scholarship student, works hard. How much did they give you for scholarships, anyway?"

"I don't know," Sami said uncomfortably. *Not enough*, they thought.

"Don't even know how much, huh?" Tom said, a hint of scorn in his voice. "Must be nice."

Sami could feel the pull of wanting to please Tom: *of*

course I know how much. But they knew Mom wouldn't want them talking about finances. The silence stretched.

"I told Alan, you could be getting those scholarships too, you know? If you worked harder." Tom put his hand out for another pole. Sami gave it to him. "But he doesn't listen to me. He's still watching cartoon shows, can you believe that?" He wiped his hands together.

"Anyway," Tom said, admiring his work. "I'm hoping you can be a good influence on him, right?"

Saying 'yes' would feel like a betrayal of Alan, so Sami made a 'huh' noise instead. Not that it mattered. Tom was reaching for the tent covering now, putting it on.

"Pull on that piece," he ordered, and Sami reached for the canvas, automatically doing exactly what Tom wanted.

"I FOUND SOMETHING," Alan said when Sami returned to the beach. There was a strange light in his eyes. "Come check it out."

"What is it?" Sami called after him, but Alan wouldn't answer. He'd walked to the massive bounders at the beach's edge and was clambering up, using his hands as well as his feet to traverse the massive slabs of sandstone. Sami followed him, the stone rough and cold under their palms.

The rock sheet at the top of the boulders was uneven, cracked and pitted with the occasional pool of green water. On the slope Sami had to crawl on all fours, clinging to outcroppings as their runners skidded on the sandstone.

"Here," Alan said jubilantly. He was pointing to a strange, triangular indentation in the rock. "Doesn't that look like an arrow?"

Sami looked at the triangle. "It's definitely cut out," they said, dubiously.

"That's what I thought," Alan said. "So I followed it

back." He pointed in the direction of the 'arrow', toward a lichen-crusted pillar of rock at the edge of the trees.

"Here," Alan said triumphantly. He pointed to a line on the face of the rock. "Doesn't this look like writing?"

"Maybe," Sami said. To them it looked more like the beginnings of a weird geometrical pattern. Alan's excitement was obvious, but something about the conversation with Tom had soured Sami's stomach. They couldn't recapture the feeling they'd had on the boat, that anything could happen.

"We should dig here," Alan said. Sami looked at the rock beneath their feet, baffled. "Or around here," Alan corrected. "In the woods on the other side."

"We don't have shovels."

"What are you," Alan scoffed. "Lazy?" There was a note in his voice that Sami hadn't heard before. "We'll use pieces of wood." He scrambled down the rock into the scraggly line of trees, not waiting to see if Sami would follow.

Sami followed reluctantly. This was kid's stuff they were doing, pretending magical things could happen just because you wanted them to. There was no treasure here; just pine needles and dirt. But Alan wanted them to stay, and Alan was their only friend at Carnarvon, so that meant Sami had to scrape uselessly at the dirt with a piece of bark until Alan got bored.

Alan didn't get bored. He wanted to try a new scraping every few paces, for no apparent reason. Sami didn't know what time it was—they'd left their useless phone on the boat for safekeeping—but the light was fading from the sky.

"We should go back," Sami said. They'd left it as long as they could. The sun was low on the horizon; the birds were calling in the branches around them, warning of nightfall. They didn't want to clamber over the rocks in the dark.

Alan threw his branch down in frustration. For once, he looked like his dad.

"I can't believe you're just going to give up on this," Alan said. "This could be really cool."

"It could, but it's not," Sami said, and they knew as soon as the words left their mouth that they were making a mistake. This was bitter Sami coming out; the Sami who hated everything. Nobody liked that version of Sami; not even them. "We've been looking around for over an hour because of your dumb lines. There's nothing here."

"Are you calling me dumb?" Alan sounded angry and also pleased, like he'd been looking for an opportunity to get mad.

"No," Sami said. "Of course not." But Alan didn't care.

"Just because you're a scholarship kid, you think you're so smart," Alan said, the words coming out in a rush. "But you're not. You don't work harder than me. You've been looking for an excuse to quit digging since we started." He kicked a rock. "So go back to the boat," he sneered. "I'll finish this."

"Finish what?" Sami said. "Looking for buried treasure in the dark? That's—" they wanted to say 'dumb' but steered themselves away in time. "Crazy."

"I'm not crazy," Alan said. "Aren't you the one who got kicked out of your last school for going nuts on people? *That's* crazy."

Sami couldn't breathe. "That's not what happened," they said after a moment.

"Whatever." Alan turned away from Sami, dismissing them.

Sami walked to the beach in a rage. The sandstone seemed to recede under them like a dream.

"Oh, you're back," said Alan's mom. She peered over Sami's shoulder. "Where's Alan?"

I don't care, Sami thought, but of course they couldn't say that. "Coming," they said, and walked over to help Tom with the fire.

～

IT WASN'T CRAZY, *what happened at Grayson,* Sami thought. When people called you names every day, when they made fun of you and pushed you against lockers, and asked if nonbinary meant you wanted to cut your dick off, it wasn't crazy to hit one of them. Just one time, in the bathroom. Not one of the bullies either, one of the ordinary kids who thought they could get away with it because making fun of you had become the normal thing to do. One of the kids who used to be your friend. And it wasn't crazy to keep hitting them either, because you're bigger, and know you will win this fight, because it can feel good to see fear in someone else's eyes for a change. And after, when you wipe the blood off your trembling hands, when you look in the mirror, you think: See. I'm not different after all. I'm *mean.* Just like you.

"Did he say what he was doing?" Alan's mom said. To Tom she said: "I think we should go look for him. He doesn't have a flashlight."

"He's got a phone," Tom said dismissively.

"It doesn't work out here," Mrs. Gotter pointed out. She looked toward the cliffs. "I'll go look for him," she said, but her feet didn't move.

The night above them prickled with stars. The temperature was dropping quickly and the forest around them rustled in the wind. The anger was ebbing out of Sami. In its place, unease was setting in. What if Alan didn't come back? What if he'd fallen in the dark? The cliffs weren't very high but the rocks were slippery. It could be easy to hit your head, or turn an ankle in one of those crevices. What if—

"I'm back," Alan said triumphantly. He was limping slightly. He carried something with him in his left hand. At first Sami thought it was Alan's phone, but no—the phone was clutched in Alan's right hand, its flashlight blazing.

"Great," Tom said. "You missed dinner."

Alan shot Sami a look as his mom fussed over him. "You left too soon," he said, and smirked.

"What?" The unease in Sami's chest had changed to something different.

"Look." Alan held the object in his second hand up, illuminating it with his phone. "I found it under a slab of rock. Near the writing."

"Writing?" Tom leaned forward, peering at the thing in Alan's hands. He began to laugh. "Seriously, kid. You never seen a beer bottle before?"

Alan's mouth turned into a firm line. "It's not a beer bottle." He held it up further. "I found it buried near these weird markings."

The bottle did look old. It was made of dark glass, too thick to be a beer bottle, or at least any Sami had seen. They turned it over in their hands as Alan tried to convince his parents.

"The book said the Egyptian cult buried spirit bottles around here," Alan said. "It was part of their defences for their treasure." He gestured at the bottle. "We found this near a pillar with writing on it." Tom laughed.

"Sami saw it too," Alan insisted. He looked to Sami for support. Sami shrugged.

"Didn't look like writing to me," they said truthfully, the bottle cold in their hands. Was it normal for a glass bottle to feel this cold? Like ice was radiating out of it.

"We should go back tomorrow," Alan said desperately. "I can show you guys exactly where I found it."

"We have to leave tomorrow, sweetie," Mrs. Gotter said diplomatically. "We can't miss the tide. You know that."

"That's right, son," Tom said. He checked his watch. "We should turn in."

"Fine." Alan took the bottle out of Sami's hands. Sami felt a sensation of loss as the bottle left their hands, but, the bottle wasn't Sami's after all. They had given up too soon. "I'll go back myself. Before we sail."

～

SAMI WOKE FIRST. The early morning air was chilly and bright, and they could no longer wait in their too-warm sleeping bag. Beside them, Alan was still snoring. The Gulf Island history book he'd been carrying around had a section on cults; a lot of it crazy stuff, like Tom had said. The bottle cult Alan had mentioned only appeared once: *"The breakaway Ket Cult claimed to retain possession of several bottles containing genies, which they would use to defend their island."*

Carefully, Sami picked up the glass bottle from where Alan had stashed it on top of his clothing. It looked like an old medicine bottle, stoppered with an ancient cork. Holding it to the light, Sami could see something at its bottom: a pile of twigs, maybe; or a clump of hair.

"What are you doing?" Alan was leaning on his elbow, watching Sami.

"Checking out the bottle," Sami said, because that was obvious. "It isn't a beer bottle, for sure."

"I already knew that." Alan pushed himself out of the sleeping bag and held out his hand. "Give it back."

I want to keep the bottle, Sami thought. It wasn't a wish. Just a thought. Alan's face clouded over.

"On second thought, you keep it," he said. "I'll need both hands to climb, anyway."

A chill ran up Sami's spine. "You can take it," he said, offering the bottle to Alan.

"Nah," Alan said. "You should stay here," he said before

Sami could say anything. "I need you to tell my parents where I've gone."

"Won't they be mad?" *Won't your dad be mad,* Sami meant.

Alan shrugged. "Dunno, don't care." He turned away from Sami to dress.

A few minutes later, Tom's voice cut through the space between them. "You kids are up? Great. You can help me take down the tents."

Alan seemed to sag into himself. There was no way he would stand up to his dad in daylight, Sami knew. There was no way either of them would.

"Moving slow, Alan!" Tom said. "Watch Sam here. He's a smart kid. He knows what to do." And Sami stood in the spotlight of Tom's attention, pulling apart the poles while Alan looked on miserably, hating Sami for something they didn't want.

I'm going to lose Alan as a friend, Sami thought. Maybe they already had. Because Sami was secretly crazy, or weird. But also because Tom liked setting the two of them against each other. Though Sami didn't want Tom's attention, here he was, doing exactly what Tom wanted, because things were safer that way. And there were still two days to go.

Alan was quiet as they returned to the boat. He said nothing as they sailed away from the island and whatever-it-was he'd found. He forgot to ask Sami for the bottle back.

That night, Sami lay on his bunk and examined the bottle in the light of his phone. It was an old bottle left behind by a previous group of campers, nothing more.

Still, as night covered them, Sami reached out for the bottle in the dark, feeling the icy cold of its surface. *I wish Tom would stop bothering us,* they thought impulsively. But Tom wouldn't. It wasn't in his nature. Nor was it in the nature of kids at school to stop bothering Sami, or Aunt Magrid, wanting them to conform to their idea of a proper young man. Even Mom, wanting Sami to come on this trip in the first place. *I wish they'd all leave me alone.*

The night washing over the boat was thick and black and full of the smell of sea. In the fragment of a nightmare, Sami thought that they knew what the inside of the bottle smelled like, now: seaweed and old rage, stoppered up. And then their thoughts stalked off, leaving Sami behind, to dream and wait for day.

~

"HAVE YOU SEEN DAD?"

Sami squinted at the light. Alan was standing on the other side of the bunk door, phone in hand. It was early morning.

"No?" Sami rolled over, trying to make sense of things. Their head hurt.

"He must have got up in the middle of the night to check the anchor." Alan swallowed, his face pale and worried. "We can't find him."

That didn't make sense. There wasn't anywhere to hide on this boat. Then Sami came awake and realized what Alan was saying. This was bad. Really bad.

They got up and stumbled through the cabin. The floor was wet and everything reeked of seaweed. Had the boat sprung a leak? No, the water would be seeping in if that was the case. This was water like someone had walked into the cabin in wet boots, trailing sand and weeds in their wake.

The deck was empty. The boat rocked at anchor, the sun seeping across the horizon, and everything was terribly peaceful. Except near the helm was a dark spot of liquid that looked a bit like blood.

Mrs. Gotter came up to join them. "I guess we should call the Coast Guard," she said after a moment. "That's what we should do, right?" When Sami and Alan didn't say

87

anything, she walked over to the radio and started punching buttons. "Do either of you know how this works?" Alan, white-faced, went to help her.

Sami went back to their bunk. The bottle was still lying there, ice-cold but innocent looking. They put their hand on the bottle, trying to quell the panic rising inside them. Who else had they thought about last night? Tom, sure, but also the kids at school. Also Aunt Magrid. Also—

I don't mean it, Sami thought desperately, wrapping their fingers around the bottle's neck. *Whatever you did, undo it. Bring them back.*

Alan poked his head into the cabin. "We got the Coast Guard," he said. "They're going to send someone."

"That's good," Sami said, but the sense of dread was still rising inside them. The bottle was so cold. How did it count wishes anyway? Had Tom been wish number two?

"Hey," Alan said from the deck, his voice excited. "I have a cell signal! Check your phone, Sami. Maybe you have one too."

Numbly, Sami reached for their phone, which flared to life. 16 missed calls, all within the last 6 hours. They didn't recognize the number.

This is a wrong number, Sami thought desperately, as they opened their voice mail. *It doesn't mean something's happened back home. It doesn't mean something's happened to Mom.* But the icy feeling in their stomach was growing stronger, saying that whatever this was, it was bad, very bad.

As usual, that feeling was right.

FANCY DAD

DAVID NICKLE

SAFFRON HAD A THEORY, AND SHE CONFIRMED IT WITH A
quick search on her phone, at once concealed and shaded
with a cupped hand. No protection here on the north side
of the river. Not from the blinding glare of the late afternoon, late summer sun. Not from detection, from the
improbable occupants of the table across the Dockside
Pub's nearly empty upper patio.

The woman sitting across that table from their boss was
not a mistress.

"See?"

Saffron passed the phone to Rick, and he did see: a
photo of the two of them, dressed for dinner at the Board
of Trade's annual award ceremony from two years past—
which would have been just after the acquisition, when
Farcomm went private.

Rick tapped the link to the board's website for more
details, and sure enough, the cutline read: *Incoming Farcomm
President Fred Perkins and Judy Perkins.*

Beyond the shared surname, it did not specify their
relationship.

Rick thought she was a daughter, given how much

younger she appeared, but Saffron guessed, given the plunging neckline of her gown and the jewellery she was wearing, that she was a wife.

Rick wondered aloud if she was either of those, why it was that Fred Perkins looked so ....

"Furtive?" Saffron suggested.

"Like he's got something to hide," said Rick.

"Waiting for his indictment."

Rick nodded. "Like half of Muskoka."

"You'd know about all *that* better than me," she deadpanned, and Rick laughed, hard.

He must have laughed too hard, because the mysterious Judy Perkins looked over at them and waved. Fred asked who she was waving at, looked over, and after a moment of confusion, broke into a broad, delighted smile.

"Saffy!" he hollered. "And ...."

"Rick," said Rick. He had started with Farcomm three months ago, and Saffron had only worked there a little longer. But Saffron was an assistant to the CFO, and had sat in on enough meetings that Fred would know *her* by sight.

Fred snapped his fingers. "Rick Edmonds! From ...."

"Legal," said Rick.

Fred stood. He wore green khaki shorts and a blue golf shirt that hung over shoulders much narrower than Rick would have guessed, from the round face and chubby cheeks that he presented on those Teams meetings. Below the neck and without a suit jacket, Fred Perkins' body was a bony jumble—a wraith of a man, nearly skeletal.

"Saffy and Ricky!" he said. "Fancy seeing you two all the way up here! We thought we were doing so well, hiding out in Huntsville."

"*Family,*" said Judy, with a big smile. "But now the jig's up. Care to join us?"

Rick pulled a chair over from their table and brought

their drinks, thinking at once what an excellent idea, and also a terrible idea it was to come over and sit with Fred Perkins and his ....

His wife? His daughter?

There *was* a similarity in their round faces, something common to their eyes that suggested lineage. Didn't some married couples come to mirror one another over the years? Didn't, for that matter, the children of all of Canada's old-money families look a bit alike to begin with? She was young—very young—but monied old men and very young women sometimes did that, get married.

Judy skidded her chair around the table to make room as Saffron sat.

"I'm Judy," she said, and Rick would have said "I know," and the jig would've been up, if Saffron hadn't saved him.

"I'm Saffron Willis," she said. "This is Rick Edmonds."

"Hi," he said.

"Saffy and Ricky, summering in the Muskokas." Judy offered a half-smile. "And you both work at Farcomm?" She wrinkled her nose. "Better call H.R." she said.

Fred Perkins tucked his bony knees back under the table and waved a hand dismissively.

"I won't tell if you won't."

Saffron smiled. "Lips are sealed," she said.

Judy looked at Rick, tipping her chin up as though regarding him through the bottom of bifocals.

"So you're the lawyer," she said, as though a lawyer was just what they'd been waiting for, and turned to Fred. "Should we get another jug?"

Fred picked up the nearly empty bottle of white, portioned off the rest into his and Judy's glasses and waved it at their server as she came up the stairs.

"Two more glasses for our friends here," Fred said. "They'll be joining us so everything on one tab."

The server nodded. "Have those burgers in a jiff," she said to Rick.

He sipped his beer as Saffron answered Fred's questions about what they were doing here.

"We're hanging out with Rick's aunt at her place on Boynton Lake," Saffron said, and when Fred asked why Rick's aunt wasn't with them, explained "She's coming up tomorrow, so we thought we'd eat here before heading over and opening the place up," and then added, "We haven't actually," when Fred asked whether she'd yet met Rick's aunt. "Not face to face."

"So this is a new thing," said Judy. "Between you two. Meeting the *family* for the first time. *Tra la la.*"

"Not that new," Rick said. "Saff and I knew each other in high school."

"It's true," said Saffron. "We even dated a bit."

"But this is our first time up north together," Rick said and Saffron smiled.

"My first time up north, period," she said.

Saffron and Rick's burgers arrived with the new bottle of wine. Fred poured generously, and Judy made a toast to office romance, and Fred added one to warm September nights. Rick hadn't finished his beer yet but set it aside and raised his wine glass.

"Boynton Lake, eh?" Fred topped up Judy's glass and then his own. "That's out by Dwight, isn't it?"

"That's right," said Rick. "Just the other side. My aunt has a cottage there. Right on the water."

"Nice," said Judy.

"Nice-ish," said Rick. "It's pretty primitive—runs on a gas generator. No indoor plumbing."

"Cell service?" asked Judy and Rick shrugged, made a see-saw motion with his hand.

"She must have had that place for a long time," Fred said, and Rick nodded.

"A very long time," he said.

Saffron interjected: "You have a place up here?"

"Dad does," said Judy.

Ah. Rick took a bite from his hamburger.

Judy Perkins was a daughter. The twenty-something round-faced daughter of the seventy-something round-faced president. Oldest child? Middle sister? Rick washed the burger down with the dregs of his beer: hunger, thirst, and curiosity, all satisfied.

"Which lake is your place on?" asked Saffron. "There are a few very fancy ones nearby, aren't there?"

Fred set his elbows on the table, braided his fingers like a hammock and rested his chin there. He made a show of batting his eyes.

"Rousseau?" He pronounced it the French way—Roo-Sow, the way you'd talk about Jean-Jacques the French philosopher, rather than Ross-Owe, the way everyone referred to the fanciest of the blue-blood, old-money cottage lakes nearby.

"Oh stop messing with them," said Judy, and then to Rick: "It's not Lake Rousseau." She picked up the bottle and topped up her glass and Fred's. "Whatever you might think. Dad's not *that* fancy."

Judy hovered the bottle over Rick's half-empty glass. He smiled and shook his head. "More for us," Judy said, and filled Saffron's glass before she could stop her.

Fred sat back and lifted his wine glass in a toast. "To Fancy Dad!" he shouted, and Judy raised her glass too.

"To Fancy Dad!"

Saffron held her glass up and Rick raised his, and they clinked them together as Judy and Fred drained their wine and slammed their glasses on the table. Fred's glass survived, Judy's did not.

"Where did the wine go?" Fred poked the neck of the

near-dead bottle, while Judy regarded the broken stem of her glass.

"Fancy *that*," she said softly, "fancy Dad."

"To hell with him," said Fred, and with that he lifted the bottle by the neck and tilted it back to drain the rest of it, to kill it. "To hell with his goddam *brood*."

It was then that the server caught Rick's eye.

She was standing at the top of the stairs, holding a card reader, and when she saw him looking she tilted her head and motioned with the reader to come over. Rick pushed his chair back and excused himself, and followed her a few steps down the stairs.

"Sorry," he said when they faced each other. She waved it off.

"Nothing to be sorry about," she said. "I ought to be the one apologizing to you." She lifted the card reader, so Rick could see the little paper printout tucked underneath. "I'm bringing up the bill."

The poor woman looked miserable here in the shadow of the stairwell: exhausted, a little embarrassed ... and Rick couldn't be sure, but she seemed more than a little bit afraid.

"I just want you to know it's not you and your wife," she said. "It's those two ... the things they're doing. The *talk*. We're a family restaurant, you know?"

"The talk?"

"Oh yeah. Last couple of tables cashed out at the bar downstairs."

Rick climbed up a step and looked back, and confirmed: the upper patio wasn't just sparse—it was empty, except for the three of them. One slouched back in his chair, one turning the bell of her broken wine glass on the table—between them, Saffron, her back to Rick, her shoulders raised into that shallow 'V' shape of coiling tension Rick had seen just often enough.

What were they saying to her now, to make her flinch like that?

"They were here long before I came on shift," she continued. "If I had been, I tell you I'd have been sure to cut them off long ago."

"How much have they had?" Rick asked, and when she showed him the bill he whistled.

"That's nearly a grand," said Rick.

She looked at the bill, and turned the reader over in her hands.

"So here's the thing," she said. "Those two have to leave."

"Of course," said Rick.

"And neither's safe to drive."

"Can't you call them a cab?"

She shook her head. "Cab company won't take those ones."

"That bad?"

The server met Rick's eye. "They have to *go*," she said, and Rick put it together.

"You want *us* to drive them?"

She didn't answer, and didn't break eye contact either while Rick worked out the rest.

Someone on the day shift had over-served a couple of patrons, and here on the afternoon-evening shift someone else had over-served them again. Over-over served them.

And there was the source of that fear in her eye.

What was more terrifying than a threat of liability? Not much, he thought.

"Sure," Rick said, "we'll get them home."

The server waited for Rick to get back to his seat before she came out with the bill. Accompanying her was a tall blond-haired man with a thick moustache and more than a bit of a gut. Fred demanded to know why they couldn't have another bottle of wine and Judy asked if it was about the broken glass and said she'd pay for it. "We don't want to go home," she said, and Fred said, "Not yet," and Judy said, "Not ever!"

The man stepped in closer as the server stood firm and set the bill on the table.

Fred picked it up, squinted at the number, and sighed, took the card reader, set a tip, and tapped his card.

The tall man waited while the four of them gathered themselves together and followed as they made their way down the stairs and through the crowded bar. He sidled up to Rick.

"Thank you for getting those two away," he said, "for getting them *home*."

"No problem," Rick said, and the tall man said: "If you say so."

Saffron was near enough to hear and cocked her head curiously. Rick explained what he'd agreed to. Her nostrils flared and her shoulders rose, but she nodded. What else could they do?

The tall man stood at the door while they made their way into the parking lot, watching as they caught up with Fred, making for a blood red Tesla—Saffron on the left, Rick on the right. The lights flashed and the door started to open, and Saffron put a hand on Fred's arm. She whispered something to him, and he shook his head.

"I won't show up with some ... some other, someone else ... driving that car. He wouldn't ...." Fred paused. "*That* wouldn't do."

His voice trembled as he said that, and when Saffron pressed him on it ever so gently, his eyes squeezed and his face reddened. Rick wondered if Fred was ashamed of bringing the car back to the house ... or Judy ....

Maybe she *was* a mistress?

Whatever she was to Fred Perkins, whatever the cause

... it seemed to Rick as though here in the parking lot, the prospect was enough that the old man might actually cry.

But he did not.

When Saffron interjected and said he could ride in their car, they both could, Fred took a breath, and that round face of his brightened; and when Rick said, "That's right," Fred nodded, as though he had just worked something out.

"We drive with you," he said. "Leave the family car here!"

"Someone can get it in the morning," said Saffron. "If you like, we can pick you up and drive you back for it."

Rick felt the cool touch of Judy's hand on his forearm.

"That won't be necessary" she said.

Rick looked back to see the pub door swing shut behind the tall man. He delicately pulled his arm away. "I don't think either of you should drive," he said and Judy laughed.

"Not what I meant," she said, and leaned over, her shoulder tight against his. She looked at him with a squinting smile and whispered close to his ear:

"Maybe we'll just *leave it here*. That's what I meant." She made another grab for his arm, but he pulled back fast enough that her nails only scraped his elbow.

"*Forever,*" she drawled.

"I like this idea!" said Fred and put his own hand on Saffron's shoulder, gave a squeeze. "Judy and I'll ride in the back."

"A clean getaway!" Judy exclaimed.

Laughing, Fred pulled his hand away and Judy steadied herself, and they made their way across the lot to Rick and Saffron's rental car.

"Where to?" said Rick as he started the engine, and from the dark behind them, Fred answered: "I'll tell you on the way."

~

"Turn right," said Fred, "and north," he demanded at the next intersection, and "east" after they'd passed through the northern, newer end of town, and "keep going," as the lights of town faded behind them and night bloomed.

"Are we really going to do it this time?" Judy sounded far away and sleepy, like a child on a long car trip.

"Looks like," said Fred, his voice just as distant, but tremulous and old.

In the mirror, Rick caught a movement, and when he looked he saw the back of Fred's head, silhouetted briefly by headlights. He sat back as a truck overtook them. "Can you go a little faster?" he snapped in a notably sharper tone.

Obediently, Rick tapped the gas and the car shook with minuscule acceleration, and he flinched at a touch on his leg before he clocked it as Saffron's hand. The dashboard glow caught a sidelong smile as she met Rick's eye and tilted her head back to ask Fred:

"Is it much farther?"

"I don't imagine," Fred said.

Judy leaned forward between the front seats. When she asked, "How far is Lake Boynton?" Rick's mouth went dry, as he considered what should have been obvious from the start.

"Not far. We'll pass it in a few minutes."

"Then we're not far at all," she said, and as she put a cold hand on Rick's shoulder, Fred added: "You know the way from here, Ricky."

"The way to where?" asked Rick, knowing the answer before Fred said it:

"The way to your auntie's."

~

RICK KNEW the way to his aunt's place very well. He had travelled it long before he had driven it, the first-time riding in a child's car-seat behind his parents, fast through Dwight, past the General Store, past the campground ... and after what seemed like hours but was only minutes, slowing along the two-lane blacktop to find the narrow dirt road to Boynton Lake where it pierced the forest's edge.

By the time he was old enough to take the wheel, he knew to take that skinny little road from the highway slowly. Even in daylight, Rick knew to take the rutted drive to his aunt's cottage slower still.

In the dark of night ... with his boss looming at his back ....

"No rush," said Fred when Rick apologized for the slow crawl over the rocky, root-choked drive to their cottage. "Just get us there in one piece."

Rick pulled the car up next to the tarp-covered woodpile across from the cottage, and he turned off the engine, and the headlights too, and darkness closed in.

"I'm going to have to get things started up," said Rick. "There's a generator in the shed and when I get it going, we can get some lights on. Do you want to wait here?"

"Let's just go inside," said Judy, and Fred said: "Don't bother with the lights."

Rick undid his seatbelt and got out of the car, fished his phone out of his pocket and turned on the light. It cast a weak glow that didn't carry far, and he saw by a blue-white firefly flare across the hood of the car, that Saffron had done the same. Her phone light winked and shifted along the car-length.

"Mr. Perkins?" she said, and the light disappeared behind the car. "Fred? Judy?"

Rick swung his own light, until it flashed on the rear driver's-side door.

It hung open, and when he bent to look inside, he confirmed: the back seat was empty. They were fast, those two.

Rick shut the door and carefully made his way around the back of the car. Saffron met him at the trunk. He put his arms around her, held her tightly enough that he couldn't tell which one of them was trembling.

"I'm sorry," he whispered into her ear.

"Sorry for what?"

"For laughing too loud."

Saffron laughed, but softly.

"Then 'twas my wry wit that did us in," she said.

"I ruined our trip," he said. "Your first trip up here."

"Don't sweat it, love. The pub was nearly empty. There they were. There we were. And Fred's our *boss*. We were trapped."

"From the start."

"There was no saying no," she said.

And somewhere in the dark, glass shattered.

Saffron and Rick raised their phones, casting dim blue glare on the tangle of pine branches between the car and the cottage. Rick took her hand and led them along the path. He called out: "Is everyone okay?" and Saffron called out: "Mr. Perkins?"

Their lights found the kitchen door to the cottage closed, and when Rick tried it, locked. He pocketed his phone, fished the keys out, and undid both lock and bolt.

Saffron's phone-light flickered across his aunt's old kitchen: the propane stove, the hand-pump faucet over the sink basin ....

The ancient refrigerator, its curved single door open— the bent back of Judy Perkins, the top of her head, peeked around its edges.

"It's not even on!" she said, and from somewhere in the

dark beyond the fridge, Fred answered: "What did you expect?"

Judy stood and shut the refrigerator door, her face like a moon as she turned to the light.

"Oh hey. Got anything to eat?"

There were some groceries in the trunk of the car, along with a case of beer, a bottle of gin and three bottles of wine they'd picked up on the way out of the city that morning.

"Nothing," said Rick. He stepped around Saffron into the kitchen, then gave Judy a wide berth as he moved into the great room. The ceiling was high and there were tall windows and French doors opening onto the deck. Across the lake lights flickered, but there was no moon, so the A-frame outline of the opening was barely visible and the living room was a black abyss.

"So this is the Edmonds ranch."

Fred Perkins was lying flat on the couch, death-pale legs crossed, his feet propped on one arm while his head rolled toward them on the other. He squinted and his lips pursed as though tasting something bitter.

"Mind turning that away, Saffy? Better yet, off?"

Saffron dropped her hand to her side so the light played across the floor.

"This is the cottage all right," said Rick. "How did you get in, if you don't mind my asking?"

"Ah, you probably heard. Made a bit of mischief."

Rick stepped toward the window and just by the French doors, felt the crunch of broken glass underfoot. The pane next to the left doorhandle was empty, and Rick felt shards at the edge. The door was still off its latch, and Rick pulled it shut.

"You were in a hurry, I see," he said.

"My bad," said Judy.

"We *were* in a hurry," said Fred, "to get inside. Now Saffy my dear, I meant what I said."

"I'm sorry?"

"Turn that Goddamn light *off.*"

Saffron fumbled for the off switch, and in the second or two it took her to find it, light flashed across the rest of the place: the shelves of books and boardgames, the steep ladder to the sleeping loft, the doors to the two spare bedrooms ... the shattered window, and finally, the constellations of broken glass that sparkled on the floor around Rick's feet.

"Thank you," said Fred in the fresh dark. "And thank you, Rick, for putting us up, seeing us safe. Very lucky to've run into you both today."

Rick looked at the lights across the lake. He wondered, were they new? The far side of the lake was pretty wild as he recalled. Rocks and cliffs on the shore and a thick mane of forest on top ... going back for *miles.*

"Sorry about the window," said Judy. "You're not going to sue us, are you?"

She was beside him—not touching this time, but close enough that she could get the message when Rick shook his head.

"Thanks," she said. "You should come back from the window."

Rick shook his head again, looked back out at the water.

"Huh," he said aloud.

Another mystery solved: The lights across the water weren't new cottages that'd somehow gone up on the cliff over the summer. The lights were moving. There were three of them, not far off the water by their shimmering reflections.

"No really," she said. "Hide yourself."

"What is it?" said Fred, and Rick heard a familiar creaking of the springs in the old sofa.

There came another sound across the lake: a splashing,

as from paddles. The lights spread farther apart, then grew nearer one another. Now Judy's hand did fall on Rick's arm, and she squeezed hard above the elbow and their feet crunched on the glass as her cold, sharp fingers tugged him backward.

In the dark behind them, Fred Perkins let out something like a moan.

Rick did not look back.

They *were* torches. At the prows of boats—long row boats. They made a rasping sound as one after another, they hit the rocky beach in front of the cabin. Someone climbed out.

"The old man found us," whispered Judy.

"Don't let him hear you call him that," whispered Fred.

The old man, then.

Rick thought he was tall, or would have been were he not bent so. Because of that, it was hard to say exactly how tall.

He held a torch in one hand—in the other, a long paddle, blade dragged through the shallow water and onto the beach. But paddles and torches came in many sizes, and while these ones seemed like toys in his grip ... who could say?

The torchlight fell on his face. It was a round face, and maybe a giant one. Like the face of a moon, half-lit by the late-summer sun at the end of that torch.

His hair was bone-white, or maybe really as red as the fire made it look ... cut close to his skull, the ends flickering like tiny, flaming suns. His mouth a pinched sphincter, eyes angry black stones under tangled brows, in that huge, ancient face creased and cratered by decades ... by eons, maybe.

He looked to the cottage, and that tight little mouth unfolded into a thin, toothless smile.

"Oh father," wailed Fred, and Judy wailed along with

him: "Dad!" and as the old man drew closer, as the other boats emptied of the rest of his round-faced, dark-eyed young, the light of their fires grew to a luminous, annihilating blaze.

~

THE MORNING SKY was dark in comparison.

Pillows of low cloud covered the late summer sun, and the wind off the lake was icy enough for fleeces. Saffron was surprised at the chill. Unlike Rick she had not spent much time around the lakes and woods north of Barrie, had no sense of the old rhythms of this land and its seasons.

Rick made coffee in the French press, found old plastic plates and mugs and a tray for them. They took their breakfast through the wreckage of the night's abduction— the re-acquisition—in the great room and onto the deck, sipped coffee and watched the steel-grey water where it began to ripple.

"Brother and sister," said Saffron, shaking her head. "Huh."

"Should have guessed," said Rick.

"Would have been a long shot, given the age difference."

"Maybe she's older than she looks," said Rick, and Saffron said, "Maybe hard living aged Fred," and when she tried to check birthdays on her phone, she huffed, "Still no signal," and put it away. Saffron frowned.

"How old would their ... dad have to be?"

"Fancy dad," said Rick as the ripples spread and water rolled, and a familiar form rose from Lake Boynton. "It's a proper Muskoka mystery."

Saffron started to laugh, but it caught in her throat when she followed Rick's gaze to the lake.

"But you know," said Rick, "Auntie's been up here *forever*."

He waved, and as she shook the skunk weed off her shoulders and spat phlegmy algae onto the shore, Auntie waved back.

"I'm sure she can shed some light."

THE BLACK FOX

DAVID DEMCHUK

I SHOULD START BY SAYING THAT I DID NOT CARE FOR MY younger sister Helen. She had been raised by my father to be loud and rude and selfish, and heedless of the feelings of others. Even so, she was my sister, and we endured each other as siblings often do. After our father abandoned us and I took a house on the other side of the lake, she would visit every Sunday for dinner and tell me of the goings-on in the nearby village, the fits of temper and petty dramas and not-so-secret affairs. I avoided the village. I kept to myself. I had no interest in these people and their little lives, but I let her tell her stories. They were no different from the serials on the radio that we overheard as children when our parents thought we were snug in our beds. She took great delight in telling them, acting out their conversations, the way that Father had delighted in telling us stories from the war, the men he killed, the women and girls he had raped, the children he likely sired. He and his men kept a collection of fingers, taken from the hands of the living before they became the hands of the dead. He grinned as he told these grisly tales, soup dribbling from his lips to his chin. We had brothers and sisters out there, children of women who had suffered in shame. The thought of all this disgusted me, but I kept my silence, as our mother kept hers. Besides, what was there to say about crimes so long in the past.

Helen and our father were cut from the same cloth, just as I took after our mother. She had vanished first, years earlier, leaving her things and leaving us, her brutish husband and her two children, to head off to a new life, or perhaps an old one—back to her family in Budapest, I always assumed. Then ten years of just the three of us: my father and Helen and me. And then he disappeared as well. A few months of half-hearted searching from the local constabulary, with patronizing reassurances that he would return. I quietly hoped he wouldn't, and he never did. Helen stayed in the old house, with the radio and rose-patterned wing chair and mother's piano, and I moved to my little cottage with the vines of roses and violets painted along the ceiling edge and the wood fires that coughed smoke into the house whenever birds tried to nest in the flue.

One Sunday in midwinter, after a few evenings of gentle snow that had frosted the pines and crusted along the edge of the lake, Helen confided a curious thing between bites of the roast that I had prepared. "I heard cries from outside the house last night," she said. "I looked out the window and in the moonlight I saw a fox, black as the night, not twenty feet from the door. If it weren't for the snow, I would never have seen it. It stood there, staring at me, then it turned and trotted back toward the lake." She fiddled with the green silk scarf around her neck threaded through with whispers of gold. It had been mother's. "I should never have worn this, now I'm afraid I'm going to soil it."

"You could always leave it here with me," I replied. "You know I'll take better care of it." She smiled smugly and sipped from her wine glass. I shrugged, lifted a spoonful of peas from my plate. "Are you sure it was a fox?" I asked. "Not a lost dog from one of the farms?" Foxes were rare in our part of the country, and black ones even more so. I had never seen one myself.

"I know what I saw," she said, slicing off another forkful of beef, the red juice pooling on her plate next to the potatoes. "Besides, we know all the dogs from the farms around here, and they know us. Do you think it was a sign from Father?" While never a religious man, our father had been fiercely superstitious like his father before him, attributing every bad turn in his life to witchery and the evil eye. Our mother's departure was the work of the devil, or so he always believed.

"A sign, after all these years?" I replied. "I doubt it. Don't go near it though. 'If a creature comes to you after dark, feed but never follow,' that's what Mother always said. Toss it a carrot and it will be on its way." As children we were told many tales of woodland spirits that made mischief in the guise of forest creatures. We grew older and heard darker tales of souls who were wronged in life and who used such means to return for revenge. Our father never shared in these stories. I think they frightened him.

"I'll chase it off with a broom, thank you, and keep my carrots to myself." She swallowed the morsel of beef and washed it down with wine. "I suppose you think it's a message from her."

"From Mother? Don't be silly," I said. But I wondered, just for a moment: who else might it be?

TWO NIGHTS LATER, I was heating myself a cup of bone broth to warm me while I sewed, when I heard a shriek and a yowl from just outside the door. It was like a child being skinned alive. 'What in God's name,' I sighed, then set down the ladle, moved the pot off the fire, and peered out into the darkness. At the end of the walk, in the clear white light of the waning moon, I saw a small slender animal, etched out of coal, with gleaming gold eyes. The black fox. He clenched something wet and raggedy in his mouth.

I hesitated, then moved to the door and opened it. The fox did not stir.

"Hello there," I said. "I'm told you've been to see my sister. What brings you here?"

He sat himself down on the snow and waited, staring at me expectantly.

"Oh, how silly of me," I said, more to myself than to him, then hurried to the larder and brought out a large yellow parsnip that had started to soften. "Here you go," I said and tossed the parsnip to the fox. He dropped the ragged thing from his mouth and caught the parsnip firmly, then turned and ran from the house, out towards the lake.

It was a blustery night, gusts of wind tossing sprays of snow hither and thither. I threw on my coat and stepped outside, careful to prop the door open so that it couldn't slam shut behind me. I scurried out to see what the fox had dropped, prepared to find a rabbit or a pheasant. Instead, I was surprised to see my mother's green silk scarf that Helen had worn to dinner. 'She must have lost it on her way back home,' I thought. It was just like her to care so little for something that I could love. I brought it inside and laid it out flat on a large clean cloth. It didn't look too much the worse for wear. There was a small spot of blood along the edge, she had stained it during our dinner after all. I sighed and dabbed at it with a few drops of salted water, smoothed it out and folded the cloth over it, then poured my cup of broth and sat down for the evening, embroidery in hand. Not even an hour passed before I could barely keep my eyes open. I doused the fire, dimmed the lights, and bundled myself into bed.

~

I AWOKE to a morning crisp and clear, the sun shining brightly off a new dusting of snow. I peeked out the front window to find the fox's tracks gone. Had it been a dream? I looked at the cloth on my table, tugged at the folds. The scarf was nestled inside, dry and undamaged, the spot of blood now faded to a dusty pink. It was real, so the fox must have been real as well. I thought to call my sister about her carelessness with the scarf, but decided I could chide her at our next meal instead.

The day itself passed without event. I had several altar cloths from the village church that required repair to the fabric and decoration. Two of them had been made by my mother, I recognized her handiwork as soon as I saw them. The priest had sent some vestments that also required mending. I cut up some lamb sausage and tossed it in a pot for stew with a few potatoes, carrots, and leek, then perched myself down by the fire to start my work. By the time I finished, the sun had crept down past the horizon's edge, casting a fiery red on the wisps of cloud in the west. I set aside my work and went about preparing my meal. The moment I sat down to eat, the scream of the fox once again pierced the silence, startling and unsettling me. It was closer than the night before, its screech like that of a baby being torn limb from limb. I poked my head into the larder, found a pair of beets tinged with powdery mould, then opened the door. The fox indeed was closer, halfway up the walk. Once again it held something in its mouth, something that caught the light and glittered.

"Hello again," I said. "What's that you have there?" I held up the beets by their greens so that he could see them. "Perhaps you'd like to trade?"

He seated himself like an obedient dog, then moved its muzzle to the ground and dropped the shiny trinket on the snow. 'He's bringing me gifts,' I thought. 'Like a crow would. Very strange behaviour for a fox.'

"What a clever lad," I said, and tossed him the beets. He let them land nearby, then nudged them up against each other, picked them up by their stalks and ran off with them swinging from his mouth, hurtling back towards the water as if I might give chase.

I approached the spot where he had sat and saw a woman's ring nestled in the snow, a finely wrought band of buttery gold set with a large orange topaz. My mother's ring, one of her favourites that I hadn't seen for years. Not since before she left us. "What does this mean?" I shouted after the fox. "Where is my mother? Where is my sister?" I almost ran after it, out into the dark and down to the water's edge, when I heard my mother's voice in my ear.

Feed but never follow.

I stepped back inside my little cottage, picked up the telephone and dialled my sister's number. The line rang and rang but no one answered. It was far too late for me to try to walk to her house, and the weather too uncertain. I decided she was already asleep. I calmed myself, sat down and ate my stew and wiped the bowl clean with a piece of crusty bread. I set the dishes aside and went to bed early, my mother's ring under my pillow. I barely slept. Whenever I closed my eyes, I imagined the black fox waiting outside my door—watching, listening. Hungering for something more than parsnips and beets.

THE NEXT MORNING I phoned my sister again. Still no answer. I called the church and asked if they would be kind enough to send a car for me. They knew I had no vehicle, and it was urgent that I see my sister. An hour later Father Miroslav himself pulled up in a black Ford sedan, helped me into the passenger seat and started off down the gravel road to my parents' old house. I was so surprised, I assumed he would have asked one of the church workers to attend to me, yet he seemed happy to come out to the lakeside. I asked him to go slowly so that I could see if something looked strange or out of place; however, the fresh-fallen snow and patches of ice made everything seem unfamiliar. The road was sometimes hard to detect, and he struggled to keep us out of the ditch, but eventually we arrived at the driveway that led to the front of the house. I saw no footprints, no sign of anyone entering or leaving. We pulled up in front of the porch and Father Miroslav honked the horn. The house remained silent and still.

"Would you like me to go in with you?" he asked. "I can at least help you up the steps."

"No, thank you," I replied. "You stay here where it's warm. If I need you, I will come for you." He clasped my hand kindly, and I stepped out of the car into the shrill white sunlight. I shielded my eyes as I walked up to the front door, knocked, waited, knocked again. I turned the knob, gave a little push. It was unlocked. I swung it open carefully, peered inside.

"Helen?" I called. Nothing, not even a sigh.

I stomped the snow off my boots and entered, walked from room to room. I wondered for a moment if I had just missed her, if we somehow passed each other on the narrow road to town, but I could soon tell she had not been in the house for several days. Her bed was made, her nightgown draped over a nearby chair. A window was cracked open, and a swirl of snow collected on the white wooden sill. A stack of supper dishes sat in the sink unwashed. The bathroom was tidy, the shower curtain pulled aside, the towels and facecloths dry to the touch. The lid was closed on mother's piano. The wing chair had a slim hardcover book half-open, face-down on its seat: a British murder mystery, with a circle of empty chairs on the cover, one knocked down to the ground. My mother's name was written in the top corner of the title page. I tucked the book into my coat pocket and continued my search. I hoped to find a note, or an appointment marked on a calendar, but no such luck. I did note, however, that Helen's coat and boots were gone.

I left the house and locked the door with my spare key, then explained the situation to Father Miroslav. He suggested we call the police and ask them to search the area, then wondered himself if she might not have spent a night with a friend or taken an unannounced trip into the city. "I suppose it's possible," I told him, though it seemed unlikely. He kindly drove me back to my home, waited till I opened the door and then I waved him on. He waved back and said he'd call me later. I felt foolish involving him in our family issues, but grateful for his assistance. I resolved that I would wait one more day before calling the police, in case Helen had done something spontaneous and uncharacteristic for the first time in her life. As the day wore on I felt a knot of worry tighten inside my chest. I knew the fox would return at nightfall, and I dreaded whatever new gift he would have for me.

I set about making a light lunch for myself; cold salted chicken and buttered biscuits, and by the time I finished eating I was exhausted. I remembered the mystery novel I'd taken from Helen's chair. I pulled it from the pocket of my coat, looked it over, sat down and started to read it. I was two pages in when I felt the need to rest my eyes. When I opened them again, hours had passed and the room was bone-achingly cold and shrouded in gloom. The wind wailed and battered the windows, shaking them in their frames.

I went to stand and found my legs had tightened and cramped. I moved about the room slowly, switching on lights and fuelling the fire, when a screech came so loud and sharp, from just outside the door, that the storm seemed to hold its breath in fright. I wrapped myself in my coat, grabbed the battery torch from the front closet, and threw open the door. There was the black fox, a few feet away, the snow all around him spattered with ruby droplets. In his mouth he held something fleshy and bloody. I held the torch up to see more clearly, then gasped and recoiled. It was a finger, a long slender finger, chewed off at the knuckle.

I couldn't move, couldn't speak. I could barely understand what I was seeing. Was it my mother's finger, or Helen's? Or was someone else out there on the ice, wounded or worse? I thought of my father and his horrible story about the trophies that he and his men had collected. A sharp icy pain seized my hand, and I glanced down to see that my forefinger was gone. I blinked, and it was back—but how? Then the fox turned and ran, ran out into the night, into the snow and down towards the lake.

I screamed. And then, I couldn't stop myself, I ran after it, trying to keep it in the torch light, following the dribbles of blood bright against the snow, *feed but never follow*, the wind like knives against my face, I slipped and slid but still I ran, closer and closer to the lake, the spot of light from the torch bobbing wildly, until I reached the water's edge. The fox tracks stopped, but there was no fox to be seen. I shone the light off to my left where the pine trees stood in silent judgement. I shone it over to the right where dull dry grasses and shapeless bushes crouched together, smothered in snow. I shone it straight ahead and down into the water and, disbelieving what I saw before me, I moved closer and bent forward, aghast.

There was Helen, under the water, in her coat and boots, eyes glassy, mouth agape, hair floating out from behind her head, hands reaching uselessly towards me.

Clutching her waist was our long-dead father, eye sockets empty, flesh gnawed away from his face and arms, in the flannel work-shirt and heavy grey overalls he wore when working the fields. Wrapped around them both were the skeletal remains of our vanished mother, draped in tatters of cloth that I remembered as the dress she had worn at my last birthday party. Had they all followed the fox down here? Is this how they met their doom?

I crouched down, looked closer at Helen's hands, at my father's, my mother's: each of them missing a finger from their left hand. Before I could even fully form the question in my mind, a brutal blow landed squarely in the centre of my back and knocked me down into the water, my face fully submerged mere inches away from Helen's vacant stare. I tried to pull myself up, but whatever clung between my shoulders dug in its claws and refused to move, it pushed me down deeper into the water so that Helen's useless arms were floating up around my neck and shoulders. The black fox, it had to be. *Feed but never follow.* I screamed and shouted, bursts of bubbles exploding out of me, and then choked as I breathed in icy water. I twisted and flailed and convulsed but it was hopeless. Bright lights shimmered and dimmed behind my eyes, I croaked out one last tiny sound and then slipped into unconsciousness.

SOMETHING STRUCK me across the face, and then struck me again. I howled, gagged, vomited. I felt hard heavy hands push into my chest, felt a rib snap, howled again louder. *She's alive!* somebody shouted. Was it Father Miroslav? *She's breathing, she's moving!* I felt someone turn me onto my side and I vomited again, coughed up water and blood and bile. I shivered all over and then couldn't stop shivering, I couldn't stop crying. My wet clothes were stripped away and I was wrapped in a coat or a blanket, lifted up off the ground and bundled into a car, red flashing lights, men shouting, frosty blasts of static, sudden lurching movement and then the scream of the siren.

A moment later, or maybe longer, I couldn't honestly tell you, a voice close to me called out, *Something's happened, she's bleeding, there's blood everywhere.* Then another voice, older, a few feet away: *Don't stop the car, we've got to keep going, turn on the light.* The light snapped on, blinding, I winced my eyes shut. *I'm looking, I'm looking, I—wait, here it is. It's her finger, something's chewed off her finger.* Someone seized my hand, turned it sharply, wrapped it tight in flannel or wool and clutched it close, afraid to let me go.

I realized then that this was how my father's victims had come to us across land and sea, how they had hunted us down to our doors. The black fox. It was the substance of their souls, an engine of their rage. And, strange as it sounds, the finger had been a taunt, a lure, a trick of time, an inkling of my fate. They wanted me to feel their fear, to follow, to see what they had done. They wanted a witness to their revenge. I shuddered all over and the grip on my hand tightened. The car dipped and rose with the heaving curving road, the siren wailed mournfully, the men around me murmured and sighed, their words lost to me.

I turned my head away from the light and my breathing slowed and grew heavy. I fell freely into a deep dark chasm of sleep. As I did so, I saw the black fox running in front of me, his mouth bloody, his eyes bright, darting through the snow, dancing across the ice, so close I could almost touch him but always, always, just out of reach.

THE KEY TO BLACK CREEK

RORY SAY

THEY HAD NOT BEEN AN HOUR ON THE ROAD WHEN Roland fell quiet and sank down in the back seat. Just as well, thought Adelaide, her nerves somewhat calmed by the sound of restful breathing—a diversion from her better judgement. Still, she couldn't help but turn now and then from the wheel and look back at her blanketed son, as if needing to make sure he was still there.

By the time they passed through Nanaimo, she'd cracked her window and begun to smoke. Another rule broken. She kept her arm outside in the mild night air, but still Roland stirred and sat upright. She turned to him.

"Go on back to sleep," she said. "We're still a ways away."

Ignoring her, Roland put his face to the window and watched the black wall of pines rushing by at their side. Adelaide eyed him in the rear-view.

"Aren't you excited to see where Mom grew up?"

Her son kept quiet, his forehead pressed to the glass.

"Roland?"

"I thought you hated it."

"What?"

"I thought you hated where you were from. I thought you ran away."

Adelaide flicked the end of her cigarette out the window. "Did Dad tell you that?"

Roland said nothing, his attention still held by the outer dark.

"Because I don't want you listening to what Dad tells you about me. Or about anyone else. I know I've told you that before."

"So it isn't true?"

"Is what not true?"

"You don't hate where you're from?"

Adelaide took her eyes from her son and fixed them to the silver patch of highway lit by her headlights. "You know," she said, "there can be good reasons for running from a place."

"Like what?"

"I'll tell you about it some other time."

"Why not now?"

"Because it's your bedtime now. Lie back down and I'll wake you when we get there."

They drove in silence. Every so often a logging truck barrelled by in the opposite direction, nightbound for Victoria, but the road ahead was all their own, at times bereft of streetlights for a stretch of kilometres. Adelaide reaffirmed her grip on the wheel. It was possible to move forward only by neglecting to think about turning back. Luckily she'd had practice; as ever in life, her plan stretched only so far as the moment in front of her.

"What else has your dad told you about me?" The question came out unbidden, voiced as soon as it crossed her mind. Roland gave no answer. He had disappeared again from the rear-view, and when Adelaide looked to the back seat she found his blanket-covered bulk lying there, peacefully breathing.

~

SHE'D SOLD it to him as an overnight journey. An adventure. "Let's pack you a bag, young man," she'd said as she boxed up the rest of the pizza they ordered every Wednesday evening. Their only evening. "I have a little adventure in mind."

He'd looked at her a moment, warily intrigued; their allotted time for the week was up. "What kind of adventure?"

"How about the kind that takes you away from school?" The brightening of his face meant no backing down.

And she hadn't. The rest, so far, was easy—clothes thrown in a gym bag and the bag in the trunk. She had some stowed cash and enough credit on her card to last until they were settled somewhere on the mainland, or until the uniformed hounds Derek was sure to unleash by this time tomorrow dragged them both back to the real world, where she could look forward to another, longer stint in Vancouver Island Correctional.

But what if Derek instead kept quiet when he discovered them gone? What if he—?

Adelaide failed to stop this train of thought. Fears raced through her head like hunted deer in a dark wood. She recalled threats Derek had made that at the time she hadn't considered, but now they resurfaced, bubbling to the forefront of her mind as she stared at the vanishing road, her eyes sore for want of blinking. At least you knew what you'd get when you dealt with cops. All bets were off if her once-beloved gave chase on his own.

This was what she wrestled with as they left Courtenay behind and turned onto the back roads leading to Black Creek. The first sign she saw bearing the name made Adelaide reach again for her cigarettes.

She'd forgotten to what depths night could reach

this far from the city. By now the streetlights had petered out altogether, and all her high beams revealed was a distant mass of swirling darkness. As the narrow road straightened out and stretched on, she was struck for a moment by the uncanny sense of being suspended, of moving interminably in place, from nowhere to nowhere, an infinite span of road ahead and behind.

The car lurched to a stop. Adelaide returned to herself only after the fact, her foot still pressing the brake to the floor.

"Mom?" Roland's voice in her ear was bleary and frightened.

"It's okay," Adelaide said. "I told you I'd wake you when we got there."

And somehow it was true. Dark surrounded them, and yet out the window to the right could barely be seen the foot of a drive, beside which a signpost displayed the illegible address. Adelaide took her foot from the brake and eased them off the road.

"I don't like it," Roland said when the headlights brought into view the squat house, densely enclosed by trees whose tops were lost in the dark. "Mom, I don't want to be here. Can't we go?"

Adelaide heard the tears in his voice. "Be brave," she told him. "We're only here till the morning and then we're off somewhere else. An adventure, remember?"

She got out of the car and opened the back door. Roland let her lift him from his seat, but still he whimpered as he clung to her. These were the moments she never missed.

The dark about them was all but perfect, moon and stars curtained off from the world. Though she wanted its flashlight, Adelaide was wary of turning on her phone, mindful that Derek might already be trying to trace her.

Instead, she groped ahead with one arm as she led Roland across the gravel yard to the front door.

Searching her shoulder bag for the key, the awful thought came to her that it wouldn't work. She'd still had another month in the can when she learned that the Followers of Angelic Light had at last made their ascent. A guard had given her a copy of the *Times Colonist*. "Suicide Cult Claims Eight Outside Courtenay", the headline had read. She'd felt nothing but relief at the time, and she felt the same now. The key to Black Creek was hers upon release. She hadn't yet gotten around to organizing an appraisal, and nor had she until tonight paid a visit herself, despite intermittent harassments from the executor.

But the key worked. Adelaide breathed relief as she stepped from the dark into the dark and flicked the nearest switch.

"Shit."

Of course. What had she been thinking? Roland began to moan as she felt her way along the wall to the kitchen, where the lightswitch was just as useless.

"It's okay," she said, whispering for some reason. "There's nothing to be afraid of. I'm right here with you."

He was crying in earnest now, begging to be taken home. She didn't need to ask which home he meant. Still, for a few seconds she wondered if it might not be a bad idea, if the drive here was adventure enough. The word *kidnapped* had only crept into her consciousness in the last hour, and it frightened her. Maybe if she had Roland back by morning she could explain to Derek that—

But no. There was no reasoning with Derek, who'd assured her on more than one occasion that if she pulled any more of her tricks then she'd never see her son again. He'd make sure of that. To go back now would be to lose her Wednesday nights, and possibly worse.

"We're spending the night here together," she said to

Roland, taking him in her arms and holding him close, "and then we're leaving in the morning. I'll be with you the whole time. I promise."

He tired himself out after a minute. Adelaide took his hand and brought him to the kitchen, guided by the pointed flame of her plastic Bic. The room, revealed by slow degrees, looked eerily unchanged from when she'd last seen it as a teenager—the spotlessly clean mint-green linoleum countertops; the same red-striped breadbox beside the same ancient toaster oven; plates and glasses she'd handwashed countless times stacked in the sink's drying rack—everything neatly kept in its rightful place, almost as if, she thought queasily, it hadn't really been abandoned by the dead.

Taking her hand from Roland's, she put her bag on the counter and felt for the old shoebox in the cupboard above the fridge. It was still there, along with a collection of partially melted candles.

"Here." She handed one to Roland and lit its wick. "Careful you don't burn yourself. And watch for the hot wax."

The boy smiled, forgetting his fear at the novelty of being given fire. He held the candle in front of his face as he led the way to the living room. Adelaide followed.

This room hadn't visibly changed either, the same plain furniture among the same neat sparsity. Still no TV. It was as if pains were taken to preserve what she would rather forget.

"Who's that?" Roland held his candle to the enlarged photograph of the old patriarch himself, Vissarion Stair, adorning the far wall. It was the only picture in the room. At once the warmth of the man's deep voice returned to Adelaide, the leathery smell of his skin, the roughness of his hands when in the dark he—

"Luckily no one you'll ever meet," she said.

"Why won't I meet him?"

"Because he's my grandfather. And he's dead. Like the rest of my family."

As her son studied the picture by the light of his candle, Adelaide fought the impulse to pull him safely out of reach.

"Why didn't you like him?" Roland asked.

"Because," said Adelaide, "he was a bad man."

"He doesn't look like he's bad."

Adelaide almost laughed. But it was true. Her grandfather did not look like a bad man. In fact he looked like what he had been—a leader. He had the sort of firm, strong-boned face people find it easy to put faith in; a gentle, friendly air at odds with his broad shoulders, full chest, and imposing height. He had always dressed well, kept his thick, dark hair neat and his person presentable.

"Looks don't always tell you the whole story."

But it seemed Roland had lost interest. He had moved to the couch and begun to yawn, his candle spilling liquid wax on the armrest. Adelaide took it from him and blew it out.

"Let's get you to bed," she whispered in his ear.

IN THE BATHROOM they took turns standing watch by the toilet. Adelaide offered to get their things from the car, but Roland loudly refused to either go outside or be left in the house. They argued, but not for long; toothbrushing could wait until morning.

On entering her old bedroom, Adelaide didn't know whether to be surprised to find that no trace of her remained. In place of the few belongings she'd left behind there was nothing but the empty cleanliness found in every other room of the house. A neatly-made single bed and a small side table, like the hollowed-out ghost of a bedroom, one that might never have been slept in at all.

Good, she told herself. It brought her some comfort knowing that, as promised, she had died in the eyes of her cult-enslaved parents, that running from this place had enacted a banishment no longer in effect. She thought spitefully of the smug assurances her father had made when she used to threaten her parents with the idea of escape. There was a special room in hell, he'd tell her, for those who spurned the light. No matter where she went or how safe she felt, it would be waiting for her at the end of the road. So long as she ran, it would always be waiting.

Roland tugged himself free of her and crawled on the bed. Adelaide joined him, helping him undress and dropping his clothes in a pile on the cold hardwood. She wanted the bag from the car but had to wait for Roland to fall asleep. More crucially, she needed a smoke.

"Do you still want to know what Dad says?"

"What?"

Roland lay curled under the covers while Adelaide sat atop them.

"In the car you wanted to know what Dad says about you."

"I thought you'd been asleep when I asked that."

"Maybe I was. I can't remember."

"Well, you don't have to tell me. I don't want to know anymore."

It was the truth. Just now the thought of Derek gave her the urge to carry Roland out to the car and put even more distance between them. What had his rage looked like, she wondered, when he'd found out they were gone? But it was better not to wonder. Safer to place trust in the tried-and-true tactic of self-suppression.

"He says that when you were away you went to a place

where the bad people are kept from the good people. Is that true?"

Adelaide's heart heaved. She clenched her eyes shut. Fucking Derek. The one secret he'd agreed to keep from their son.

"It isn't as straightforward as that," she said. "Just because you do a bad thing doesn't make you a bad person."

"What bad thing did you do?" Roland asked.

"Don't worry about that," said Adelaide. "And for God's sake, don't listen to another word your dad says about me."

They fell quiet. Adelaide was sure Roland had fallen asleep when suddenly he asked, "Is it some other time yet?"

"I don't know what you mean."

"You told me in the car that you'd tell me why you ran away from here some other time. Is it some other time now?"

Adelaide smiled, then yawned. "The only time it is now is time for sleep."

"Please."

"I don't think it's something you'd want to know about."

"But I do want to."

Idly, she began stroking her son's fine hair, wondering how long it had been since the last time she'd put him to bed. She took a breath, then plunged.

"Once there was a little girl," she said, "who lived with her family in the middle of nowhere."

Roland turned on his side, pressing his spine into his mother's ribs.

"And this little girl's family had a strange way of looking at the world, different from everyone else."

"Different how?"

"Hush. Go to sleep and I'll tell you." Adelaide waited a moment. "The little girl's family believed that the little girl's grandfather was—special. They believed he could see things no one else could see. Angels, for example, and they believed these angels spoke to him. They believed this because he told them so, and they believed whatever he told them. And what these angels said when they spoke to him was that if he, as well as anyone who followed him, lived their lives in a certain way then they wouldn't really die when they died, but live on forever as spirits in this world while their souls rose to become stars in the sky. But there were problems. In order to make this happen they had to do certain things in life. Things the little girl's grandfather told them to do. Bad things. Things that I ...."

Adelaide's voice died in her throat. What in the world was she telling her son? She sat stone-still against the headboard, wishing she could retract the last few minutes—the last few hours—when the sound of Roland's sleepful breathing reached her. Thank God.

Carefully, she shifted off the bed and crept from the room. In the kitchen she took her smokes from her bag and began to light up as she slid the back door open. Let the car wait till she'd had a single moment of peace.

WHAT STRUCK her as she stepped out into the overgrown backyard was how utterly the night had changed. She could now clearly see by a silvery light the ground ahead, and when she craned her neck she was met with a glinting tapestry that froze her in place. Her cigarette fell to the grass.

Among the numberless stars fixed in the sky were ones that tumbled brightly through the dark, visible for all of a second on their journeys to extinction. And how many of them there were, falling star after falling star, as if the extinguishing of one ignited the next in an endless succession Adelaide recognized as both natural and miraculous. She could neither move nor look away. The idea came to her that she should wake Roland and show him the sky, but now she lay flat on her back in the wild grass and could not stand. All she was able to do was watch the burning movement above, ceaseless, visible and yet unimaginable, the cold white stones of the heavens dismantled at last before her eyes.

Perhaps she slept and awoke without knowing it. Suddenly an iciness spread in her bones and she noticed with a small shock that the night had changed again. The stars, lately so innumerable and luminous, now appeared twice as rare and distantly faint, hardly there at all. Nor did those that remained glint in the slightest or appear to emit the merest light, leaving Adelaide to wonder if any of it was real, if she were not looking at false stars in a false night. There was no moon.

A piercing sound from inside the house brought her to her feet. She fell twice in the renewed dark but was through the open back door and down the hall in seconds. Roland sat screaming in bed. She couldn't see, but when Adelaide went to her son and held him she felt him trembling breathlessly. His high keening blanked her thoughts.

"I'm here with you," she said, running her fingers through his hair and stroking his back. "It was only a dream, Roland, and I'm here with you now. Nothing can hurt you so long as I'm here with you." She wouldn't permit herself to consider whether she was telling him the truth.

All the same, Roland fell quiet after some minutes. Then he said, "It wasn't you that was here." His voice came as if from far away, his face buried in Adelaide's lap.

"You had a bad dream, Roland," she said, her ears pricking at some inaudible sound. "I'm sorry. I went out for a moment but I'm here now."

"Please can we go home?"

"We're leaving in the morning."

"No, now. Please can we go now?"

A sinking sense of defeat kept Adelaide from responding at once. The damage was done even if they left this minute, but it would only be worse if they didn't. In the back of her mind she knew exactly how much worse it could get.

"All right," she whispered, "we can go out to the car and I'll take us home. Let me help you get dressed."

But Roland stayed where he was, a dead weight in her lap. Adelaide sat as calmly as she could, trying to match his even breathing with her own, but she'd become too anxious at the idea of leaving. All about her was a charged stillness, as though she were the subject of motionless observers standing unseen in the dark. She kept herself still and listened, half expecting the quiet to be broken by the sound of sudden movement or the clearing of a throat, a cough. The faces of her family came to her, as did their voices that had so often filled this room.

She needed to leave.

Sliding her legs out from under her son, she placed his head lightly on the pillow. Best to try and carry him while he was still asleep, she decided, but first she collected his clothes from the floor, which she'd take out to the car before returning. She prayed Roland wouldn't wake as she left the room, grabbed her bag from the kitchen, and made for the front door.

The night seemed to have deepened. Adelaide walked blindly down the drive until her feet found the road. How had she missed the car? She turned and walked more slowly back toward the house, feeling the empty air ahead with her one free hand. Finally she dropped her bag and Roland's clothes to the gravel and searched for the car with her lighter's useless flame.

The car was gone.

Even once she realized this beyond doubt she would not believe it. She checked her bag for the keys and dumped the contents on the ground when she couldn't find them. Her mind went briefly black. She walked up and down the drive, frantic now, sure the car would be there the next time she turned, that somehow she'd only missed it, that her keys were misplaced in the backyard or the kitchen. But the car was never there. Her thoughts went to Roland and she ran in a panic back into the house.

He lay where she'd left him. Adelaide stood frozen by his side, wanting to wake him but not wanting him to worry, not wanting to have to tell him about the car, the keys she would not believe were gone.

It wasn't you that was here.

The memory of the words opened a hole inside of her. It was difficult to breathe. She'd begun to panic, and could think of no reason to calm herself. The car was gone, and leaving on foot in the sightless dark was just as unthinkable as staying.

Adelaide sat at the edge of the bed and rested a hand on Roland's back, feeling it rise and gently fall. Her phone had been in the bag she'd upturned on the gravel drive. She envisioned herself getting to her feet to retrieve it, but long minutes passed and she did not move. And who could she call for help?

As she sat in paralysis with her sleeping son, the story she'd told him returned to her, the story of a little girl and her awful family, who wouldn't really die when they died. What had compelled her to say such things? And why had she brought her son to this place from which she'd fled so long ago?

Silence hummed in her ears. She would wait like this while Roland slept. It was a decision she made without thinking. So long as they stayed together in this room, then morning would find them safe. She believed this because she had to believe something. Maybe even the car would be there if only they waited till daylight.

It wasn't you that was here.

She drew her legs up on the mattress, focusing on the silence in the house. How deep it was, a depthless silence that was everywhere, inside her head and out in the night. She thought of the stars she had seen, the ones that skipped in silence across the sky like shining pebbles on a pool of ink, their trails of white fire still imprinted in the black of her mind. Then the image dissolved and she thought of nothing; for the deepening silence was itself a kind of noise, one that muffled thought and rendered her fears irrelevant. Sleepily, she slipped inside of it, knowing that all she had to do was wait. She would sit with her son in the silent dark and wait for the night to end.

HOW LONG DID SHE WAIT? Long enough, apparently, that when she found the room filled with pale sunlight she had forgotten what it was she waited for. She had forgotten the house and the car and the stars in the dark, and she began to recall these things slowly and all at once, as fragments of a dream. Her limbs were leaden; a white fog hung in her head, gradually dispersing as her eyes blinked and took in the room, the bare walls and wooden floor. The emptiness.

Beside her on the bed lay the imprint of her son, a dent in the pillow where his head had rested. How ordinary it appeared, how harmless and horrifying. Adelaide looked at the pillow for a long while before it occurred to her to shout Roland's name and scour the house.

But the house was empty, its quiet broken by the stricken sounds only a mother can make. Through her tears she screamed her son's name and the name of his father. She screamed the names of her own vanished parents, of her grandfather, the names of all those—living and dead— who'd promised her a life in ruin. She screamed until she tasted blood at the back of her throat, and she swallowed and kept screaming.

Heaped in the drive out front were the clothes she'd forgotten from the night before, a pair of child's jeans and a small white shirt. She took these and held them in her arms as if for hope, searching and screaming, soon hysterical so at times she was almost frozen. The car was still gone.

Again and again her search took her back to the room of her youth, where she prayed in spite of herself she'd find her son, awake and ready to be taken home. And when each time she found instead an empty bed, one side still impressed by his weight, the shock of loss struck her as new. Her search then resumed, or repeated, and yet still she returned over and over to where it began.

In any hell that might one day house her, there would be no need for further or more elaborate torments than the sight of that unmade bed in the empty room.

THE NIGHT BIRDS

PREMEE MOHAMED

THE HOUSE WAS HOT—NOT, I SUSPECTED, FOR MY comfort, despite my famously thin and tropical blood, but for the little girl inside, who carried the winter around in her bones. Her foster carer drew me inside, a friendly blob behind my cold-frosted glasses. "Sorry I'm late," I said. "The roads are godawful—it's like we all forgot how to drive."

"Well, it's been a while," Grace said, which was true; Calgary hadn't gotten major snow, the snow of my childhood, in decades. Even a few inches these days sent everybody sliding into the ditch. "Anyway, it's fine. She just got up."

"What?"

"She ... has trouble sleeping at night." Grace's voice was carefully neutral. "She naps during the day."

My glasses finally cleared, revealing the worry in her face. "Well," I said, "let's see how she's doing."

The girl was sitting on her bed, the navy-blue blanket bunched and built up around her to form a kind of nest. Back to the wall, watching the door: it was sad how often you saw traumatized kids repeat the same actions, imprisoned in the atavistic desire to avoid a predator's ambush.

She wore pyjamas in a similar print to the blanket—dancing polar bears and reindeer. Cheery stuff, but she still looked gaunt, harried, pale to the point of translucence. At least Grace had combed and braided the girl's thin, fawn-brown hair.

Grace said, "Serbel? Do you remember Hayley Wilkinson? Your caseworker? You met a week ago."

The girl looked up from the pad of paper in her lap—her black eye hadn't healed, I noticed, but the scrapes and cuts looked better. "Hi, Miss Chan."

"This lady is going to ask you some questions. And I'll be right here, so you won't be alone. Is that all right?"

Serbel nodded. I sat at the desk chair, which put my knees almost up to my eyebrows, but I knew she'd never talk to me if I violated the safe space of her bed.

"You can call me Hayley," I said.

"Hi, Miss Wilkinson," she said without missing a beat.

I smiled. "Whatever makes you feel more comfortable. What've you got there? Can I see?"

She presented me with the pad and I flipped through it, feeling her eyes on me: blue-grey, alight not with anticipation but apprehension. I knew that look too. Kids whose parents abused them for bad grades developed a terror of any kind of evaluation, and a kind of numb resignation—a watchfulness that dissolved into dissociation when they knew they hadn't measured up and the beating was coming.

I like my job, which my friends find bizarre. But it's not as simple as liking kids, which I do, or wanting to bring a hammer down on people who fuck them up; it's also trying to solve puzzles with half the pieces missing, and figuring out how to find the other pieces. And this pad ....

I handed it back, her icy fingers connecting with a little

shock of static electricity, and said, "That's nice, Serbel. Listen—it's okay if you don't remember me. A week isn't a long time, but it can feel like it when big things happen. So I just want you to tell me what happened—why you're not with your family anymore. Can you do that?"

She stared at me; eyes huge. The room filled with golden light—at a quarter to four, *God* I hated winter—and we watched it fade, leaching the bright colours from the pictures on the wall, the covers of the books. Grace flipped the lights on: four LED bulbs in a frosted dome, like a second sun.

Serbel didn't relax; her entire body radiated fight and flight. But she steeled herself and whispered, "The night birds."

GRACE MADE tea and we sat at the kitchen island. It was so quiet I could hear each individual squeak and crunch of a car inching through the snow in the back alley.

Eventually Grace said, "She doesn't like having music or the TV on. She always needs to hear what's happening outside."

"Hypervigilance," I said. "She's talking to you?"

"Now and then." Grace sighed, wrapping her small, powerful hands around her mug. "Always at night ... it bothers her that I sleep when it's dark, so I asked her if she's always slept during the day and stayed up all night, and she said no, only now."

"Has she mentioned these ... 'night birds' before?"

"No."

"Well I don't know what the hell I'm going to put in my report," I said. "They opened up an official child intervention case, and the new process is that you start with family confirmation first." I enclosed my mug in my hands too, but didn't feel much warmer.

Kids always talked to Grace; she was a good carer, in my opinion as well as my experience. I'd seen a hell of a lot of bad ones, some so bad that the child in question needed a second rescue after their first. Bad luck: trauma on top of trauma, trauma squared. But Grace was sedate, giving, thoughtful. She was a soft surface to land on when you'd fallen unexpectedly.

And this kid—Serbel, if that was her real name—had sure taken a tumble. An old fellow had driven her into the downtown police station claiming he'd found her stumbling across the highway in the middle of the night. First thought, of course, is he's the culprit—abducted her, did whatever sick things he needed to do, and changed his mind, hoping she'd be unable to identify him. But his whereabouts had checked out, and at the hospital she had confirmed that he had indeed rescued her.

Which left us with a half-frozen little girl with no identification, unable to tell us when or where she was born, her last name, where her family was. No way to find her in any databases. A nothingness, a cipher. Barefoot and wearing only a shapeless homespun dress made of dirty white wool —not even underwear or socks. They'd whisked that away to check for blood and semen, but I hadn't heard back yet. Probably sitting in a fridge somewhere, victim of the usual backlog.

"*Serbel*," I said. "Do you know what nationality that is? Or if it means something in another language? Obviously she's been taught English, but she's got an accent I've never heard before."

"I didn't think to look it up," Grace said.

It might be one puzzle piece; it might not. There was nothing to go on, and she had been found so profoundly in the middle of nowhere. I couldn't stop thinking about it, how utterly uninhabited the place was, how lucky she'd been that that old guy had been a large animal vet returning from an emergency call at a horse farm with quite literally nothing nearby except fields and unpaved range roads and maybe, here or there, a lonely oil well. It was a blank spot on the map, the closest actual town, Okotoks, more than a hundred kilometres away.

So where had she come from? How far had she run— and how had she survived in the freezing darkness, in her bare feet, on the longest night of the year? It stymied belief. Reminded me of my parents, too, born in the Bahamas and moving here for work in the 90's, their horror at going from their warm little island to this wild, featureless expanse of grass and scrub.

"Wait a minute," I said. "I swear I read something about the residential schools and how the Indigenous kids who were forced to go there sometimes referred to the priests and nuns as crows. Maybe ...."

"You think she was with ... priests?"

"I don't know. There's a lot of tiny deranged rural cults in Alberta, we already know that, but ... maybe a church? No, I don't know what I'm saying. It's like she fell out of the sky." I gulped my tea, catching a glimpse of my reflection in the darkened kitchen window: a furious mask. "I'm sorry. I'm not mad at you. It's just that I have to find her family, and there's ... *nothing.*"

~

IN THIS PLACE
In this
In this pl
In this place there are no clocks. Day drags a plough beneath the yoke of the sun. When the sun is gone so too is the burden, and then it is time to shut the doors and ride

out the night. Another, longer burden. Time is not real, the world is not real, nothing exists in the darkness except what you cannot see: knitting by touch, counting stitches; practicing sums on a chalkboard, listening to the sounds the numbers make. Chalk sounds: *chh chh*, like claws. Like the sound of a hooked beak breaking a songbird's bones.

A liquid darkness

(*Where am I?*)

flowing like the slaty trickle between the ice cliffs of the river, thick and dull, not black, not grey, *dark*, reaching—an upper droplet meeting the lower, the stars going out one by one. Blades of feathers. Then talons, then eyes, hot and red. One final star gone wrong, supernova, a captured disaster in the wet eyes of the—

(*Of the what? Of what? Wake up, wake up, wake up, wake up, it's a dream, wake up*)

Not stars at all but reflections, no relief in the realization, a flame fluttering in the distance over a long-dead city of red ... spires and arches, domes and streets, moated with a lake of burning oil ....

MY SUPERVISOR HAD a cubicle like the rest of us. This had nothing to do with wanting to appear equitable (she reminded us) and everything to do with, verbatim, "The fact that the government never gives us any fucking money." I looked around as we talked, taking in the things she'd pinned to the beige walls: accolades, degrees, reminders, grim little cartoons with no children.

"You have a dozen other cases." Eloise kept her voice down; many of the other caseworkers and support people were on the phone all day, usually with distraught relatives or lawyers. "You *can't* spend all your time on this one. I don't mean that as a suggestion, I mean physically you cannot."

"Look, I know it sounds nuts—"

"Yes. Correct. It does."

"—but I did drive out there and I saw a bunch of trailers parked way up on the slope overlooking the refinery. Someone cut the fence to get in. I just need you to sign off on letting me at least *ask* if they're the right people. We need information about her or our hands are completely tied for family confirmation."

She watched me stonily, a big white woman in three layers of lumpy hand-knit sweater, nothing moving except her eyes. This was her great skill as a Children and Family Services employee: knowing when people were lying. And I was, of course.

I couldn't tell her I suspected I'd seen Serbel's family (never mind what else) in a *dream*; I had told her the little girl mentioned an unusual landmark, and I had figured out on my own that it was the old Lydor refinery, so it was just a matter of driving around till I spotted something unusual in the empty white landscape. The place had been shuttered for decades, oozing who knew what into the soil and rusting to bits while the legal battle went on; no one had a reason to be there.

"Get Grace to release the kid for the day," Eloise muttered. *I don't like this*, her face said, and I tried to say the same with mine. "She can provide positive ID. And I'm not signing off unless you take an escort."

"I don't need—"

"Call Benny Fisher," she said. "And see if he can get one more cop. There's something ...." She shook her head, opened the dark green file folder I'd given her, closed it again. "Nobody reported a kid with her description missing. It's been ... what, nine days? No calls from someone claiming to be dad, mom, uncle, aunt ... not even grand-parents."

"I know." We both knew what that meant; she also knew I wasn't suggesting we return Serbel to the family if we did find them. The preference *is* always to give a kid into kinship care, it's true. It's better for the kid, the family, and the government's bottom line. But sometimes that means removing a kid from one abusive relative and giving them to a different one. And that happened most often in cases like this, where they washed their hands of the runaway, where no one contacted any authorities—called the clinics or emergency rooms or the police.

I'm not wild about cops. Eloise wasn't either. And all I could give them was a few more puzzle pieces about the family: no houses, only trailers and trucks, livestock carriers. They definitely roamed as a practice, not out of panic. They knew how to find a middle of nowhere. They dressed their children in homespun wool rather than store-bought clothes. And they didn't let their kids create images. They taught them that if you were given paper and a crayon, you had to sketch lines across it and fill the intervening space with page after page of careful, precise lettering. Upper-case, lowercase. Printing and cursive. No drawings allowed.

Part of me didn't want to finish the puzzle and find out what it showed. And part of me thought about that terrified little girl and her whispered *The night birds* and my dream and how exactly we had become connected or whether her mere proximity was doing things to my sanity; and that was the part that urged me on. "We're not talking return to custody," I said, as much to my manager as to myself. "That's out of the question, given the state she was found. Just identification and initial discussions. If I'm right."

"If."

~

OVERNIGHT IT SNOWED AGAIN, making me think of the phrase *Insult to injury*, everything was slick and treacherous already, black ice lurking in the ruts between each compacted lane of snow, bad enough before another foot of the stuff.

In the rear-view mirror I watched Serbel, whom we'd tucked into the back seat with Officer Mankodi ("Call me Harry") so I could sit shotgun and help Fisher navigate. Grace had found good winter clothes—a puffy pink jacket, fuzzy boots, hat and gloves. The big white SUV had the heat up high but Serbel refused to shed any layers. Inexplicably, I felt the same—the cops were in shirtsleeves, but my body felt sheathed in ice, and I felt like if I took off my own winter gear I'd freeze from the inside out.

"How are you feeling?" I said, twisting in my seat. "Do you feel scared? Anxious? Remember what we talked about—"

"I'm all right, Miss Wilkinson," she said. Her voice was flat, and I noticed she was staring fixedly at the back of Fisher's seat rather than outside at the passing landscape. Uh oh.

"If you're going to be car-sick, that's okay," I said. "We can pull over, honey, don't feel bad."

"I don't feel sick."

I had almost said *Stop and pull over* but we were mostly stopped already, moving at a snail's pace—some accident up ahead. The two officers discussed, briefly, putting on the flashers to see if they could push through the traffic, but decided against it. There was simply nowhere for people to go, us included, except to creep steadily forward till we all got clear of the wreck.

"Serbel," I said softly. "We're not going to leave you

with your family, all right? We just want you to say yes or no
—is it them. Then *we'll* talk to them. Not you."

"Can I stay in here?" she whispered. "In this?"

"In the car? Sure."

"I'll stay with her," said Mankodi. He patted her puffy
pink shoulder. "You don't even have to get out, okay kid?
You just tell me yes or no."

~

BY THE TIME the traffic slackened we were well into the
afternoon, and Serbel was nodding off, exhausted from
staying up all night and all day today. But Fisher and I saw
the trailers still there as we crept up the long hill (*Good
vantage point*, I thought, reluctantly, tasting the violence of
it, the flavour of war. *Like a castle. Easier to defend if you've got
the higher ground.*)

The trailers, trucks, and shipping containers were
backed into a neat ring, headlights out, reminding me of
bison guarding their calves: an unbroken wall of aggression.
It seemed eerily still—no one walking around, no kids playing, the only movement the pacing of sheep behind the
slats of a livestock carrier.

The sky was leaden, the light a dull blue; Fisher and I
cast no shadows as we approached the first trailer, where in
one window we had seen the thick curtains twitch as we
parked. The snow was packed down in paths leading from
one structure to another, very few footprints between
them. A few looked strange, as if—

"What do you want?"

The door had opened while I was staring at the snow,
and I flinched, stepping behind Fisher without meaning to.

"Afternoon!" Fisher said brightly. "Officer Benjamin
Fisher, CPS."

The man in the doorway watched us, expressionless. He

looked like Serbel, didn't he? Or was I trying to convince myself of it? The same pale eyes with virtually no ring around the iris, the same skim-milk skin. He might have been in his early sixties, big and heavy, thinning brown hair framing a clean-shaven face. Real clothes though: clocked that. Blue jeans, t-shirt, sweater. You needed someone to present a public face to the world if you wanted to keep everyone else hidden.

I glanced back at the SUV, unable to see Serbel, but Mankodi leaned into the middle of the seat and gave us the thumbs-up. The tiny gesture filled me with helpless rage. *You*, I wanted to snap at the man in the trailer. *You! You did this to a little kid! What in the hell is wrong with you?*

But I was a government representative, and I knew the answer anyway. I straightened my shoulders. "And I'm Hayley Wilkinson, with Children and Family Services. Can you just confirm for us that you're Serbel's father? And your name?"

He blinked. "She's alive."

"Yessir, Mr. ...?" Fisher prompted him.

"Thruroth is the name I would give to you," he said. "Nothing more you deserve ... the true name is secret."

What *was* that accent? Where had he come from? Behind him I could see only the plywood panelling of the trailer, which, like the others, wasn't really a recreational vehicle so much as what looked like an old storage unit on a hitch. No furniture, no insulation. If they couldn't demonstrate facilities for hygiene, sufficient points of egress, and the ability to provide suitable food ... hmm. Eloise would want that in the report.

"Give her back," the man said. "She is mine; I created her. She is for the use of the gods. Not you. You had no right to take her."

"Mr. Thruroth, she ran away from what appeared to be a physically dangerous event," I said. "She had every right to try to get help. Now, the province does have a process for—"

"I degrade myself by speaking to you," he cut me off. "Even looking upon you. Either of you—and him down there. Creatures of the mud. Of the dirt and the dung. We will need a ritual cleansing. After the servants of the gods retrieve her. And *you* ...." He shrugged dismissively. "Animals may be killed without remorse."

Fisher blinked; it took me even longer than him, though I should have been ready for it. And for a moment I saw us through this stranger's eyes: I always pictured myself as merely tall and thin, but now that seemed fragile, flimsy; Fisher looked pitifully unprepared for a fight, despite boasting both a taser and a gun. And Fisher was Métis, and I was Black. And this guy didn't *like* that.

I opened my mouth, but Fisher replied first, pleasantly. "While we're here, I'm sure all you folks are up to date on your paperwork," he said. "Can't say as I've noticed any stickers or plates, though ... I'd like to see vehicle licenses and registrations. Now."

Thruroth simply watched us, unblinking, as if Fisher hadn't spoken. He seemed to be receding into the doorway somehow, though his boots remained on the threshold. No —he wasn't moving at all. The *sun* was moving, microscopically yet indefatigably, unnoticeable until it dipped below the hill.

And the night birds came for us.

~

AT FIRST IT seemed like winter and night had suddenly allied themselves against us, but that wasn't so. It was already winter. It was already night. But *something* slithered across the ground faster than any animal, faster even than flowing water.

I wasted the first seconds staring instead of running. Fisher did too—and the stream of darkness got him first, flicking up like switchblades, two then three then a half a dozen, shapes formed from the sharp edges of absence: feathers, beaks, talons, eyes. Their legs were long and thin, like waterbirds, but their feet bore the black claws of extinct beasts.

Fisher's scream broke my paralysis—three of the things closed on him, pinning him in the snow. I scrambled backwards, running for the SUV, hearing footsteps *no they can't be real I'm hallucinating this it's not real* pattering after me, inhumanly quick.

They were real. Real enough to hit me from behind, slam me into the ground hard enough to knock my breath out. Fisher's screams gurgled into silence. I didn't dare look back, only try to get up, protect my head, get something between me and them—

"Hayley! Stay down!"

Black claws scuffled near me in the snow—then fell back at the faint sound of pops, Mankodi shooting but the sound impossibly muffled, even though he was a few steps away. Something kicked me in the side, and I went down again, bright spots dancing in front of my eyes as my chin hit the snow.

Serbel. Alone in the back seat. Get her—if I can—

It seemed even her father would not approach while the things were out here, and would wait—as he said—till the killing was done. The slaughter, *like animals*, of the people he had never let his family even look at, realize the existence of: no need to see it now. As I crawled toward the pale shape in the darkness, the gunshots stopped and the screaming began.

The birds beat me to it, encircling the SUV as if forgetting me, their tall gawky forms suddenly still. Saying grace before a meal? No, they would take her alive. It was not a prayer but the touch of gloves before a boxing match.

The huge beaks descended, slamming into the roof of the vehicle, each blow denting it further, crumpling the metal around the windows.

"Serbel!" My voice barely carried over the metallic hammering. There was Mankodi, his navy-clad body no more than a slightly darker shape in the snow. More importantly: his gun. I dove for it, rose, feeling the weight—he had had time to put in one more clip, though I had no idea how many rounds remained—and shot wildly at the dark creatures.

If I hit them, if they noticed, I couldn't tell—I saw no signs of impact, no puffs of feathers or blood. They turned, eerily as one, each head swivelling identically on each neck, each pair of legs rearranging themselves, like a dance, and stared at me.

"Serbel!" I screamed in the sudden silence. "Get out, run!"

Once I spotted the pink form slithering out of the back door, I flung the gun at the birds and ran after her, scarcely hoping to outpace them. They didn't pursue us at once, instead splitting up to flank us, stalking between the motley vehicles, splashes of flat darkness against rust and grime and metal and wood.

Serbel was sliding in the snow, clumsy in the unfamiliar boots; I caught up to her and we half-ran, half-slid where she was pointing, behind the sheep trailer. Their frantic bleating meant I couldn't hear the creatures approaching, but it also meant, I hoped, that they couldn't hear us. All around us loomed the deep blue twilight and soon we would lose even that, and we would have nothing—no streetlights, no headlights. Only the unsteady hairs of candlelight peeking between heavy curtains.

"The night birds are *real*," I whispered, more for my sake than hers.

"Of course they are." Tears glittered on her cheeks in the last of the light. "Father calls them. For the ceremony."

"The ... that's what you were running from?"

She nodded. "I am ashamed," she whispered. "I knew it must happen. Last year they took my sister. I am not allowed to say her name now that she is a bride of the night birds. But when my time came ... I wasn't strong. I did everything wrong. Father was angry, they were all angry. All I could think to do was run."

I inhaled deeply. Cold air, mud, diesel, sheep shit, lanolin. Under that the sweet soapiness of Grace's donated clothes. *I did everything wrong. Everything.* I saw my father's face clear as day, twisted with rage, fumbling for his belt. How many times had I heard it, growing up? How many times had he hit me? Told me it was what had to happen, what *needed* to happen? How long before I finally realized he had become an old man incapable of harming me, instead of the monster of my childhood? *You did everything wrong.* And I had never escaped. I stayed and took it. And no one I told believed me.

"You cannot be a bride of *anybody*," I said. "You're a child."

"No, eleven solstices," she said. "Father arranges all the joinings at eleven. It is a meaningful number."

"If we get out of this, I'm gonna ...." I muttered. "Come on. Stay with me."

THE ONLY WAY I could figure was the one way they weren't expecting, and it all relied on doing something I'd only ever seen on TV. I figured it was about a fifty-fifty chance that the bullet blew back and made the gun explode in my hand, versus shooting the lock off the trailer, but the shot punched through the metal like paper and Serbel and I burst inside, leaving the door swinging behind us.

For several seconds no one moved. My eyes took things in like a camera: the bullet hole in the floor, black and comma-shaped; the candles shuddering in their tin pie plates. The woman sitting against the wall, her lips wired shut, not bleeding but oozing clear fluid onto the embroidery on her lap. The three children huddling under the table. Thruroth rising from his chair, hands empty. He needed no weapon. His weapons stalked outside, their footsteps croaking in the snow.

All the same, we were indoors—safe, for the moment. And only a moment. One shove and we'd be back out there, at the mercy of the night and the creatures and the cold.

Or no. I would. His child he would take back. To complete the interrupted ceremony that had claimed her sister ....

As if reading my mind, Thruroth smiled, revealing strong, chalk-white teeth. "Yes," he murmured. "You will not be a sacrifice. Sacrifices are holy ... they serve the gods. They make possible the new world to come. You, a creature of filth, an animal covered in its own dung, you will be only ...."

"Call them off," I said. "Let us go. Two people have died already—two *cops*. You think they'll leave you alone now? If you add a ... a woman and a child to it ...."

"Not a woman." His smile had not budged. "Not a person. And they do not know the child exists. We keep to ourselves."

His boots creaked on the floor; outside, the stalking monsters made nearly the same noise. Waiting for me. Birds made of night. I had watched it happen—coalescing from this terrifying, primeval darkness, miles from any grid. *Birds made of night. Light them up.*

I lunged past Thruroth and snatched at the first candle I could reach, splattering hot wax on my hand, sweeping it down first to the stacked sheets of crayoned writing on the table, then scattering the burning pages down to the rag rug.

Thruroth looped a forearm around my neck from behind, throwing me to the floor, but loosened his grip when Serbel forced herself between us. Her screams were in no language I knew, but he reacted as if slapped, and flung me aside to reach for her instead.

The children were shrieking, the mutilated mother making muffled noises, and while there wasn't much furniture inside the trailer, piles of books and clothes were vanishing in sheets of yellow flame. Already the heat was unbearable.

"Get away from her!" I wrestled Thruroth away and grabbed Serbel, jumping clumsily back out into the snow. He couldn't stay in the flames—he'd *have* to tell the things to back off—there they came, the three kids in their white woollen sacks, then the woman with her mouth freshly bloodied, where the hell was—

We had barely made it a dozen steps before he ran into me from the side, sending both me and Serbel sprawling. I grunted something like "Run!" or "Fuck!" This time she didn't—only scrambled to her feet, then cried out.

I rolled over, the flames of the burning trailer illuminating the towering birds, no phantoms, no effect of light or illusion, very real, white gouges on their black beaks where they had hammered the roof of the SUV. And Thruroth, regaining his feet for another lunge.

As a child I was so locked-down and helicoptered that I never learned how to fight; in my job, it comes up less than you'd think. People take swipes at me sometimes. Aim a kick, point guns. But I don't *fight*. So this wasn't much of one: the man snarling and thrashing, me covering my face and getting in the occasional knee in the crotch. The birds stood back, watching us fight. This was something he wanted to do himself: kill the animal that desecrated his property.

Serbel was still screaming, the only sound in all the darkness. I willed her, with all the power of whatever connection we had made when I had first touched her hand, with whatever power created and called the night birds, to *run back to the road*. She didn't move.

What happened next happened in moments. Thruroth got his hands around my throat, his fingers slipping on my scarf; my own flailing hand touched something sharp, and seized it even as I hissed with pain at the contact. Close enough to reach my throat was close enough to reach his.

I swung the thing—and in the fading light of the fire I glimpsed that it was a shard of broken plastic, not ice as I had thought—across Thruroth's face, meaning only (I told myself later) to make him release me. Instead it slid into his throat, almost without effort, disappearing into the flesh.

I rolled away in time to avoid most of the blood, catching the edge of the spray across my glasses, and backed away on my hands and knees. He died without a sound, crimson gushing across the trampled snow. In the dying light it swiftly became black.

The night birds conferred amongst one another; muttered softly, beaks clacking; stooped to examine the blood of their summoner, tilting their heads to get a closer look. A few touched the puddle with their talons, thoughtfully, as if deciding what to do next.

I threw Serbel over my shoulder and ran.

≈

"Happy New Year."

"Yes, happy New Year." Grace looked as if she wanted to hug me, but held off, hovering anxiously. "How's your neck?"

"It doesn't hurt," I said, which was true; a lingering hoarseness was all that was left, and that wasn't going to get better while I was in meetings for six hours a day as part of the investigation. Another puzzle missing most of its pieces. The measurable, physical facts: I had been attacked by someone who had left marks on my throat; I had recently fired a firearm; Officers Mankodi and Fisher were missing. No evidence had remained when the task force arrived at daybreak, not so much as a speck of sheep shit.

The story that both Serbel and I were sticking to was that her family had been identified, responded to our visit with lethal force, and killed the two officers, then absconded with the bodies. Which was, in fact, more or less what had happened. But it left a lot of questions, and I was trying to provide answers so she didn't have to.

Serbel looked up from her notepad and attempted a smile; I attempted one back. She seemed less perturbed to be smiling at a murderer, even an involuntary one, than I would have guessed. The conversations we must have later could not be held here. I had questions for her; she would have questions for me. We might not have any answers for each other. *I know*, she seemed to say, moving one shoulder minutely, a helpless shrug. What had we prevented? What had we set into motion? How much of all this was in our heads—or the head of her father?

"I'm so sorry," I said. "This isn't the way anyone wanted this to go."

"I think it will be all right," she said, sounding uncertain. "This is ... better. I think it's safe."

"It is," I said. "It is safe. Grace will ... she'll keep you *so* safe."

Serbel set aside her crayon and carefully tore off the top sheet, then handed it to me. "This is for you. It took me a long time to do the sky."

I turned it around: yellow moon, dark blue sky, and a half-dozen tall black things that could have easily been mistaken for trees (except what trees had two narrow trunks each?) wreathed in orange and red flames. The night birds, burning. "This is beautiful," I said. "Thank you."

"You are welcome," she said. "Will you come back, Hayley? Maybe draw pictures with me?"

"I will. I promise." I turned the picture over as Grace returned from the kitchen. "We have ... a lot to talk about."

THE CHURCH AND THE WESTBOUND TRAIN

DAVID NEIL LEE

DUMONT DISMOUNTED AND WALKED HIS ANIMAL INTO A Batoche he had never seen. The village was never as still as this. Church, stores, a few clapboard houses, barns, and stables—their foundations were built onto the flanks of a green valley that was itself a living thing. The town existed because of the freshness of the river, the murky waters of the spring melt, the banked energies of prairie summer. The fertility of the earth here. Batoche, and all the people in and around it, every living thing that was its citizen, swelled and exhaled with the seasons but tonight— although Gabriel tasted the air, found it barely freezing— something in the night had it locked solid. The earth was no longer in charge, something else had taken over.

Dumont knew the source, but not the cause. It wasn't something he'd seen or heard or smelled in the night air as he approached the silent village. Last Monday the west-bound train had unloaded in Saskatoon. Tuesday night brought the first storm of the fall, in a country where snow squalls don't necessarily bring winter: they just warn you it's coming. When winter brings eight-foot drifts, and forty-below temperatures, a late-October squall, even if it kills livestock and leaves travellers with frostbite, only trumpets that worse things are on the way.

Since the railroad had gone in, twenty years before, everyone in Batoche, and everyone around it, was attuned to the Monday train, the westbound train that stopped in Saskatoon, fifty miles to the southeast. The Friday train was eastbound and that was important, bringing salmon from the BC canneries, rice from Japan, tea, and silk from the Asian continent. Batoche was changing and growing. If once there were hopes that it would become the capital of a future Saskatchewan, those hopes had faded because of the westbound train. Already the Carlton Trail conducted only local traffic: hunters and families on foot, horses, cattle, and ox carts. It was the westbound train that was shaping and reshaping the countryside, bringing in forces that nobody was able to control—not Dumont, not his friend Louis Riel, not the people, not the priests.

The westbound train came from the eastern metropolises: Montreal and Toronto and also of course, Ottawa. "Satan's shithole." Even Père Dupuis stopped censoring Dumont's language when it came to Ottawa. Granted the victory at Batoche two years before, the new Métis nation still had to suffer the embargoes of the federal government. Embargoes either official and written, or unofficial and unspoken; to Gabriel Dumont, who couldn't read or write but spoke seven languages, the written and the unspoken were the same thing and he treated them with equal suspicion. Even so, much as Dumont despised anything from Ottawa, like everyone in Batoche he was increasingly dependent on whatever came on the westbound train.

What came on the train came from the big cities, or through the big cities from the smokestacks and fields and sweatshops south of the border. Or from the Atlantic: smoked cod, whale oil for lamps, rum from Jamaica, and even from the great continent beyond, the imperial culture: books, magazines, bibles, musical scores, the town piano. All of it paid for with wheat, whitefish, rye, and other grains; beaver, fox, mink pelts, and the hides and horns of the last of the prairie bison.

Dumont knew in particular that the wagon driver, Lenny Garnot, and his swamper Michel Gaudet, had struggled through the squall, had feared losing their way as they battled the plummeting temperatures, the clinging, wet snow, and the dangers on this long unlit trail—barely discernible at the best of times from the surrounding prairies. Even though they knew the route and the places where they could dig themselves in and hole up until the morning. But the word was, there was something in this shipment—something sent from the East—that they had to deliver, had to get off their cart and far away from before sunset. Five long crates—barely room on top to secure the few sacks and wooden boxes that made up the rest of the shipment. Garnot and Gaudet drove all night and arrived at the Hryciuk barn at ten o'clock in the morning. The barn had been patched and repaired especially to receive this shipment, fitted with a set of great double doors secured by chains and an enormous padlock to which Lenny had been given the only key by the spitting and stammering station agent in Saskatoon. With orders: "Drive all night if you have to. D-d-drive as if your lives and souls depended on it. Unload and get out of there by sundown, and lock those doors behind you, secure those chains so that no one can get in and nothing can get out."

But someone or something had gotten out, and whoever and whatever it was, a great dark stain was spreading through the town, turning Batoche; turning it so that within Batoche the seasons had stopped; turning it so that it was no longer a living town, but a frozen monument to a town that had been.

The horse was nervous; it wanted to turn and go back, but Dumont guided it into the stable behind Xavier Letendre's general store and found a stall where it would be out of the wind and comforted among other nervous horses.

He bounded up the store's familiar back steps but stopped dead at the door. For the first time he could remember, Xavier had bolted it. Dumont took off his mittens and knocked with his fists. He stood and listened to the night. He heard something stirring but it was not from the inside storeroom but from the outside. Somewhere out there, in the vast prairie dark embroidered with whirls of snow, something had heard him knock and out there something moved.

Shaking his head, Dumont reached into his coat and fingered the silver crucifix that hung inside his wool shirt. A prized possession made in Italy which, he understood, was very close to the Holy Land itself. Replacing the wooden cross that his aunt had carved for him when he was a boy, the crucifix was something that had come, years ago, on the westbound train. It wasn't a gift, but Riel had helped him get a deal on it from a shop in Saskatoon.

He let go of the crucifix and went down the steps and around the store to the front. If the church piano was the town's pride, so were the large frames of the plate glass windows at the front of Letendre's.

"They look merveilleuse," Xavier always said, "but they sure let in the cold." Dumont peered inside and saw movement at the back of the store, the glow of a lamp. A shape moved out of the dark to the front door and he heard a bar being lifted off its brackets.

Dumont went in, hearing whispers, "It's Dumont, Dumont is here. Look, it's Gabriel," and even the phrase he dreaded the most:

"Dumont—he'll know what to do."

He recognized everyone grouped around the dampened light of the lamp. Xavier of course was in charge, but Dumont's eyes were drawn to the small figure crumpled on a Hudson's Bay blanket behind the counter. He went onto his knees, feeling the cold of his heavy coat against his thighs.

"Lisette," he said. "What happened?"

"I told her to go before dark, but she never listens." Catherine's voice shook. "She went to lock up the chickens for the night. And when she didn't come ...."

"Petite Lisette—is she alive?"

"Look at her throat."

"The lamp—bring the lamp my way." Shadows stretched and shifted against the merchandise shelved and hanging on the store's walls.

Dumont pulled the girl's collar back from her neck, gently as he could. "Something has bit her." He touched the girl's face, feeling heat through his fingers, and then touched her hand. "Is it a fever? She's hot and cold at the same time."

"She's breathing," Catherine said. "I'm not afraid she will die."

Dumont stood and looked at the people gathered around the injured girl and the amber glow of the lamp. He spent so much time alone on the prairie, as a hunter and in recent years, as a diplomat and envoy and warrior. He knew that in his heart he was a hermit—but he also knew when his people needed him.

"We've got to take her to the church."

"But there's no heat at the church," Xavier said. "Here there's the woodstove. The father went ahead."

Dumont looked at the girl, hearing the mother's voice in his head. *I'm not afraid she will die.*

"When did Dupuis leave?" he asked. "Surely it's warmed by now."

"He went almost an hour ago." Catherine wrung her hands in exasperation. "He said he'd come back soon."

"Catherine, you know why I want to get her to the church." Dumont gestured to the night outside. "You know we won the war with the Canadians. And now we are at peace with them, so-called. But MacDonald has sent something else. Something else is coming for us."

The girl, Lisette, moaned as her mother scooped her off the floor. Catherine and her husband Serge whispered, and Serge took Lisette in his arms.

"We've got to get her there," Serge said.

"It's the only safe place," said Catherine.

"I have to go to the stable," Dumont said. "Be ready to break for the church the instant I get back. Wait for me."

"Gabriel, there's no need," Xavier said. "I have my shotgun under the counter."

"Leave it there. Wait for me." Dumont had been in Letendre's so often that even in the dark, he easily threaded his way through the bolts, boxes, and barrels of the storeroom. He unlocked the door and slipped back out into the night.

A freshening breeze was blowing wisps of snow from the roofs and eaves of the besieged village. The night's forces were arraying around him. In the stable Dumont found his saddle bags, slipped a few rifle shells into his pocket, and pulled Le Petit from the scabbard where it rode beside him. In moments he was at the back stoop again. This time, as soon as he tried the door it opened and Xavier hustled him into the store. Dumont rejoined the group and stood among them until they fell still.

"D'accord," he said. "Allons-y."

Xavier opened the door and the group hurried down the steps into the snow, Dumont taking the lead, looking around for danger, hissing "Vite vite vite."

The church was just outside the village; they had to go

to the last house on the street, and then cross a hundred yards of field. Fresh snow started to fall, lightly at first, but by the time they rounded the corner of the last house it was coming down with a vengeance, and the way ahead was a dense, featureless whirl.

"The good father helps us," Dumont said. "We can follow his tracks." He pointed down.

The priest wasn't a large man, but there would be plenty of time for them to reach the church before his footsteps, close together in the existing snow, would be obliterated.

"Attendez," Catherine said. "What happened here?" She pointed at the track ahead of them. The regular prints stopped and made a kind of a circle. Then they continued, the prints farther apart this time, heading across the field.

"He saw something or heard something," Dumont said. "He stopped. Then he began to run." He waved his arms at the group's stragglers. "Come on, let's hurry up."

Dumont forged ahead of them. His heavy boots had once belonged to a Canadian soldier, and they made the huge tracks of a much larger man.

"And then ...." Dumont pointed into the dark. "What in heaven?"

The priest's footprints stopped. The group looked about for some sign that he was somehow there in front of them—perhaps he'd fallen, and in the brief period since he'd left the store, the snow had covered him. But the snow was a vast and featureless blanket over the field, with nowhere the contour of a man's body.

"Vite vite vite." Dumont hurried the group ahead of him. "I'll catch up." He watched the group push ahead towards the corner monument of the church graveyard. Snow or not, once you spotted the graveyard, it was easy to get to the church's front door. "Don't worry about Père Dupuis."

What bullshit, Dumont thought. He was very worried

about the priest. Cradling Le Petit in one arm, he circled around the spot where the tracks ended. Where did the man go? No one had heard a gunshot—and who would want to shoot Père Dupuis anyway, and if he'd been shot, where was his body? Did a wild beast take him? If that had happened, where were the creature's tracks?

Dumont saw movement at the edge of the graveyard. At the base of a tombstone, something dark tugged itself out of sight. Reluctantly, he trudged through the deepening snow. He didn't want to walk among the graves—not at night in the snow, when he could feel the evil that was billowing like a shroud over his village.

He never liked la cemetière to begin with. Batoche was a new town. In its first years, there had been only three or four graves in the cemetery. Then, when their requests to Ottawa had branded them rebels, John A. MacDonald had sent in the troops, and the graveyard had started to fill up —mostly with Dumont's friends and relatives. Thanks to Macdonald, la cemetière was full of people Dumont knew and loved.

He walked past the first monument and saw something move in the shadows. It was the priest, his arms around the base of the Denys LaMontagne cross—a crucifix seven feet high, carved from granite, that LaMontagne had made in Quebec and lugged around the prairies for decades. Denys was gone, but the crucifix still had a use.

"Gabe," the priest gasped. "LaMontagne—he saved me." Dumont looked up, saw a flicker of light from a church window. The others had made it inside and they were lighting candles. Dumont tried to turn over Dupuis and the priest screamed.

"I'm broken," Dupuis gasped. "He broke me."

Clearly, Dumont had to go into the church and fetch his friends. They would need to find a blanket and then, gently as possible, ease the priest onto the blanket and, each gripping a corner ... Dumont shook his head, clenched his jaw, shouldered his rifle, and threw himself onto his knees. The priest cried out as Dumont scooped him into his arms, stood erect, and began threading through the tombstones towards the door of the church.

The group inside fanned out to let him enter carrying the priest. Dumont knew there was a cot in the little back vestry, but when he got there it was—as he should have known—given over to little Lisette. He bellowed, "Get blankets, for god's sake." A blanket was spread on the floor, and the unconscious priest laid out there. Dumont bent over him.

"He's been hurt," he said. "Broken ribs, but he breathes. I don't think he's punctured a lung."

Through the open door, he could see that a fire had been lit in the church woodstove. As he watched, Catherine laid out the stove poker and shovel on top of the stove to make a kind of crude grill, and stooped to lift onto it the bénitier, the ceramic bowl that held the church's holy water.

"What in god's name are you doing?" he called. "We need hot water to clean wounds, not holy water."

"We need holy water." Catherine came into the vestry and looked until she found a cast iron tea kettle. She filled it with water from a jug, and went back out to the stove.

"We don't need hot holy water, Catherine."

"I'm not heating it," she replied. "I'm thawing it."

Of course. With the change in weather, everything in the church would be frozen solid.

"She's doing the right thing." The priest's voice was barely heard. "Turn me over. I must get onto my knees."

Dumont hated every move of turning Dupuis onto his stomach, hearing him cry as he was helped up so that he could kneel at Lisette's bedside.

"Bring it now. Vite!" Catherine brought a bowl of

melted holy water and a rosary. Dupuis reached down and looped the rosary around the girl's neck. The child's eyes opened, feral and suspicious, and she struggled as Dupuis recited the Lord's Prayer and sprinkled her with the consecrated meltwater. "Délivre-nous du mal ...." Lisette moaned and writhed. Dumont raised his head: outside in the snow, he heard shouts of outrage. Then Lisette closed her eyes, and the night went silent.

Catherine leaned over and touched her daughter's face.

"She sleeps," Dupuis said. "To be honest, I don't know if she will live or die."

Catherine shrugged. "One or the other." Dupuis slumped out of the way and Catherine replaced him at her daughter's bedside.

The room shook: someone was pounding at the front door. Dumont heard a man's voice.

"Help us! Let us in! The storm ... and something is out here!"

Serge headed towards the door. "No!" Dupuis croaked, and Dumont began really to understand.

"Serge, stand back," he ordered. "Père Dupuis, help me."

Dupuis shook as he supported himself against the bed. Dumont wondered, given his condition, how much more the priest could stand. Dumont lay his rifle in front of him and took three bullets from his pocket. The hammering at the door grew louder along with the shouts of the man outside.

"It's cold out there," Serge insisted. "The wind is rising. He could have kids with him."

"Don't you dare go near that door. Bring me a candle so I don't cut my fingers off." Someone laid a candleholder on the floor, and by its light Dumont used his pocketknife to scratch a horizontal line across the lead tip of each bullet, and then at right angles, crossed that line with another.

"Ask yourself, Serge," Dumont said as he worked. "The door is not locked. Whoever is there, why do they rave and shout? Why don't they just come in?"

The priest prayed over the bullets as fervently as he had over the injured girl. Dumont thanked him and loaded the cartridges into Le Petit. When he looked, Lisette was sitting up on the edge of the cot.

"Angel, let's put a blanket down for you." Catherine led her daughter from the vestry into the church. "Let Père Dupuis have his bed."

Dumont helped Dupuis lie back on the cot. "Something lifted up our good priest," he said, "like a forkful of hay, and pitched him to the ground. Something that left no tracks in the snow."

"I fought," whispered Dupuis, "but he can't be knocked over, because he does not truly stand ...."

"Lie down, my friend," Dumont said.

"... he just IS ...." Dupuis closed his eyes.

"This is inhuman ...." Serge shouted. "For god's sake, help these people." Before anyone could act, Serge ran to the door and threw it open. "Come in, mes amis."

Wind gusted through, unimpeded by the man who stepped inside. He wore a black hat in the style of European visitors and like many of those visitors, was oddly beardless. He was dressed all in black, although Dumont couldn't tell if it was black fabric, skin, or fur. His suit seemed tailored from blackness itself. He stretched his arms towards the assembly and grinned.

Lisette looked up and screamed. The man wheeled around and grabbed Serge. Dumont raised Le Petit but didn't want to hit Serge or any of the people who had come forward to help. Catherine for one, had seized the heavy ceramic bénitier, and was rushing to the front of the church. The situation was out of Dumont's control—yet it was up to him to solve this, to save his people. He lay his rifle on a pew, pushed past the woman, grabbed the black arm of the intruder, and pulled the thing off of Serge.

The creature turned, looked Dumont in the eye, and in the candled room the amber light went dark. Dumont was in the eye of a prairie dust devil, the living world whirled around spiralling gushes of unbreathable air. He had surprised the thing, might as well have lassoed a grizzly bear, or dived into a river at full flood; and the thing struck back. Dumont felt a force that far outweighed his, yet he didn't lose his grip. He gritted his teeth and held on, pushed the thing away from Serge.

And it grew as powerful as a storm cloud, as a starless sky sparked with lightning. Dumont heard the priest's voice —he cannot be knocked over because he does not stand, he just IS—and knew that his hands grasped a force that could darken cities, lay waste to forests, crumble empires. He did not let go.

The thing hissed like a bull snake, its neck swelled into a great darkening hood, Serge cried out in fear, and Dumont felt himself shoved to one side—not by another man, but by Catherine. He still hung onto the creature as Catherine raised the ceramic bénitier in her arms. Only a small part of the ice had been melted for Dupuis' ministrations; using the bowl like a sling, Catherine flung the half-globe of ice at the intruder's head.

The ice struck and the thing's head exploded. Not into blood and brains but like a burst puffball, swirls of darkness erupted from the thing's torso. The creature staggered backwards, headless, Dumont leapt to the nearest pew and seized Le Petit. He aimed the rifle and fired once, a consecrated bullet into its chest. The mantle of dark swelled and filled the room with the stink of a corpse, the cold room became a vacuum, sucking air from lungs and light from every candle.

And then the candles flamed again.

"Close the door," Dumont ordered. "Bolt it." He checked on Serge.

"I was helpless." Serge was dazed and breathless. "He squished me like a bug. And then Catherine ...."

Someone lit another candle, and then another. The door stayed closed. Dumont sank onto a pew.

"Catherine!" he exclaimed. "Next time I'll stay back at camp. And leave it to her." His mind was already racing. The priest had saved the girl. Now, if they worked hard, they could save the priest. And then ....

"What was that thing?" Serge asked. "Where'd it go?"

Dumont looked around. "That's bastard MacDonald's revenge. His revenge on a free people. His Yankee Gatling gun and his soldiers couldn't kill us, so he sent that."

"Is it dead? Did we kill it?"

Dumont shook his head. "It takes all the combined forces of nature, man, and heaven to kill such a thing. But I swear my friends, I will kill it—but only if it comes again. Meanwhile, let's give it another chance.

"At first light we'll go to Hryciuk's barn and find the place where that thing sleeps. If we hurry, there's time to load it onto a wagon and get it on the next eastbound train. We'll send it back to Ottawa, make MacDonald—that drunkard with a loaded rifle—make him pay for it C.O.D."

Dumont shivered. "Let's build up the fire, and watch Lisette, and help our father make it through the night. And from now on, we'll watch very carefully, and look very hard, at whatever comes on the westbound train."

THE FRAGMENTS OF AN EARLIER WORLD

CAMILLA GRUDOVA

1850s or thereabouts, Canada.

A WEEK BEFORE OUR COUSINS WERE DUE TO ARRIVE FROM Scotland, I had a lump removed from behind my ear. I was calm and didn't scream though I was terrified of a scar. Teresa, my younger sister, asked if she could keep the lump, but the doctor, disgusted, refused and threw it into the fireplace. The doctor never liked Teresa, or I, because our mother was Catholic. Our invalid mother didn't trust the doctor, and preferred to rely on her sister, our aunt. Our mother wept bitterly when our father forced her to be inspected, our aunt praying over a rosary in a corner of the same room. As the eldest daughter I ran the household duties for mother—looking over the menus for supper and talking to the kitchen and servants. Our mother and aunt lived in their own wing of our house—the first house in Canada to have running taps, toilets, and gas lamps installed. Father liked modern conveniences as much as he liked history. It was on the edge of the town of Hamilton, looking out over the lake and forests beyond. The style of the house was Greek, which was fashionable at the time it was built, an architect from Edinburgh designing it, but everyone in Hamilton called it The Castle.

No one knew how the toilets flushed at first, and they filled up with waste until our father had to go around to all seven and pull the flush chains. One of us, no one was sure who, continued to not pull it, even after father gave us all a lesson, and I found filth in the toilets again and again, sometimes mixed with blood and hair the family colour. The gas lamps made the house smell of farts, said Teresa. It was true, though I didn't tell her I agreed. We made the servants leave the one in our room off and continued to use candles.

Father was a government minister for our province and wanted everything to look grand and perfect for the arrival of our cousins, including us; though they were poor, father was very proud of his ancestry and said our family could be traced back hundreds of years in the Scottish borders and the visiting cousins were in the direct line of nobility. He had etchings of the family castles, crumbling piles of stone, and one of a tall tower, where our cousins were said to be born. There was an unmarried son, and our father had only daughters. Teresa said to me, it is because our mother is ill, father will soon want a second wife, and one of our cousins was a young lady. She had a way of saying unpleasant things which I couldn't help believe were somewhat true. Teresa was twelve, with a strange face and unlike the rest of us, had dark, almost black hair. She spent most of her time running around outside in the garden, or by the river. She went into the tunnels under the house, which were forbidden, and there before the house was built. They had been used by soldiers during the war of 1812 and she sometimes came up with old bullets.

Nobody watched in case Teresa got near to drowning except me. I suspected no one else would care. When we did embroidery samples, she spent the time pricking her own fingers and watching the blood. She didn't concentrate in lessons, but taught herself ancient Greek which seemed wicked especially as she wrote the letters all over her arms with her quill. She sang like a crow, and during Scottish country dancing, which our father was so fond of, she would stomp her feet and wave her hands manically. She slept not with a doll, but a toy cast iron stove named Barnabas, made out of real iron, the size of a cat. She fed it lumps of coal stolen from the kitchen. Her sheets were always covered in coal dust.

Once, sitting behind a woman wearing a feathered hat in church, she removed the feathers one by one with a penknife, quietly enough the woman didn't notice, and those surrounding us were too polite to interrupt the service. Teresa then stuffed all the feathers in her mouth, swallowing them. When we were home, in the privacy of our bedroom I slapped her and told her never to do such a thing again—she could find dropped feathers in the garden.

She hid many of her treasures—dead animals, four leaf clovers, her milk teeth, in mother's apartments. Mother herself had a saints fingerbone in a jewelled box, which Teresa coveted.

OUR MOTHER HAD AN INFECTED BREAST, it was large and lumpy, so she wore a shawl around her chest to hide it. She blamed it on Teresa, the first and last child she fed, as no wet nurses were available when she was born. I had seen it once, by accident. It was blue, green, and hairy.

Our mother and her sister had boxes of hair from relatives which they braided and turned into flowers kept under glass. Our aunt, who wore a lace bonnet and had a moustache so thick it covered her mouth, seemed greedy for our mother's hair, which was long and red. She kept scissors in a sewing bag secured around her waist, and I knew once mother died she would use it to cut off her plaits. Father married her because of it, though she was Irish, not Scottish. When they met she said her family was from Galway and he thought she meant Galloway in Scotland, though he had never been, and did not find out until after their engagement, when he looked at a map to find it. They had a Catholic altar in their wing of the house, and were taken to the Catholic church in town multiple times a week. We were in the church of Scotland, like our father. Mother had Teresa baptized Catholic to cure her wickedness as a baby, as she howled all the time and bit mother's chest, and our father thought this just made Teresa more sinister in the end. My name was Flora, after a Walter Scott character.

Our cousins arrived unexpectedly early, in a butcher's cart, sitting on lambskins, with a bunch of dripping, fresh meat meant for the meal being prepared in their honour. They did not know a carriage would be sent for them from town, they said. Father had planned to serenade them at the front of the house with bagpipes, but here they arrived, by the kitchen door, smelling of flesh. Teresa and I did not have on the dresses ordered for the occasion; silk patterned with the family tartan. We were astonished to see three cousins, not two, as had been written to us by their mother, who died not long before they left and whom our father had been in communication with for years, though they had never met.

Robbie, our male cousin, had black hair, worn long, as did his sister Iona. Their faces were narrow and sallow, their eyes dark and little but had something noble and beautiful, yet also sickly and evanescent, about them. Robbie had a thin moustache above his lip and wore an old-fashioned cravat and a long black coat, pulled around him in the cold, for it was March and I didn't believe they were used to such strong winds. I thought he looked as I believed a poet would, though I had never met one. I blushed at the sight of him. The third was a child, for he was small, with very large feet, and a large wide strange face, and unseeing, watery eyes under black hair.

Father arrived to greet them flustered, having thrown on his kilt and sporran but no time to prepare his bagpipes. I was relieved, as I found the sound abhorrent. Though we had many chiming clocks, Father woke everyone up in the house every morning by playing them at dawn on the roof of the house. He looked confounded at the strange boy.

"This is Alasdair our younger brother," said Robbie, setting the boy down from the carriage, his hands on his shoulders, guiding him forward.

"Mother is ashamed of him, but we are not," replied Robbie with a chilling frankness we were not used to, for he could see what we were thinking in our eyes. Father's eyes went from the monstrous boy to Teresa, shiftily, seeing a thread between them.

"All the places have the same names as places we know in Britain. It is eerie," said Robbie.

Our cousins had taken a boat to Halifax, and from there, many carriages over a weeks' time. Before I could suggest to father they should rest, they were brought into the parlour—a room with tartan wallpaper and a painting of a stag—and father said to Robbie, I will bring you hunting. Robbie replied that he was not fond of it but would like to meet some of the native peoples he had read so much about before the journey, to which father replied there were no more in the area. He opened his liquor cabinet and offered Robbie a dram which Robbie took and downed before our father could make a toast. He was promptly poured another one. There were two paintings in the parlour, which like our cousins, were shipped over from Scotland; an earl, dressed in black with white frills and the same sandy hair as father which sat upon his head like a disintegrating cloud, and one of a highland warrior, a dead hare at his foot, a gun in his arms. Robbie went up to the portrait of the earl and said, "This very painting terrified me as a child. Father, who was alive then, had it moved to the kitchen so I wouldn't see it." He drew a finger across the portrait's face and showed us a brown and dusty fingertip. "Mutton grease," he said and put the finger in his mouth.

❧

MOTHER DID NOT COME DOWN to the dinner. She never did. She ate only porridge, oysters, and weak tea. Neither did her sister, in order to keep her company. No one else liked to be in her presence when she ate, for she expelled gas from her mouth and bottom, loudly and frequently like some sort of machine.

All the distinguished families in our town were invited to the welcoming supper. There was no place for Alasdair at the table, but Robbie had bathed and dressed him for supper, and brought through a chair from another room without asking the servants.

They were sat across from myself and Teresa, who had been silent and staring since they arrived. I was considered to be the only one with any control over her, though it was only that I was kind to her. When she brought strange rocks from the garden, shaped like livers and hearts, or bird's skulls, I looked at them with interest. Teresa rolled up the sleeves of her dress. I saw she had covered her arms in Greek letters and made-up symbols with ink. She put her elbows on the table, so Robbie could see. He did not ask her about the Greek, though he surely knew the letters.

"I see, Cousin, you are intrigued by my brother's eyes," said Robbie, looking at Teresa and speaking quietly enough only those of us in front of him could hear. "They are made of glass. His real eyes were gouged out by cruel children."

It did not frighten her, only made her look more keenly at Alasdair. Robbie fed him, bringing forks and spoons to his mouth. Alasdair chewed with his mouth open, bits dribbling down his chin. It was a meal of turnips, carrots, lamb, an approximation of haggis father had the chef prepare, along with the usual fare of jellies and chicken, of white soups and fish. The combination, with great quantities of wine, put my stomach in knots.

Iona was sat beside father. She had no proper dresses for the evening with her so was lent one of mine, purple tartan which was too big on her frame.

"Tell us of our ancestral house," father said, loudly to Robbie from the other side of the table, silencing the scattered conversations.

"We have lived in Edinburgh with mother for many years, sir. The castle is too draughty and we could not afford to heat it."

I saw father blush; I had never seen him do so. He had sent money to their mother for many years.

"I also attended university in Edinburgh, the Royal College of Surgeons and Physicians," added Robbie, sensing the embarrassment he caused. A friend of fathers made the comment that he heard it was one of the best medical colleges in the world and the conversation turned to medicine. A woman remarked what wonderful accents our cousins had.

OVER THE NEXT MONTH, Iona was put into the company of Teresa and I. She rarely spoke, and when she did she said something vague, soft, and agreeable. I thought her nose too long, and her teeth too big. Father took her for walks around our gardens, or into town to buy things, finer dresses than I, Teresa, or mother had. I noticed father giving this special attention to her, especially as Robbie did not, as expected, share so many of father's interests. He did not hunt or play any musical instruments. When father asked him about Scotland, he did not speak of the glens and castles and famous battles, only the poverty and filth which surrounded Edinburgh Castle, the scandal of body snatchings from fresh graves and Godless enlightenment philosophers who looked like toads. His taste in literature was vastly different from all of us too—he said the truest Scottish writer was James Hogg who none of us had read, but generally he preferred the work of the English poets— Shelly and Keats and the Brontë sisters. During our nightly readings of Robbie Burns and Walter Scott he paid no attention, only drank the whisky and tea that went with it.

One such evening, as Father read:

> Our Loud should Clan-Alpine then
> Ring from her deepmost glen,
> "Roderigh Vich Alpine dhu, ho! ieroe!"

Robbie snored, his hand still around a whisky glass. There was a moan from Alasdair, and the parlour filled with a smell like burnt porridge. I tapped Robbie on the shoulder to awake him and let him know. He took Alasdair from the room. Iona ignored them both, not offering any assistance to her soiled brother, but her eyes still focused on her embroidery, though I noticed her neck and ears turned red. She was sewing an image of a purple thistle.

One evening, gathering for our reading from father, we found a mess—library books were all over the floor, pages ripped out. Etchings had been taken down from the walls, their glass frames smashed, the images stolen, the feathers plucked off a taxidermized exotic bird.

Teresa had used these to create the most craven playing cards—pictures and words cut and collaged together with ink scribbles overtop. She had used the etching of the family seat in Scotland, the dear draughty home of our cousins.

Father was so furious he intended to make her sleep out on the roof in the cold, and to whip her twenty times, but Robbie intervened.

"It is my fault uncle, I showed her my tarot cards I purchased in France ... she is easily influenced, as a child."

He showed us his own pack of cards and explained to us how they could see the past, present and future; father told him to put them away. I believed, if they were Scottish instead of French, he would have allowed it, but I was comforted, as I believed Robbie's frankness would only tell horrors and misfortunes for us all. However, over the course of the week, after he showed us the cards, I noticed one member of the household to another suddenly downcast. The cook, the housemaids and the gardener, he had read all of their fortunes, leaving them in despair though they wouldn't say what he revealed exactly.

ROBBIE WAS the primary caretaker of Alasdair. Our servants were frightened of him and Iona pretended he didn't exist, though more and more Robbie spent a great amount of his time in our library, drinking, or outdoors, inspecting plant species in the garden which were new to him, or going into town, to look for natives to learn about their medicine he said. He was aimless, he made no talk of setting up a medical practice in Canada nor did he try to win the affection of me—which surely father had meant him too—only vaguely talked of Scottish medical reviews in which he could write of medicine in Canada. As Robbie became more and more distracted, I found Alasdair wandering the halls of our house alone, humming, or in one of the bathrooms, covered in his own filth. Teresa followed him like a shadow, and so I followed Teresa. My intuition she would cause harm to him was correct.

One morning, I came across Alasdair crying in the library, his hands over his face. When he heard me, he took his hands away. His glass eyes were gone, leaving red pockets filled with puss. One socket was filled with blood, which dribbled down his face. He came close to me, screaming, his mouth and his eye sockets smelled of rancid milk. I screamed, and I screamed for Robbie, who came with a number of the servants.

Teresa came out from behind one of the curtains, smiling at the sight of them all.

"Where are his eyes, Teresa?" asked Robbie. She didn't answer.

"Only one of his eyes was glass. He was blind, but I hadn't removed that eye as it wasn't infected," he said in a low voice beside me. His breath smelled of whisky. He lunged towards Teresa and shook her. She spat an eyeball onto the floor. From the sound it made on the wooden floor we knew it was the glass one. He hit her across the side of the head, which made me scream again and Teresa ran from the room. I picked up the glass eye, hard and grey, still warm from Teresa's mouth.

By the time we found Alasdair's true eyeball in my and Teresa's room, it had been smashed, ruined, like a piece of abandoned fruit.

I held Alasdair as Robbie put the glass eye back in its socket and cleaned the whole area with peculiar smelling spirits from his medicine bag and a felt cloth.

Alasdair's hair smelled and was spotted with lice he must have brought from Scotland. I told Robbie we must bathe him. Robbie said he had to immediately write to specialists in London, to Toronto and New York, to order a new eye. I was left with Alasdair myself. Our bathtubs were narrow and framed in dark wood. They looked like coffins and frightened Alasdair who screamed and shouted as I scrubbed his ears with tar soap. He had scars and welts all over his body. His member shrunk in the water; it was the first I had ever seen, a strange curl of flesh, dripping with cream like seed. I touched it, briefly, to see the texture and whether it was similar to a finger or not. It wasn't. I borrowed some clothes from the male servants promising to replace them, to dress him in. I sewed an eye patch, to hide the ugliness of his other empty eye.

We could not find Teresa anywhere in the house, she did not come to dinner. I did not tell father how Alasdair came to be wearing an eyepatch for he would surely beat Teresa.

When Teresa was not found in time for bed a household search party was sent into the gardens, the field, the town, and the forest beyond the lake, led by our father. She wasn't found for three days, and was ill with fever, cold and dirty, with blood down the front of her dress and pinecones and burrs in her hair. Father didn't call his own doctor, saying it was a delicate matter, but asked Robbie who tended to her in mother's apartments. She needed surgery Robbie said, she was badly injured inside. When I was let in to see her as she recovered, she was awake staring at the tartan ceiling. "Teresa," I said, and she turned, looking at me blankly. Her eyes, once blue, were now grey.

I tried to touch them, to feel what her eyes were made of, but she turned away from me. I asked Robbie what he had done, and he told me she could see better now, see the things she wanted to see. I tried to tell father I believed she was blind now—look how the colour has changed!—but they both said nonsense, as did mother and auntie, who said Robbie had cared for Teresa so tenderly and brought her back to health.

Alasdair's new eye had arrived, in the same parcel as Teresa's I assumed. It made no difference to his behaviour, for he had already been unseeing, but the new eye was a vivid green, and looked slightly too big for his socket, as if it were about to fall out.

The next time I went to visit Teresa she was holding something beige and square. She brought the thing to her nose, smelling it and rubbing it against her cheek. "Robbie gave it to me in exchange for Alasdair's eyes" she said. "It is a patch of skin belonging to a man who was hanged in Edinburgh." She held it up. "Tell me what is on it." There was an indecipherable, dried tattoo on it. I replied, "Nothing, it is only pigskin." I tried to take it from her—it was no toy for a child, but she clutched it tightly.

Whenever I tried to ask Teresa about her eyes, she said they were *her* eyes, and no one else believed me, they only liked that Teresa was less destructive, more subdued. Even the servants said how much improved she was. Yet she spilled tea when she tried to drink it and no longer read. Robbie and Teresa seemed to make their peace. She followed him, with her now awkward gait, bumping into the furniture and breaking windows, at a short distance, as he explored our gardens.

Now and then, he turned to Teresa, and asked her a question about one of the herbs or flowers he was examining, describing it to her. If she did not know the answer, she told a lie. She went with him on excursions to the forest, Robbie holding her hand. They returned with heavy bags of mushrooms and leaves and roots. It seemed to do Teresa good, remarked father.

I cared for Alasdair, as if Robbie and I exchanged charges. He threw tantrums more and frequently soiled himself. If I read to him, he threw things at me (he had long been quietly banned from our evening readings). In the bath, I hit his bottom and his member with my tar soap as revenge. I was so bruised and scratched and tired by the care of my cousin, I confronted Iona, who I found in a parlour, wearing a new dress my father had tailored for her. I told her it was her Christian duty to help care for her brother.

"He is not my brother, or any relation of mine!" she screeched, then turned her voice to a whisper. "Robbie bought him from a poor family in Edinburgh while at the university and declared we must all call him brother. As the boy could not speak and is simple minded, he removed his eye as an experiment at the royal college of surgeons, though it wasn't infected at all, and made the other eye blind with chemicals, and for this he was expelled. I have stayed silent, for my true brother's sake and the family's reputation. I ask you to do the same. We have nowhere else to go."

I kept quiet, though I was repulsed by the body of Alasdair, no longer my blood, but a strange young man.

Mother became much sicker. Father sent for the doctor but mother refused to let him in. Robbie said he could tend to her, and to my surprise she let him, though I begged auntie not to. She said Robbie had cured Teresa and would cure her too.

I waited outside her bedroom, Teresa beside me, until late at night when Robbie emerged, our aunt behind him and said:

"She has passed."

There was blood on his collar and he held a surgical implement of some sort I didn't know the name of. I could not tell our aunt's expression as her lips were hidden by her moustache, but she had her scissors in one hand, and held mother's hair plaits in the other. Leaving Teresa with our aunt, I wandered the house, looking for father to tell him. I heard his voice in the library saying "good, very good," followed by the sound of pouring water and a female laugh. I opened the door quietly and saw by the fireplace, Iona naked, crouched over a chamber pot into which she urinated, father standing near her, wearing his kilt. I shut the door and turned to leave. Robbie was behind me, a bottle of spirits in hand. When he saw me, he said, his voice thick with drink:

"I have raised Alasdair, since he was eight years of age, I took him in when I was a student, his parents did not want him, his eyes were covered with scabs. I shared my scholarship to feed, clothe and educate him, shared my lodgings with him. He is good as a brother to me, more family than the inhabitants of Dundurn castle, more family than Iona is to me now."

Robbie was gone by morning. He had taken Alasdair and Teresa with him, along with many rare books and other treasures of father's. Teresa had left our bedroom in the night, while I slept, tired with grief. I found on her bed, near the pillow, one of her tarot cards, a ruined Scottish castle decorated with garish feathers.

Father, instead of making effort to retrieve her or advertise that she was kidnapped, had her declared dead and an empty coffin buried, the same funeral as mother's. He proposed marriage to Iona.

Cleaning out mother's things, I found a silver dish near her bedside, a last forgotten meal. I took off the lid, and there was mother's sickly breast, rotting with embroidery pins stuck in it, and four bloody eyeballs, withered yet still blue. I was sick on the carpet, a stain which would haunt me for the rest of my days.

BANQUETS OF EMBERTIDE

RICHARD GAVIN

UNLIKE MOST SMALL NORTHERN TOWNS, WHITE BIRCH IS not a tightknit community. Its residents restrict their activities to their drab houses, or to the fields on which those houses stand. Though earthy and obtuse, these people lead the sort of cloistered, spartan lives one usually finds only in hagiographies.

The breadwinners of each household earn their keep outside the town limits, for White Birch has no industry to speak of. The few lingering storefronts on main street have long been boarded-up and neglected, like jack-o'-lanterns left to rot after Halloween.

An annual banquet at the town hall is the only tradition significant enough to draw White Birch together. The unspoken consensus is that this feast is held in honour of Christmas, but its true nature remains a secret that the townsfolk guard fiercely from everyone, especially from themselves.

Many Decembers ago, a butcher who'd gotten too deep in his cups had interrupted the entertainment. He'd hollered grisly speculations about the town's Embertide custom, demanding to know why this queer supper always fell upon the longest, darkest night of the year, and why no one ever thought to connect it with the atrocities that subsequently plagued White Birch each winter. The details of these atrocities vary according to the storyteller, but all are united on the fact that they were so ghastly children had cried and the elderly had covered their ears.

Every version of this account ends with the butcher being forcibly ejected from the hall by furious neighbours, and with his body being discovered several days later in the vineyard behind his home. The coroner's report allegedly cites exposure as the official cause of death, but the butcher is consistently rumoured to have been discovered with his eyes and his left foot missing. His mangled remains are said to have been interred in an unmarked grave in another county. Whether he'd found the answers he'd so rudely sought at that year's banquet is a riddle best left undeciphered.

This year, on the appointed day and at the appointed time, the locals migrate to the town hall. No invitations are required. (No one has ever been brave or foolish enough to seek out the identity of the host or hosts of these yearly fetes.) The cardinal rules are to arrive before nightfall, and to ensure that everyone obeys the proper etiquette.

It is a frigid evening, but autumn stubbornly refuses to yield to winter. For weeks the lands have been ossified and fallow. The foliage that litters the mud has lost both its colour and its perfume of decay. It makes everyone feel dismal, eager for a cleanse.

The great walnut doors of the town hall are pressed shut just as stars are beginning to stir in the cloud-swept sky. The atmosphere inside is cold, both in temperature and in lack of affection. Long tables have been veiled in white cloth and laid with precisely enough settings. Tented cards written in a filigree script indicate a mad seating plan: siblings are stationed at opposite ends of the hall, high school athletes are placed beside hopeless old maids, wives sit nowhere near their spouses. Upon every plate rests a green linen napkin ingeniously folded in the shape of praying hands. These resemble polluted glaciers upon their little seas of glazed bone china.

A tedious span of anticipatory stillness follows the seating. The faint hiss of guttering wax within the oakwood candelabras and the wet rumble of bellies calling for nourishment are the only noises. Someone sneezes but no one whispers a blessing.

A rustling from the blackness of the vaulted ceiling notifies the guests that the evening's entertainment is commencing. Those who opt to look up witness iridescent cords unfurling from the joists and beams. Their pulsating descent is akin to serpents uncoiling after a period of rest. The lowering of these bright garlands extinguishes the flames of the candelabras. The hall's luminescence now comes in lurid shades of coral and yellow.

The far end of the hall is inlaid with an impressive arched window. The heavy velvet curtain covering this window is hoisted. A trapezoid of moonlight stretches across the narrow stage.

Eventually the entertainer makes his appearance, shuffling unceremoniously into the lunar spotlight. The man is attired in a rumpled suit of midnight-blue wool. Piled dust nests inside the suit's many creases, suggesting a rich baroque design that the fabric does not actually possess. The man also wears an ugly crown, a novelty of cheap tin that is too small for his skull. Its edges slice into the delicate, aged skin of his brow.

A wedded seamstress at the rear of the hall flinches under a wave of unpleasant recognition. The man onstage is familiar to her. She'd grown up knowing of him only as 'the widower.' As best she can recollect, the widower had been condemned to the bedlam after his beloved had been committed to the earth.

The seamstress's anxiety mounts as she ponders the chilling scenario of the widower escaping his padded cell. She longs to share this insight with her husband, the carpenter, but he is seated at the foot of the stage, between the fisherwoman and one of the many local tillers.

The widower starts to fret, suggesting a lack of rehearsal, or possibly stage fright. Each jitter of his longish body fills the room with the cloying stench of camphor. A gormless child loudly retches and is paternally reprimanded by the man nearest to him.

The widower's expression turns apologetic. He fishes through the pockets of his dusty suit and retrieves the stub of a cheroot. Striking a match against his bruised thumbnail, he ignites the cheroot. It fumes out thick ribbons of smoke. Though everyone is expecting the pungent stench of cheap tobacco, they are instead greeted with the sweet musk of frankincense, the finest the world has known since Balthasar had carefully borne it as a holy gift.

Having perfumed the chamber, the widower swallows the still-burning incense cone; the first in what is to be a series of marvellous illusions. Partway through these charming glamours the man suddenly halts. His signal for silence is so desperate, so urgent, that tension surges through the crowd. The tears that fill the widower's eyes sparkle like polished gems under the hall's peculiar iridescence.

He leans forward and cups a hand over one of his large ears. He listens intently.

Something in the darkness is moving toward the hall. Everyone takes a frantic mental attendance check. The fact that all residents are present only serves to worsen those plodding sounds of approach.

"What is coming? What?" hisses the widower. His voice is

the gurgle of brackish water leaking through a clogged drain. The noises without grow louder, and although the barricade is solid and true, everyone is heartsick with the sense that this intruder is now darkening their door.

The thud of the iron doorknocker causes many to cry out.

"Wait!" the seamstress shouts. Instinctively, she leaps from her seat, nearly upsetting her place-setting. Realizing her breach of decorum, she clasps a hand across her mouth as a gesture of penance before sinking back into her chair. The revelation that inspired her outburst was that her initial memory of the legend had been inverted: it was not the widower who had gone mad after his wife had gone into the ground, but vice versa.

"Something foul is knocking at the door to our world," explains this man who is no longer the widower. *"We must be brave!"*

The knocking abruptly ceases, but the crowd's relief is short-lived. A moment later, the thing from without pushes effortlessly through the bolted doors, slipping through the barrier as silkily as smoke.

This unbidden guest reveals itself to be a great absence, a thing (or rather a no-thing) of darkness, a negation whose absolute stillness permeates all.

"It is the grave, my friends! That is what has come here! It has lain hungry for too long," the crowned man explains sotto voce. *"Like all of you, the grave has come here to feast. And we know what food it craves, don't we?"*

Once the grave proceeds to glide noiselessly between the long tables, the townsfolk can no longer maintain their mute civility; children wail, men sob quietly, and women loudly demand a halt to the proceedings. But their revolt is aborted almost as soon as it begins, for whomever the grave floats nearest to is paralyzed with shock and left in a state of inhuman grace.

The oblong pit passes through all objects in its path yet disturbs none. The grave has no qualities whatsoever. It holds no odour of the soil from whence it came, nor any traces of its previous occupants. In fact, nothing about it is inherent. Where one person feels a shudder of revulsion in the grave's proximity, another experiences a sense of peace.

"She is seeking Her next disciple!" the crowned man declares. To many, the notion of the grave being feminine rings true.

The crowned man then claps his hands several times as if to summon his royal subjects. The noise of this breaks the catatonic spell caused by the sailing grave. The people turn their attention once more to the stage, where yet another visitor moves into view.

A stone catafalque comes meandering into the moonlight. It has been lavishly carved to feature flying buttresses and arches worthy of the finest cathedrals. Its movement comes courtesy of the stone goat legs that have been chiselled into each corner of the oblong stone. Though crooked, these legs of living stone are nimble and strong. Their cloven hooves clack against the floorboards as they ferry the catafalque closer to the crowned man.

The grave makes one last patient pass of the hall before finally stationing itself at the only exit.

"There is no escaping Her. One of us must learn Her lesson. Who is it to be? You? Or you, madame? How about you, sir? If not you, why not the kindly-looking child beside you?"

Stifled pleas ripple through the hall. This din of helplessness brings a smile to the entertainer's face. Someone points a quaking hand at him while another person warns of bleeding.

The crown the man bears is melting into a corona of dark steam. This weepy new form is shapeless yet somehow even more regal. It halos him in burning shadows. Rivulets of crimson stream down the man's face. They fill the creases in his flesh and the wrinkles of his suit, creating a map of some new circulatory system, an externalized mask to convey the secrets of the blood. The atmosphere ripens with the aroma of cooking meat.

The king lies down on the catafalque.

In response to this, the origami praying hands uniformly unravel, as if flowers parting for pollination.

The open napkins reveal the tools secreted within them. The guests find themselves faced with a keen needle and spindles of coarse embalmers thread. There are small cellars of salt and phials of pungent oil. Two lucky children each discover matching pennies for the eyes. One unfortunate guest has been gifted an ancient scalpel of Turkish obsidian.

WAN daylight is pouring through the great window by the time the citizens finally lift their groggy heads. The settings have been cleared away. Everyone feels sated, though they intuit that the only thing fed last night was the grave.

Torpidly, the citizens rise and depart, as if summoned by the tolling of the bells from the bedlam on the hill. When the doors are finally opened, some gasp at the sight of fresh snow covering the landscape. This cold white shroud, they know, will linger for a long spell, not yielding until the sparrows return from afar and the first green sprouts of spring disclose some of the secrets that circulate beneath the surface.

THE BREATH OF KANNASK

HIRON ENNES

Every year, or twice a year if we're truly unlucky, the lights come down to Bronfeld. During the darkest months, when the cold whittles the daylight to thin, sharp minutes, they erupt over the foothills, casting a pestilent green glow across the prairies. And with them, as timely as the lights themselves, come the spectators. From the south, from the university towns where the frost is half-hearted and literacy is rampant, carriages rattle up to chase them; from the north, where shelter is sparse, the dogsleds come down to flee them.

Physicists and scholars flood Bronfeld's single inn, hauling brass telescopes and chittering spectrometers from carriage beds and the backs of braying mules. Students make pillows of their books in the lobby, while adjuncts tap at the windows, hopeful for a vacancy. The old lodge makes its years' worth from a few weeks of hosting the brave southern academics. The rest of us, as the old treaties demand, host the dogsledders.

They make kennels of our garages and camps of our homes, but they are fine guests most years, facilitating a mingling of dialects, economics, genetics, and all the other exchanges that make feasible the existence of their migratory lifestyle and our stationary one. Compensation for a sturdy roof is offered by the yard, in wool spun from canine fur and dyed with the brilliance of melted plastics. They furnish us with deerskin coats, with scavenged machine parts, with baubles rescued from ruins only accessible through the fragmented ice of high summer.

Every year, in exchange for a month or two in the room I keep above my tavern, a young weaver offers me a tapestry. This year he's threaded copper wiring into his patterns, framing his ornate geometries with bottlecaps and glass lenses, little weights that chime as a breeze or ghost passes by. He lays his gift over my bed with great care, ensuring every wrinkle is smoothed out before we crawl under it and warm ourselves until dusk.

Afterward, he stands half-dressed on the icy balcony, casting his gaze to the crests of the knolls, where the physicists assemble their equipment.

I wish they wouldn't do that, he says.

A smouldering spliff passes between us, staving off the chill. He tolerates the bite of the wind far better than me.

Do what? I ask.

Try to fight it.

What harm can they do? I say. My grip on his dialect is strong enough to convey that I'm kidding, but too weak to convey that I'm not.

He replies in a whisper, out the side of his mouth, so the sky can't hear him. They tempt God, he says.

OLD AYBEE, as my grandma calls them, have always glowed over our little town. Even back when they were harmless, when they were nothing more than flickers of the sun's sidelong glance, Bronfeld had been the best place to watch them. We had clear air and a rare, broad sky unsullied by satellites, advertisements, or other flotsam set adrift from ages past. Before the Francoglot migrations—before the oil sand wars—we hosted thousands of abyss-gazers every year, or so say the placards unearthed from nearby burial sites. There are some human traditions not even apocalypses can change.

Some years are worse than others. Some years the lights pass us by with nothing but a brush of their thin, massless fingers along the treetops. Other years, they bring (or only *portend*, as the scientists say) misfortune, blight, or a winter so dark the moon won't rise until spring. The worst years are the ones they spawn, shedding little parts of themselves and seeding them across the plains. Wriggling curtains of light will peel from Aybee's periphery and scintillate between chimney tops, cold and keen as knives. Watchful, hungry, they might circle the town for a month or more before vanishing into the night.

My grandma likes to tell of a particularly bad spawning, a winter of seven straight months of darkness, three seasons smeared into a single, terrible night—no starlight, no glint of moon, nothing but Aybee on the horizon, on *every* horizon, casting their electric nets over the sky. That year was the coldest on record. Fires, when they did not sputter out entirely, burned blue and listless. Boiling water froze as it exited the kettle. Icicles formed along Aybee's field lines, dripping into slick-jawed traps over doorways, or crawling upward along the snowy sidewalks, waiting to bite a careless foot. Everything metal in the town, from toasters to snowmobile treads, began to ring, painfully, in pulses, and in a register only dogs and babies could hear. No one slept for the crying and howling, and that alone drove half the town murderous.

The only way to survive the night, my grandma says, was to board the train. Entire families climbed into the parlour car of the old Breath of Kannask, dragging luggage and supplies and bewildered pets. My grandma, then just a girl, lay under a table and cuddled her toiletry bag while the adults reinforced the rattling windows, building shields of wood and wire and body heat. Still, she saw the fields stretch beyond the glass, shrieking to thin, blurred lines in the green night. She remembered so vividly the juddering of the wheels, the chorus of screaming metal. At first she was sure she would die. She had never felt something so otherworldly as a rocking train.

Where did it take you? I asked.

To Aybee's blind spot, she answered. And then on to springtime.

She recounted every detail of the ordeal, how entire families snored in their seats, heads bent at every odd angle, and how, when the storms calmed, the children dared to dump the latrine bucket from the rimy deck of the caboose, dreading an unfortunate gust. How her father's affair with the schoolmistress had been unearthed when they attempted to copulate in a luggage compartment. She would spare no particular in her accounts. The only thing she wouldn't talk about was what they found left of their town after they disembarked, and the people who stayed behind.

Pray you don't have a year like that, she said. For what good it'll do you. There's only one God in Bronfeld that listens to prayers, and it's not the one you want.

THE PHYSICIST IS A YOUNG WOMAN, but not too young, and a decent drinker. She frequents my tavern every year, when light and temperature allow. She usually brings her mentor with her, an aging professor whose knees, she tells me, could not make the trip this year (nor the rest of him, she adds). She still brings his old apparatus, a monstrosity of a telescope tested, tinkered with, and retested every winter. She is adamant, like he was, that through a long, convoluted trap of mirrors and lenses, Aybee can be ensnared and subdued.

She leans at the end of my bar, explaining her theories to a devoted cluster of students. This year, according to her astronomical codices, will be a spawning year. This year she will capture a piece of those damnable lights. Caged in a contraption of reflectors and currents, she will bring a sliver of their young, vulnerable offspring back to her labs. Dissected with her microscopes and interferometers and incantations, Aybee, like all natural phenomena, will be stripped bare, examined, and finally brought to heel.

The weaver sits at the other end of the bar, nursing his creamed whisky and rubbing static between his fingers. He lowers his cup and says something I can't hear. The physicist turns, ears pricked, and asks him to repeat himself.

He does. Quietly, urgently, he corrects her. Aybee is not a natural phenomenon, he says. His words are heavy with Franco, and with wine, but he does not stumble in their recitation. They have been repeated hundreds of times around fires, between children tucked into dogsleds, between matriarchs meeting in the abandoned lobbies of obsidian towers. Aybee, he says, is a travesty molded by people like the physicist, a failed attempt to tame the last untameable beauty on Earth. Scientific efforts to domesticate the lights had turned them feral.

The physicist lets him speak. Then, with her half-smile of superior knowledge, she tries to explain the mechanics of the lights to him, the complex net of ley lines they follow, the angelic moans they emit when caught on wax cylinder. Half lecture, half retort, her students listen in awe. She doesn't fear the lights, not like the weaver's people do, who claim the ruin-rich lands in the north and still hide under southern roofs when winter rears its head. Little slaves to the sky, running like their dogs wherever the lights herd them.

Then catch it, the weaver says. Make bait of yourself; it will eat you alive.

Her eyes flare, irises streaked with glints of copper. She has a wide face, tanned and freckled—one that has seen the sky's tyranny south of the university towns, south of even the fungus geysers. She has known a sun that burns and blinds, a judge and executioner under whose searing gaze criminals condemned to death are staked without shade. What is the soft touch of a few chilly lights compared to that?

~

THAT NIGHT, the weaver moans beside me. He lies perfectly still, pinned on his back by a net of paralysis. Sweat gathers on his face, crawls down his cheeks, his shoulders, and ribs in thin, straight lines, darkening the sheets under his back. The tapestry rattles and chimes, staving off the worst, but his hair still stands on end, from his scalp to his pubis. When I run my palm over the trail at his belly, trying to smooth him down, he sparks against my skin. His mouth opens in a soporific gasp. In the garages under us, his dogs howl.

He has always been sensitive, his matriarch told me once. It is what makes him so good at weaving. He knows the intricate agonies of a field of intersecting lines; he can feel the sting of a billion minuscule forces, electric warp and magnetic weft. He can feel Aybee bend his vision, his dreams, his blood. Sometimes his tongue, and sometimes so strongly that he will wake, terrified, babbling in a language he does not know.

Tonight he babbles only in Franco. Freezing hot, he

clenches in his sleep, while green light spills through a crack in my curtains. I slip from bed and creep to the window, peering through the tinted casement. The lights pulsate a soundless rhythm over the town, injecting blue and green and pink into the flurries of snow blown from sloping roofs. The flares lick toward the chimney tops, teasing, testing. Across the street, from the inn's attic, a row of dormer windows glows. One of the casements flips open and a long, thin barrel of a telescope crawls out.

Before I retreat to bed, I fetch my grandma's sewing pins and close the slit in my curtains.

IN THE MORNING, when the dregs of sun cast blue-pink dawn over the snow, the innkeeper finds the body. He tells us, when we show up with our useless shovels, that he had expected a few deaths this year. He could feel it in his gouty toe. He just didn't expect the first to be so early.

The young man lies facedown, fingers curled in blue, bare fists. A spectrometer sputters next to him, ejecting long, inky strips of paper. When we call the physicist to identify her student's corpse, she kneels beside the apparatus and examines the output. She is saddened, mostly, to see the graphs are less than comprehensible. Another death, and no data of use.

He had been one of her braver protégés, she says. He often strode too close to the lights, seeking higher and higher ground, staying out late, even as the moon slipped past the horizon and the stars disappeared, leaving no light but Aybee. Last year she caught him out near dawn, thermos in one mitt and brass dials in the other, beet-red nose poking from a parka dusted with frost.

Last night, says the physicist, when the lights descended, he was wise enough to come inside with the others. God knows what compelled him to go out again. He forgot something on the hill, a notebook, or some vital piece of equipment. Or he heard a faint scratching at his window, as we sometimes do during the brightest depths of winter night.

We examine the body from a few paces away. Only the physicist dares to touch him, turning him on his back with a thick mitten. He is stiff, blue, mouth frozen wide as his eyes. A small knife of pale light rises between his lips, barely visible in the dawn. It ripples above his face for a moment, taking us in, then evaporates.

The physicist releases a breath, and I can't tell if it's horror or relief.

I told you it would be a spawning year, she says.

WE LEAVE the student where he is. He will stay there all winter, an offering to the skies. Animals won't touch him, and we won't bury him until we're sure a stalk of Aybee's light won't spring up from the ground where he lies. We don't need to fight a battle on two fronts, especially vertical ones.

A few of his colleagues, the younger adjuncts and members of his cohort, take issue with the decision. A pair of first-years attempt to reclaim his body and fail, unable to unstick him from the ice, caught in the frayed ends of Aybee's electric net, paralyzed and pained until they are forced to retreat. More out of respect for a fallen colleague than actual suspicion, the scholars jab accusatory pipes at the weaver, citing his challenge to the physicist. His *curse,* they insist. They're educated men. They know witchery when they see it.

The weaver ignores them. Instead, he speaks with his matriarch, who has set up camp in the machinist's garage with her nipping, white-furred pack. He sits among her dogs, exchanging a glottal conversation that only grows more intense as the day progresses. I bring them mulled wine for breakfast and hot whisky for lunch, a pretense for eavesdropping. Their words are swift and heated, but a few I can make out. Depart. Hunted. Under.

They are not talking about the scholars at the inn. They have nothing to fear from them. Their pointed fingers are only human flesh, their threats are formed with human tongues. Their violence, if it comes to that, will be fathomable.

All night, the lights curl their fingers around the knolls. Aybee rakes across Bronfeld, sparking fires in some places, drawing blood in others. My walls bend. Cutlery clatters helplessly in the kitchen drawers; sewing pins align and shiver upright. The weaver and I also contort, twisting into shapes of least resistance. Pierced with wires of stinging cold, we attempt to shield ourselves with one another. We wrap ourselves around ourselves, each attempting to dig deeper inside the other, bending our backs, cracking, crying out. Icy moisture traces field lines in perfect, parallel streaks down our skin, but in the dim green glow I can't tell if it's sweat, or blood, or something else.

We spend ourselves, utterly, torturously, and still cannot sleep. And so we throw on the tapestry, plastics and glass tintinnabulating in the waves of intersecting forces, and sit at the window, watching the scholars battle the sky.

Across the street, the inn's dormer windows open. Rows of armaments crawl into the freezing air, then retreat. Astronomers aim the sights of their telescopes, engineers fire columns of magnetism into the night. The physicist and her protégés, bent on vengeance, brave the street with their looping apparatus and their wind-whipped notebooks, frantically calculating the angle at which Aybee could slip into their trap. Their mouths move soundlessly as they shout over the electric winds; the ink in their pens freezes before it touches paper.

On the horizon, Aybee thickens and churns. Slender proboscises of light slither downward. The descent is slow, protracted over an hour or two, and eventually the threads converge, gesturing to the ground where the student's body lies. My view is obscured by a nearby rooftop, so I do not see the lights make landfall. But I can see the photonic appendages split and entwine and split again, glowing boluses bobbing up and down like elongated, swallowing throats.

My stomach turns. I can't tell if Aybee is eating, or inseminating.

~

WE'RE GOING, says the weaver. Before the nights get longer. We have to go. We're moving on.

His mulled wine shakes, slightly, in his hands. His hair stands on end, thick with static that even my roughest touches can't rub away.

South? I ask.

Deep, he answers. There are tunnels out west, in the mountains. Mines. Quarries. Places where a man and his dogs can run safely, under a few hundred metres of rock.

Aybee will follow, I tell him. You won't make it. Board the train instead. It's safe there, in the Breath.

He hesitates, turning something over on his tongue.

It's a spawning year, I continue, and I can't keep the hint of sorrow from my voice. It'll be bad.

I know.

You'll die.

So will you.

We sit, wordless, for a while. Outside, something like a cannon fires into the night. Streaks of green light branch across the inn's window, pulsating, probing, searching for cracks.

Stay here, I say, just as he says, Come with us.

In the ensuing silence, we mourn the inevitable.

~

I WAKE ALONE, and freezing. Instinctively I reach for him, straining my ears for the sounds of dogs down in the garages. The place is utterly silent. I have overslept. I have missed his departure.

Pre-dawn light peers through the curtains, and I fling myself from bed. I throw on a few layers, wrap his tapestry around me and descend into the street, empty except for sled tracks and injured astronomical equipment. Uselessly, I call after him, my voice echoing unanswered in the brightening sky. As I make my way down the town's main boulevard, I find nothing of him. Only the scraps of nocturnal, mathematical warfare, bent wires and broken glass and discarded notebooks steadily chewed away by tepid, green flames. A student, or at least the leg of one, pokes out from under the snow by the stables.

A chill deeper than cold crawls down my spine. The tapestry's baubles begin to chime and sing. Behind me, dawn breaks free from the knolls. The prick of pain on my back tells me it's not the sun that rises.

I know why I run. That much is obvious. But I don't know why I run in his direction. Maybe lovesick desperation, maybe because I know how to heed a warning when it's given. Maybe I am only swept helplessly forward by the invisible mesh of Aybee's will. Either way, I don't return home, I don't turn to the nearest shelter, as I should. Instead, I make my way westward.

Sparks flicker between my layered jackets. My throat tightens, my sweat runs against gravity, each droplet sharpening to a fine, frosty blade. My breath crystallizes as it passes my lips, millions of tiny needles glowing in Aybee's light. I lean into a sprint, skin opening in minuscule, parallel streaks, and will myself not to cry.

I don't stop running until I'm at the edge of town, where the fields begin, where in the distance, on good days, one can see the chipped teeth of the mountains saw at the sky. Striped with bloodied sweat, lips cracked under hoarfrost, I come to the collapsed train station. Broken brass lamps sprout from fissures of crumbled brick, angled toward carvings of routes long severed. Just beyond the platform, engine slumped nose-first into the frozen earth, is the Breath of Kannask.

The old war train lies half buried in snow; long tail of cars strung askew on broken tracks. The wheels are paralyzed under a thousand years of rust, yet the plated armour of each car remains intact, serviced by a staunch bloodline of Bronfeld machinists stretching back to when the train first limped up from the oil fields, fleeing something larger even than itself.

I shove open the parlour car door and climb inside. The atmosphere is more ice than air, solid, dead, perfectly still. I heave the door closed behind me in a hiss of flurried snow and make my way up the stairs; I imagine others will follow me as the day deteriorates, bringing food and bedding to add to the stockpiles in the luggage compartments. I crawl past rows of cushioned seats, reinforced and repaired over the years, and sink onto a stool at the bar. Slowly, my hair eases back downward, my breath returns to shapeless, colourless condensation. My heart slows, and I glance to the western window, where generations of Bronfelders have patched and barred the glass, scrawling messages of encouragement with pen knives across the metal sills. Here and there, passengers have left presents for their future selves, for their children. A well-worn book. A good bottle of liqueur. A toiletry bag filled with toys.

Outside, the fields shed sheets of green light. A granular mist shudders upward like uncanny, reverse snowfall. As I watch the glow rise, I pray for the swift feet of dogs and for the resilience of my weaver, who knows his way through a maze of perpendicular lines. I pray for the endlessness of his freedom, and for the stability of my metal cage. I pray I will see him next year, I pray there will be a next year; I pray for myself, and my tavern, and the physicist, and my grandmother, and I pray out loud, though I know Aybee is the only one listening.

As I spin my plea, I can almost feel the lights respond, clenching charged fingers around the parlour car. I can feel them grope blindly along the train's metal skeleton, this way and that, sweeping a pattern of herringbone as they search for gaps to slip through. And I feel, heavy as the tapestry around my shoulders, their infinite, invisible threads netting the sky, stretching taut, ready to snap.

JANE DOE'S TONGUE

LYNN HUTCHINSON LEE

PEOPLE DRIVE UP THE HIGHWAY TO THE DARK SKY PRESERVE *and peer with their telescopes into the black veil of the night. Awed by the mystery, satisfied and safe, they finally get back into their cars and drive home. If you live (as I do, or once did) in this lowland of silent roads and swamps and shadowed forests, that same veil may at any time lower itself over the trees and enter your quiet garden.*

At first you may be unaware.

The night draws you into its loop. It walks behind you as if down a dark hall. You can't get out. There is no beginning, no end. Only the coiled dark path like the ouroboros swallowing its own tail.

∾

WHEN LIO WENT OUT to the road at dusk, intending to look for mail in her mailbox, she saw a rounded shape in the ditch where there should not be a shape. *Body?* she thought. She nearly always saw things at this time of night, when the shadows of young cedars or sumacs or tree stumps coalesced into half-human shapes. When she called out, she heard no answer.

Her road was abandoned when they put in the county road, and then they closed the county road and built the highway, and the mail stopped coming. But she consoled herself: *There is always hope.*

These days everything was over the internet. A shipment of seeds. An order of inks or paper dropped off at the edge of the road by an unseen hand. Still. It was the reassurance of seeing her name on a package, evidence the world and its people were still out there.

She studied the ditch. No. There was no body. Only the shadow thrown by a clump of dogwoods. She was certain of this. Yes.

She longed for anyone, human or otherwise, no matter how amorphous or fleeting or damaged. *I'm open for anything,* she said to the ditch.

The shadow was body-shaped. A curled fetal heap, as if knees were drawn up to a chin.

She opened the mailbox (empty) and closed it again, not taking her eyes from the ditch-shadow. *Are you there? Are you real?* There seemed to be a substance, a mass to this shape.

A cloud briefly hid the light from the moon. She looked around. Bats swooping in the breath of the night. Wind high in the pines around the mailbox, night clicks and whines of insects. The cloud passed, and moonlight streamed into the ditch.

A body. Not a shadow hugging the low curve of the ditch, but a body.

A kind of scream came from Lio's mouth.

The body was small, fragile, twiglike. It could be a girl. Beside this body, this girl, was a shopping cart filled with sheafs of cardboard, a sleeping bag, clothes. Things in plastic bags.

When Lio started stirring around, not sure what she was looking for, the body shuddered, and sent her heart flipping like a fish in a net. An arm shot out and there came a hoarse cry. Who was crying here? Lio? The girl? The cry came again, clearly from the girl. *It's okay,* said Lio. *I'm not going to touch anything. It's okay,* knowing it wasn't. *I can carry you. Will you let me carry you? Who are you?* The girl didn't answer. *Who are you, girl?*

Under the overturned bowl of the night, Lio gathered the small twiggy arms and legs and lifted the girl light as a cat into the shopping cart.

How did you get yourself here? Lio waited for an answer, but none came. *Did you come down off the old county road,* she said, *or along the highway to Ottawa?* She found herself aching for conversation. *There's that one bus stop up on Highway 7 at the Actinolite Diner with its caged bear. Did you see it? The bear?* Did the girl register, or even care, what Lio was saying? Were there not greater priorities right now? Lio's tongue would not stop. *Nobody comes by here, really, except people who've strayed off the highway. I think they must have got lost looking for the old ghost mines around Eldorado.* How did she get started on that? The empty towns and hamlets, the haunted mine shafts in the hills, everything buried in abandon.

The girl's eyelids shivered with each jolt of the shopping cart as it lurched over the gravel and potholes of the track to the house, and her mouth opened and shut like a fish pulled from the river. *I'm going to give you a nightgown,* said Lio, *maybe a bath, you want a bath? And something to eat?* The girl did not answer.

The house was up ahead under the trees. Lio did not see the shred of darkness attach itself to the shopping cart, gliding along like a flag behind them. She shut the door. The dark drew back from the clearing and retreated to the forest.

~

LIO HAD a small bed in the seed room, where she slept from time to time when a young plant cried out for extra care. It was on this bed that the girl let Lio remove her clothes. *I'm giving you a bath,* Lio said, bringing a basin of water. The girl must have known Lio meant no harm, for she held herself still, then raised an arm and turned to help the lifting of her shredded blouse.

Lio wanted to cry out when she saw the girl's naked twig legs, breasts like dried apples, the jut of her bones, the shivering cave of her stomach. *O you poor starveling. You little sparrow.* She ran a facecloth over the papery skin. *Don't be afraid.* She lowered a nightgown over the girl's head. The girl's eyes opened and she made a cooing sound. Lio cooed back.

She brought a cup of thin broth. *Can you sit up?* The girl needed help holding the cup. She drank noisily. *Who are you?* said Lio. *What's your name?* The girl didn't answer. Her eyes were half-shut. *What do I call you?* Still the girl didn't answer. Lio turned off the light and went across the kitchen into her bedroom, and lay listening to the girl breathe in, breathe out. *Jane Doe. I could call you Jane Doe, although you're alive, and Jane Doe is what they call the nameless dead. Oh. I'm sorry, Jane Doe. I shouldn't say that. Should I.* A sigh came from the seed room. *Jane Doe,* said Lio, *Jane Doe,* floating the name over the girl's caved-in body.

~

LIO BOLTED UP when Jane Doe cried out like the coyotes in the night forest. How did it come to be morning? The sun was tipping up from the trees. The lemony light flooded her face. *You hungry?* she called. She went to the stove, trying not to rattle the pots and pans, concerned that Jane

Doe might be startled by sudden sounds. She prayed the hunters would not start shooting back in the bush, for it was bear season. *Here,* she said, finally, coming to sit on the side of the bed with a bowl of porridge. She brought the spoon to Jane Doe's lips. *Is that good? Yes?*

In the evening Jane Doe sat up, supported by Lio's arm, and sipped some tea. Then she freed herself and made throaty noises, reaching around, trying to crawl off the bed. *Is it your shopping cart? You want your shopping cart?* Lio had wanted a chance to go through its contents, hoping to find something that would tell her who Jane Doe was. She brought the shopping cart into the seed room, and Jane Doe pulled it close.

For three days, Lio fed Jane Doe with a spoon, and raised her up a little to drink tea from a cup. Each day Jane Doe ate a little more, drank a little more, and on the fourth day she supported herself without Lio's arm at her back. It took great effort for her to bring her legs to the side of the bed and pull herself up, hanging onto Lio, but she got to her feet, and they stood face to face.

Standing outside the kitchen door before bed, Lio felt something glide quiet as a falling leaf. A dark veil back there behind the trees? Or was it her own exhaustion? When she turned, trying to face it, the veil seemed not to have been there at all. She slept, but not well.

On the fifth day Jane Doe emerged from the seed room. She looked at the drawings covering the walls of the kitchen. *They're mine,* said Lio. *Some are for a book about night-scented flowers.* She pointed to the flared white petals of a jimsonweed. *These have an intoxicating aroma, although they are deadly.* She was unsure if Jane Doe understood, or needed this information.

∾

It was dusk when Lio was washing the dishes and didn't see Jane Doe open the wrong door and enter the knife room where Lio sharpened her knives. Jane Doe emerged howling, white-faced, hand clamped to her mouth. What in this room caused such terror? Lio rushed to comfort her, assuring her the knives were not a threat. She showed Jane Doe how she used one knife to ease a seedling out of its pot and into the garden. Another to cut a boiled egg into wedges. The small knife with its replaceable blades, for sharpening a drawing pencil to the finest point. Yet another to scrape the scales of the fish caught in the river, ease the white fillets from the coiled stinking innards. *These are the uses of knives,* she said. Jane Doe shook her head frantically. Her eyes rolled back and she retched into the wash basin; and Lio saw her fears were made worse.

My poor sparrow, said Lio, rocking Jane Doe in her arms, *my sparrow, my child;* and after Jane Doe's cries subsided, Lio opened another door, hoping to erase the terror of the knives. It was in this room, the drawing room, where Lio spent her days with her pencils and inks, sticks of charcoal and sheets of fine paper, giving light and depth to the flowers she'd planted among the trees of the forest and in the garden at the kitchen door. Jane Doe lifted Lio's drawings from the table. *They come alive at night,* said Lio. *That's when their scent is at its heaviest.* Here were the deadly jimsonweed, night-flowering tobacco, the white-petalled nightshade. Jane Doe pored over the drawing of veined leaves and lush long-tunnelled petals of the jimsonweed, its roots like tributaries of rivers. She shifted the pages in her fingers, bringing them close to her eyes as the dark came in.

These drawings, said Lio. *They're my life.*

Jane Doe ran her fingers over the paper.

You, too, could draw beautiful things, Jane Doe, said Lio. *You could draw anything at all. You could draw your life.* And she thought: *Then I would know who you are.*

Later, standing outside the kitchen door, she listened to Jane Doe's quiet breath. The veil appeared again far off behind the trees, dense as a seeded cloud. *My eyes are going,* she thought, but reasoned it was the night doing its work of bringing in the dark.

In the morning, Jane Doe took her shopping cart into the drawing room and shut the door.

AS NIGHTS CAME in earlier than usual, and colder, Jane Doe spent her mornings studying the drawings on the kitchen walls, and the afternoons and evenings in the drawing room, always shutting the door behind her. Lio was content to let her take over. She saw that Jane Doe had begun to recover, and seemed to have grown taller, stronger, and began to move with a self-assured grace. Even the night was affected: Lio no longer felt the menace of veils or shadows, and tree stumps and bushes were simply dark versions of themselves, and nothing more.

ONE MORNING LIO and Jane Doe walked through the trail into deep bush. It rained earlier, the path wet with leaves. The trail narrowed through swamps and low ridges of jack pine, then opened to a glade of aspen and birch. As leaves spiralled to the ground, Jane Doe held out her hands to catch them. *Isn't it beautiful, Jane Doe,* Lio said, and Jane Doe made sounds of delight.

Over the next days, the leaves of the maples around the clearing blanketed the forest floor, and the petals of the jimsonweed and night-flowering tobacco withered on their stems. The ground bloomed white with thin rinds of frost.

Lio saw the grey daylight scooped up earlier and earlier, and in the forest, night winds shook the thinning branches.

Sitting in the darkening kitchen, she heard Jane Doe move about the drawing room, sometimes humming tunelessly. She imagined the intensity of Jane Doe's concentration, the sound of her pencil gliding over the page. She needed nothing more than this.

After midnight Jane Doe appeared. She held out a sheet of paper. Lio brought it to the light, and saw the bright withered petals of the jimsonweed. They seemed to be reaching into the room. Behind them, heavy strokes of charcoal cast a violent exhalation. Like the petals, they slid off the page. Jane Doe's drawing was more than a drawing. It was the dark pivot between what has been kept alive and what is about to die.

Lio was overcome. In the lamplight she turned to embrace Jane Doe, and Jane Doe opened her mouth wide in a loud laugh. Some missing teeth, which Lio had expected. But her tongue. Where was her tongue? Jane Doe drew a deep breath and laughed again. There was no tongue. *O my beauty, what happened? What did they do to you?*

Lio felt the floor move under her feet, as if one end had lifted like a wave and then fallen. She made herself laugh with Jane Doe. She couldn't look, couldn't not look at the clipped root in Jane Doe's mouth. They stood together, each holding the other's arms, swallowing each other's breath, and in spite of wanting to cry, in spite of Jane Doe's missing tongue and her crow's voice, Lio laughed with her until Jane Doe's fingers loosened and she let Lio guide her to the seed room and toward the narrow bed.

∿

LIO TRIED to keep the horror of Jane Doe's tongue at bay. She moved her papers and inks into the knife room, and left the drawing room for Jane Doe. She liked to imagine Jane Doe at the table, and wondered if she was drawing the maples at the edge of the clearing, or more jimsonweed, or had moved on to stories from her life. She recalled the petals of Jane Doe's drawing as a blaze of white light, and the darkness a valley where no person should go. She sometimes thought to take back the drawing room, but did not want to disrupt a delicate balance.

In the mornings she awoke to breakfast made by Jane Doe. She loved to see her moving around the kitchen, the eggs carefully broken and waiting in the bowl, the plates on the table. She loved to hear the rattle of the cups, the water splashing in the basin. *My sparrow. My beauty. Where's your kitchen? Did you cook for your family, for your sisters, brothers, aunts? Or a child? Did you have a child?* Lio did not ask these questions aloud.

WHEN DID the night begin to heave and loom closer? Lio hadn't paid attention. Nor had she registered the dark shifting vault of the ceiling, or the shadows in the kitchen corners, black as the Actinolite bear. The night lowered itself over the forest. It came faster and colder. Not just a function of the moving earth or the changing season, but a movement that was purposeful, icy as winter waves breaking on a shore.

Daily chores and small pleasures came to feel like acts of resistance. There seemed scarcely any time between sleeping and waking and then sleeping again: shreds of the dark had begun to spill into the clearing. Each day it moved closer to the house. When Lio looked through the window she couldn't see the forest. As if it were walled off by the night.

As she lay in her bed, she tried not to think about Jane

Doe's tongue; but in the darkest dark it entered her dream, flying at her and fluttering around tangles of words that came out so urgently and so fast that she couldn't understand what they were saying. When she woke, she tried to find them, but they'd been swallowed by the dream.

A message came in on her phone. *Your package awaiting delivery. Please confirm.* A package. Had she ordered a package? Was it spam?

The sun. It would rise soon. She knew this. The pinkish ice-blood kiss would touch the sky before dawn.

They gathered wood for the stove, brought in eggs from the chicken coop, and cabbages and onions from the garden. Together they made soup. They ate, looking out at the forest. The trees were almost bare. They saw the bones of the land.

The afternoon quickened, and the dark slouched quietly near the edges of the clearing. A shadow settled itself into the eaves. For supper they ate soup again. Jane Doe washed the dishes and went into the drawing room. Lio let the fire go out. She went to bed. She may or may not have slept.

~

THE MORNING FLEW AROUND THEM, and too soon the veil of the night unfurled itself again over the clearing. It encroached on the dim vault of the ceiling, causing it to lift and fall, and before Lio knew it, the time had come again to sleep.

Again Jane Doe's tongue flew into Lio's dream. It was pink and tongue-sized at first, and then it grew, plumping up like the seedlings, like Jane Doe herself. It grew, and panicked, the tongue like a wing in a cage, trapped and beating at the edges of Lio's dream till it was too big, and Lio found herself sitting up in bed, soaking, heart thrashing against her ribs, and Jane Doe's tongue approached the threshold of her dream. *I love you*, it said.

Lio woke to inconsolable grief. The dream was a kind of farewell, a leave-taking. The night watched from the forest. She slept again.

She woke, checked her phone. *Your package has arrived.*

~

THE NIGHT LOWERED itself like black silk into the clearing, soaking up the fading daylight, and as the last of the light was sucked away, the dark moved in. It was close. Choking, almost. Even so, Lio was impelled to get up. She dressed and paused at the door of the seed room. Jane Doe lay on her back, snoring delicately, breath fogging the air. *Remember this,* thought Lio. *Always remember this.*

She opened the door. If not for the first luminous film of snow in the clearing and along the path, she would not have been able to see her way to the mailbox. But her errand was urgent. This time a parcel would be waiting. It could be a package of seeds, a box of drawing paper or charcoal or ink.

Her hand went into the mailbox and her fingers closed upon a small object. Sharp at one end. Sharp and then curved. The curve a friendly shape. She brought it out into her palm. The eyes of the night upon her. This thing, whatever it was, appeared to be some kind of ripping device. A device beautifully, horrifically crafted.

Jane Doe! Jane Doe! Her tongue! Lio threw the device into the trees. She opened her mouth and no sound came out. She ran, tripping over rocks and roots, and at the house she slammed the door behind her.

What were these sounds coming from the drawing room? Muffled cries, grunts, as if Jane Doe was attacking the paper, or was herself being attacked. Lio knocked at the drawing room door, rattled the handle and called, but didn't know what else to do at the moment. She sat on the bench at the kitchen door, overcome by Jane Doe's cries, the horror of the ripping device, the dark veil crouching behind the trees.

The sounds from the drawing room faded, and Lio was relieved, both for Jane Doe and herself. She had not wanted to sleep close to this voice, and imagined her own bed to be dangerous, as if infected by Jane Doe's cries. After some time, the door of the seed room creaked open, and soon after Lio heard Jane Doe's quiet rhythmic breathing. She was aware of her own eyelids closing, of the night circling like the Actinolite bear in its cage, preparing to settle.

She woke, shivering, from what may have been a dream or visitation. At the edge of the forest, the night held its breath. She felt a rip in the air. Would she, like Jane Doe, find herself walking along the remains of the road? Would she end up at another driveway, much like her own, and the woman down the road, a woman much like herself, would she be coming to look for nonexistent mail at night? Would this woman remark on the advancing blackness, as if a curtain or dark mist had been drawn across the road, as if the night was not the night but a living being, darker, bigger, swallowing the road, the trees, the bogs and fens, everything across these lowlands? Would this woman lean down to Lio, saying, *O you poor sparrow, lying here in the ditch?* Would she lift Lio into her arms and carry her up the drive, and as she walked, would the night walk swiftly behind her?

Lio opened her eyes. It was the thinnest, coldest moment between night and dawn. The veil was lapping at the edges of the clearing. The moon dropped behind the branches of the trees.

She couldn't remember leaving the bench and coming to her bed. She slept, and awoke later to kitchen sounds. Jane Doe was already up, and came to Lio with a cup of tea.

They carried in wood to start the fire, because a chill had settled in, causing the floorboards to creak.

~

THEY STOOD at the window and watched the clearing. They hadn't eaten all morning. They didn't know that they weren't hungry.

The darkness found the house in early afternoon. Lio brought out the coal oil. She cleaned and lit the lamps. Even the light they threw was dark. Jane Doe went into the drawing room and shut the door. Lio sensed her not drawing. She heard her pacing back and forth, as if in a cage.

An email from the publisher. *Your deadline was last week.* She erased the message. The veil was inside the house. It pressed against her, sending its web into her nightgown, her hair. It clung and she could not shake it out.

In the morning there was no tea and no breakfast. There was no wood in the fire. She called Jane Doe and Jane Doe did not appear. The door of the drawing room was open. The shopping cart was gone. Jane Doe was gone. *Gone? No. She wouldn't. Not without first letting me know.* Lio lay down in Jane Doe's bed and slept. It was darkest dark when her body jolted her awake. The night had sent itself into her mouth, sat perched on her tongue. *Get up, fast, move, light the lamps, make tea.* She ran into the kitchen. Yes. Lamps, hot water, tea. Cup on the table. *Drink, drink. Good.*

On the table lay a book, heavy, made of large rough pages, with a cover of bent cardboard. How had she not seen it before? Maybe Jane Doe had made the book herself. Maybe it had been sitting in the shopping cart, all this time, waiting to be finished. Could this be possible? *Draw, Jane Doe. You could draw anything at all.*

Lio opened the book, and saw a blackness swallowing the page. The black was coming from something that might have been a night sky. Clouds like fangs. Here was a bladed flying thing. Dragonfly? Helicopter? Drone? Shapes dropping. Fire, ash. Something tearing at the paper, tearing at the streets. She turned the page. Half a house with walls on the ground, a chair on its side. She turned the page. A table with breakfast or lunch or supper half-eaten on the plates. Other plates shattered on the floor. She turned the page, turned the page. A broken bed. On the sheet an unspeakable stain. *Jane Doe? Is that your house? Your bed, your kitchen? Are those your walls?*

Another page. A collection of shadows in a night room. They were busy at something. A woman on a table. She saw the twist of the woman's head against their hands. *Jane Doe? Is that you?* The shadow bodies or not-bodies were never still: bending, gesturing, examining, conferring, digging. *Get away,* said Lio. *Get away from her.* They turned. They saw her. She wanted to run at them. Get them off Jane Doe. The shadows would not allow her to move. They would not allow her eyes to look away. They would not let her save Jane Doe.

They passed a small sharp instrument among them. It glittered in the dark. The dark the dark. The page was black, with points of light. The stars. The big dipper, little dipper, pouring the dark onto the page and out into the room.

Charcoal had been worked and worked into the paper like the black curtain of night coming down coming down. The shadows did not want to release her hand. She pulled away and turned the page. She'd see to the end. The end. The pages so thick and heavy they creaked when turned.

So much black and black and black, nothing but shadow, the kind of shadow that pushed Jane Doe along an empty night road and sent her here.

Jane Doe had spoken, and these were her words.

~

THIS THIN SEAM OF NIGHT, *moonlight pouring through the knife room window, the air cracking like ice. What's this? The ripping device, on the table? Jagged blade, narrow broken edges. Smell of old metal and varnish and rust with fleshy notes, a thin meaty stain. Wooden handle painted and carved to fit perfectly in the palm of my hand, shallow grooves for fingers and thumb.*

I look at my hand. It may or may not be made to move toward the device. It may or may not be made to stop. There is a drawing in of breath, a sudden flash, a beauty, a shining, as if the whole darkness is briefly lit from inside itself. The veil of the night, or whatever it is in this moment, kisses the back of my neck and draws me in.

EVERY FRIDAY

NABEN RUTHNUM

I

FRIESEN ALMOST MISSES THE TURN, BUT THE PHONE holstered on the dash compels a right and his hands obey in time. He'd been looking for a landmark, the one he and Jennifer always hailed when they took this stretch, though he knows the place has been gone for years.

This is his fourteenth hour driving. Long enough, and mostly on highways he's driven so often, that when he looks through the windshield he sees not only what's out there, but also what he remembers and what he expects.

There's nothing where the building used to be, not even a billboard or a hole. Friesen's pretty sure everything he passed was just flat, frosted dirt. It had once been a shotgun shack that looked like a fish-and-chips shop when you passed at 30k over the posted speed, but with a yellowed plastic arrow sign advertising *Live Girls Every Friday*. They'd stopped once in the daytime, and not a Friday. A closed, empty bar, about six tables, no stage. *No pole*, said Jennifer.

It's closer to midnight than Friesen would like, even if it

is Jennifer he's dropping in on, who never kept normal hours. She'd said 'after dinner,' and in the old days, she used to eat dinner at ten or so, breakfast at noon.

It's the same dark here as it is every time you turn onto one of these little roads off 17. A dark that tells tentative drivers this isn't the road they meant to take. There are few of these turnoffs left, now. Most of the ones he can remember between here and Thunder Bay are old logging or construction roads, not paths to anywhere anyone lives.

He stopped counting the number of drives he's made across the country years ago, but could add them up if he went through his box of tour posters or his email. It's not a number that would impress a trucker, but it's high enough that he doesn't understand why he's still alive, why none of these half-awake long night hauls across these roads have ended in a ditch, a rollover, a fireball that would leave keyboards, amps, and three guitars scattered over his last kilometre of life.

Five minutes of road brings him to the place where Jennifer lives now, where she's been since she left Friesen's band and turned him into a solo project. They'd been between tours when she left, and they barely spoke in those in-betweens except to write and record. So he didn't know she had plans to leave until she told him she was done. Still didn't know why she chose this place, on this road behind the vanished bar that catered to the locals they had never seen but were now Jennifer's neighbours. The fans they had back then didn't understand why Friesen didn't have anything to tell them, assumed there was resentment, but it was just how he and Jennifer were: they played, they discussed what they played, they did the drives and shows. That was it.

He doesn't care that it's midnight anymore. He just doesn't want to go in yet. He knows this is it, the house. Jennifer doesn't post anywhere but she mailed him a photo of it, white with red trim, candy cane colours. Posted to his parents' house, the address she still has for him, where they'd crashed several times. The photo and an invitation to come. So short, more a note than a letter, and he'd replied with a date, the night he has between his gig at the Royal Albert and the one at Crocks in Thunder Bay. He didn't expect a reply but his mom had texted him a photo of a postcard he'd gotten, the only writing besides his address and hers an "OK." Mom sent him a picture of the front, too: it's a vintage postcard. A yellowed strip of border at the bottom reads *The Scenic Splendour of Northern Ontario*. Rolling forests in autumn, some red and yellow on the few leafy trees between evergreens your clue to the season. Two cars, both red, climbing the grey cut of highway in the centre of the image.

Before he arrives, Friesen wants to take some time where he's not driving, and not with Jennifer or anyone else. He turns the van around and starts driving back to *Live Girls Every Friday*.

No cars, no rigs on the road. He gets strange with the wheel, drifts across the centre line, stays in the other lane for half a minute, turns on the high beams to see if he can find the place where the place was. When he thinks he's almost on top of it, he brings the lights down to normal and heads off the road entirely, making a neat left turn onto flat cold grass, driving with faith. He feels the asphalt below before he sees it. He's in the parking lot now, and it's grown over the way places do in a jungle. It does get hot here in the summers, mosquito humid, but this still doesn't make sense. Grass and moss have taken over the whole lot, but it's still smooth under his tires. Like someone has raked micron-thin slits to connect the air and the earth beneath the asphalt, leaving it all there, making space for seed and spore to grow. Friesen doesn't want to step out onto what he's driving over, even when he is sure he's at the place, that the centre of this lot is where the shack once stood. He rolls past the emptiness where the six tables stood. He parks where the pole would have been if there was one.

When Friesen shifts into park and releases the brake the ground is gone. Not really, it can't be, but he feels the earth absent under the vehicle, the sensation of a foot floating through air where a step was anticipated. The illusion doesn't go away, the ground doesn't become solid again, even though Friesen tries to wait it out, because this is ridiculous. Not until his foot is on the brake again and he's out of the lot does the ground come back. He drives back to Jennifer's.

The building wasn't wanted there any longer; neither is anything else. That's the nonsense Friesen has in his head. To control it he begins to think of it as a lyric, starts to puzzle through what the next lines could be until he's in Jennifer's driveway.

II

"I INHERITED IT."

"The money to buy?"

"No. This place. This exact house. All the furniture. And another place in Sudbury that I sold."

"Every time we took this shortcut, not once did you tell me your dad had a place here."

"It's why I knew the shortcut. That was your clue. And it's not like I ever lived here with him, just a couple visits. No story to tell."

"That's a pretty weird way to look at things."

"Do you want another whisky?"

"Not if I'm driving."

"You can crash. So do you want another one?"

"Where's all your stuff? Nothing in here looks like it's yours. Upstairs?"

"I moved with my clothes and that's it. You must know Darren got my records. The books I left at Pulp. Drink or not?"

"Drink. What are you doing, then?"

"What?"

"You know, doing."

"Nothing. I sold the place in Sudbury so I don't have to."

"Travel at least?"

"I stay here. Right here. You want to get your gear while I'm in the kitchen? I'd like to hear your new stuff."

"You haven't kept up."

"I don't listen to anything, Ben, it's not specific."

III

FRIESEN'S OPENING the van when he sees the light behind the house. Light moving naturally. Fire. He has a Les Paul case in his left hand, and he moves a few steps to the right to see. It's not in Jennifer's backyard, but over the half-collapsed fence, in the yard behind hers. A bonfire, three men in boots at it. Flames high and hot. He can't see their faces, but he sees that at least the one closest to him is in a t-shirt.

He takes the forty-watt he uses as a preamp in his right hand. He checks that the Minimoog is where it should be; he has no memory of packing after the gig. But it's there, where his hands slotted it in automatically last night. He leaves it behind and backs out of the cargo through the smell of his laundry bag. Friesen's nose can't be getting more sensitive, but it's possible he's started to smell worse, some chemical process in his body slowing or speeding and making the bag smell the way it does. When his feet are on the ground again, he nuzzles into his jacket and inhales, finding the neutrality he was hoping for, with a trace of Pabst. But that's from a spill, not his pores. He kicks the van shut.

The conversation inside was toothy from the start, and that's Friesen's fault, unless he can blame Jennifer for how he thinks she was looking at him. They hugged when he came in, then she leaned back, smiled, and in the course of the movement becoming a smile, was watching him, no longer really here. Amused. She let her hands drop, pointed to the couch, and he started in on her about how dramatic her vanishing had been, and for no reason at all.

Touring, especially alone, it takes at least two tries to be normal when you leave the van and talk to someone from the world, someone who has nothing to do with the highway or the show. That's all this was, and Jennifer knows that reality. So she'll know why he was rude. And this time he'll be himself.

He'd left the door ajar, so it nudges open with the head of the guitar case. He hears the kitchen tap and familiar sounds that he soon understands as the filling of ice cube trays. The sound continues as he enters and looks for an outlet for the amp, finding one behind a big wooden cabinet television that itself isn't plugged in.

She's still filling ice cube trays, if he wasn't wrong about what the sound was. By the time the tap shuts off she must have done twenty, just from the time that Friesen came in the door. There's no dust under or behind the dead television, no dust on the wood floor when Friesen knees his way back to the amp and unfastens the guitar case. Everything in the room is old and clean in a way that doesn't suit it, as though the place has been preserved and relocated to a museum.

Jennifer enters with the drinks and Friesen apologizes with his back to her.

"Sorry for being a dick. My sleep has been fucked."

"Don't worry."

Friesen has the guitar strap around his neck and is wearing the Les Paul when he turns around to face Jennifer again. He takes the drink from her, sits on the arm of the recliner next to the amp. The guitar gives him a degree of separation that makes him feel comfortable in the room, with Jennifer, no matter how she's looking at him. He doesn't want to tell her that she looks the same as when she left ten years ago, because he knows he doesn't.

"You have a kit here anywhere? Basement?"

Jennifer shakes her head.

"Didn't bring anything, remember."

"I thought maybe you bought one out here with your new fortune. Hard to imagine you not playing."

"It's hard for me to imagine ever playing again."

"Why?"

"You know. I should have stopped a long time before I did."

Friesen hears more at the end of the sentence. It makes him not want to play for Jennifer.

She takes her own drink to the wall, sets it on the television, and turns off the overhead bulb. Only a side table lamp is on, the edges of its light just reaching his fretboard.

Jennifer starts pulling the curtains on the back wall open. There's a big bay window, with a cratered bench in front of it, the cushions missing.

Beyond the window is the collapsed fence, the fire, and the yard. Friesen sees the three men around the fire, and now there are lights on in the house beyond the fire. The whole second floor is lit up, and seems to be one continuous room, with curtained windows every three feet. Friesen can tell it's one room because he sees the shadows of people walking across the curtains without pause, crossing from one side of the house to the other. There are at least a dozen people. Most of them are carrying glasses, pint glasses, turning the shadows of their forearms into hammer handles.

His fingers have already put the amp on standby, the small ruby bulb glowing. The patch cord is jacked in. All of these things have happened while he was deciding not to play, because they are the things that always happen when the back of the strap is across his neck.

Friesen tunes instead of looking at Jennifer. She's kneeling at his case, and holds up the grey reverb / delay pedal and another patch cord when he finishes with the high E string.

"You don't need this?"

"My stuff has changed a little. I can just do a few songs clean for you."

"I want your best ones. Best three. So I think you should have something close to your actual rig, right?"

"That's a drum machine, two cabs, and my pedalboard is about twice what it was ten years ago, Jen, it's not going to be close. I'm just giving you the idea, right?"

"I think you should at least have this. At least."

Jennifer perches on the edge of the bench while he sets up. Friesen thumbs the bridge pickup's volume knob to where he wants it, as quiet as it can be and still get hot.

"Wait, don't start."

"No?"

"I mean, before you start. Are you really still getting something from it? And—I mean, you're here on a Friday night. Is that how the drive worked out, or could you not get a show on a Friday?"

"Both. But I would have moved things around if—"

"And are you still getting something from it?"

"I never loved the road part of things."

"Not this part. All of it."

"Yeah, Jennifer. Of course. It's all that means anything to me."

Jennifer is looking at him in that no-longer-there way, like he's a static picture on that dead TV in the room with them. He knows she's going to tell him that he hasn't answered her question, or that his answer doesn't mean what he thinks it does, so he thumbs the knob higher and digs the pick in.

When he starts to play, Jennifer looks down. She used to do this whenever he showed her a new track, usually from her throne behind the kit in their practice space, and Friesen thought it was because she was imagining her patterns under and overtop of the music. But she's doing it again here, and it's either habit or because she doesn't want to embarrass him, throw him off.

Friesen looks past her, above her. The people on the second floor of the house have stopped moving, all of them. With the curtains down and with the distance he can't be sure that they're facing him, but he thinks they are. It's impossible that they could hear, though.

He's in the middle of the second song when he feels a draft from the kitchen. A window, maybe a side door, is open. Still, not even the guys at the fire would be able to hear him properly, let alone the people in the house.

The third song is the longest, and he's glad for the delay pedal. He can do it right, set the loops, create something close to the density this piece has onstage. Turnouts have been bad this tour, and even the launch was flat. Lots of friends without childcare and others who moved out of the city to somewhere they could afford sending him hope-it-went-well messages. He sold three t-shirts. This song needs the collective intimacy of a packed, sweaty space to work. Maybe the intimacy of playing it for just one person will be enough. But his head comes up when he starts to sing and he knows he's not just playing for Jennifer, but for the men at the fire and the people in the house.

IV

THE LAST FRAGMENT of the loop dies after the third song, and Friesen waits for Jennifer to look up. She does, and sticks out her hand. Friesen thinks she's going to get up and give him a fake solemn handshake.

"Can I?"

"Can you what?"

"Grab the guitar."

"You learned to play?"

"Just give."

Friesen walks the guitar over, stands by Jennifer as she settles it over her thigh and starts to talk.

"There was nothing in the first or the third one. Nothing to salvage. But the second one, is perfect you. It gets the almost of you. Listen."

Jennifer starts to play. It's his song, the one of the three that he knows is the best, but she's changed it. There's a flat fifth in there where there wasn't before, there's a tiny modal run he can't figure out on the bridge, and when she starts to sing—which she could never do, not before—the melody is fixed, it's right. And the phrases she's singing are close, but different. Friesen has to recall something from a review of their first record to understand what he's hearing; the writer called his lyrics "placeholders for better words." Jennifer is singing the better words. They're what he meant to say, just like this music is what he intended before he wrote it. She plays right to the end of the song.

"Can I use that?"

"You won't remember it."

"I will. Since when do you—"

"It won't work outside of here. You won't be able to take it."

Jennifer lays the guitar on the floor and walks to the kitchen. Friesen's behind her, and it's not until he's at the small, open side door that he thinks to go in for his boots. When he gets back, Jennifer's at the fire, alone. Friesen crosses the yard, reaches the collapsed fence, looks up into the second floor to see if there are three extra silhouettes there. He can't tell, but they're all moving again, no longer standing still with their glasses.

At the fire Jennifer's quiet, standing in the warmth. Friesen thinks if he's patient enough, she'll drop the mystery, tell him what she's been doing with herself musically, and eventually surrender to the inevitability of making songs with him again. He waits, not looking at her, and looking past the flames. This yard doesn't seem to stop; it's a huge grass lot, and as Friesen scans it, disciplining himself to be quiet, he sees the sign. The yellow, plastic arrow sign, all of its letters missing. There are still a few bulbs, but they're all dark.

"You could never do it, Ben. You could never put it together."

"What together?"

"I just showed you. Twenty years, now. You know you couldn't ever do it, and you won't be able to. I just showed you, Ben."

"So don't just show me, come back and do it with me."

"It won't work outside of here. I can't do it either, only I didn't need anyone to tell me that. You do. I'm doing that for you now. So you can stop."

Friesen looks away from the fire and to the second floor. They're moving again, and now he can hear something from the closed windows. Something between speech and music, or an overlap: different conversations and pieces at once. It's impossible to tell from out here.

"I don't want to just quit. You shouldn't have either."

"I didn't. I came here. I stayed."

The fingers of Jennifer's left hand move in the firelight, a flutter, and they stay still for a second, as though she's forming a chord on the neck of the Les Paul again. She looks back at her house, and starts to move inside.

She doesn't invite Friesen, and he doesn't follow her. He doesn't know if he'll be able to stay there, if her invitation for him to crash was only for the night. If there's a permanent place for him it's probably in the house behind him, on the second floor or perhaps in the darkness of the first. He walks away from the fire to look for a door to try, deciding that he won't knock. The sounds from inside are clearer now: it is music, and singing, different distinct pieces, waiting to be sorted. Friesen will turn the knob; he will assume he's been invited.

DO NOT OPEN

RICH LARSON

THEY SAY HUMANS HAVE NO NATURAL PREDATORS, discounting oceanic whitetip sharks and man-eating great cats and saltwater crocodilians as opportunists or aberrations, since those fine creatures did not EVOLVE to prey on us.

They say this out of ignorance. They are unaware of the beast that has stalked us from the very dawn of history, following us down from the ancient canopies, across the marshlands that smoothed our skin, adapting alongside us to the cycles of agriculture, and I am not talking about a virus or bacterium, or making some kind of metaphor (homo homini lupus), which I loathe.

When civilization sprang up, when the great stone cities of Sumer took shape, our predator must have rejoiced —and again, millennia later, when the great ~~Nicolas~~ Nikola Tesla invented the lightbulb, tempting humans out from safety to scatter themselves across midnight streets. The unsleeping city teems with meat.

(Possible Dossier Title: THE UNSLEEPING CITY TEEMS WITH MEAT.)

~

LET us speak briefly of ants.

Ants trust chemicals over their own eyes and antennae. Meaning, a foreign attacker can slather itself in the fluids of the dead, as a dog may roll in roadkill, and descend into the nest unmolested. It puts one in mind of Little Red ~~Robin~~ Riding Hood: the guard feels the attacker's foreign body (my what large mandibles), sees their foreign coloration (my what dark chitin), and then—right this way, Grandmother!

(I have nothing against foreigners of colour.)

It may seem absurd to you, but the truth is that humans are equally susceptible to chemical trickery. There was a long evolutionary arms race between mankind and our nocturnal enemy, lost before we even kindled flame. This is why the predator's victims go all but willingly to their deaths. They are able to SEE it but not UNDERSTAND what they SEE. The French would call this an "angle mort." They are as stupid and certain as the ant in the tunnel.

As best I can tell, it has gone on like this for millennia. The predator has preyed on us with impunity, unwitnessed and unimpeded—until now. At long last, the genetic dice have colluded, and produced a throwback: a human lacking the correct chemoreceptors, or neural wiring, the predator evolved to pheromonally manipulate.

That is me. I first saw the predator when I was six years old.

~

IF YOU WERE in Northern Alberta during the winter of 1994, you might recall a sudden and vicious cold snap, which ~~occurred on~~ descended the very same day my father and I left Fort McMurray and drove east. The air that morning was thick, blank, and white, as if every last drop of moisture in it had frozen and blossomed. I recall my hands and feet turned numb during the drive, and every time my father rolled down his window to smoke, the cold felt like thorns in my eyes.

We did not stop for gas until nightfall, at a service station some ways outside Regina. On the edge of the parking lot, through the ice fog, I saw a shape. It stood higher than a man. I asked my father what it was, and he told me it was a phonebooth, and made it clear I should have known this already. (Phonebooths were a common sight back then.)

While he used handfuls of snow to clean the salt-splatter off our headlights, I jumped down from the truck and went to look more closely at the phonebooth. I ~~saw~~ found it to be a mound of pebbly black flesh, with glimpses of raw pink in the creases (I know them now to be highly elastic tendons that allow unexpectedly swift and sudden movement). Steam leaked steadily from a sort of organic chimney at its ~~top~~ crown.

When I stepped closer, with the fearlessness many children display briefly between developmental stages (after they learn autonomy and before they learn death), the predator (it was NOT A PHONEBOOTH) changed. Geometric angles forced their way out of the pebbly flesh, giving it a boxy look. Colour patterns emerged, as if an unskilled painter ~~were was~~ were trying to evoke panels of fogged glass framed by painted metal.

These changes were not occurring in reality, of course, but only in my mind's eye, as the predator increased the potency of its pheromonal ejaculations. But I had not yet studied biology at that time, and so I saw it as a wondrous ~~otherworldy~~ otherworldly phenomenon. I watched it almost fondly, mistaking its interlocking vertical maw for a gleaming zipper, and thinking it wore a heavy parka for winter, as I did.

My father paid for the gas and a carton of cigarettes, and took no notice of the predator. We drove off, and it is only now, years and years later, that I picture the doom of the clerk who worked at that station: during the midnight lull, staring out the frost-toothed window, the pheromone lure would have suddenly overcome him. Maybe he would have perceived it as needing to make a call.

In any case, it would have drawn him out into the cold, across the parking lot, all the way to the predator's maw. A moment of voracity, of sundered meat and splintered bone. Come morning, no sign of him. No sign of a struggle. No sign of a phonebooth.

~

I AM INSOMNIAC BY NATURE, and for this reason I had more opportunity to encounter the predator than most, even in my youth. Off and on, in various places and various guises—sometimes bulky and boxy, ~~all the better to~~ to better imitate a phonebooth or public toilet, sometimes tall and slender, ingratiating itself as a streetlamp or signpost. But always at night. ~~Always at night at night at night at night.~~

I accepted its presence, and the fact others could not perceive it, as a minor mystery, but certainly not worthy of obsession. Because to this point, I did not KNOW it was a PREDATOR. In contrast to the aforementioned beasts (oceanic whitetip, Bengal tiger, Nile crocodile), the sight of it triggered no reflexive terror, no evolution-honed foreboding. On the contrary, I found it oddly comforting.

I did not know it was a predator until the day I saw it kill and eat a ~~drunkard~~ man experiencing intoxication outside a metro station. I was nineteen then, and had developed a taste for speed, which was much safer and cleaner than the fentanyl-cut crank one finds nowadays. This compounded my insomniac tendencies, and I could go three or four days at a stretch without sleeping.

(It was around this period in my life I read Heart of Darkness, by Joseph Conrad, and realized that a Night Journey is fundamentally different to a Day Journey, and further realized that my life is a Night Journey.)

The metro entrance was long since shut when I arrived there; I had lost track of time. So too the drunkard, who thumped his hands against the locked doors, then cursed and staggered away. His path took him right past a predator, which was standing with its wide and heavy body pressed against the concrete wall of the station.

I had seen it earlier from the corner of my eye, but had taken less interest than usual, since the speed had sharpened my mind to a scythe that ~~wonted wanted only for~~ only wanted a swift route downtown. But now I took interest, because the predator's maw was slowly opening, which I had never seen before, and from within there ~~emnated~~ emanated a yellowish sort of bioluminescence.

I believe the drunkard saw it as a vending machine. He was rattling coins in his coat pocket as he approached it. I watched, still with no sense of foreboding, as the predator's vertical jaws opened wider. Now the pheromone lure was so strong that the man forgot even the fiction of the vending machine. He clambered inside as if clambering through a window, and remained calm as the predator ate him.

Much later, I learned that spiders are calm while the clinging larva of a parasitoid wasp gorges itself on their flesh. To this day (October 11 2003), I am unsure if I would have preferred the man to have screamed.

~

ONCE I WITNESSED its true nature, the fact I could see the predator's true form gained new ~~signifigance~~ significance. Its camouflage was that of the hunter, not the hunted, and as such it was a threat, if not to myself, then certainly to humanity at large. I felt no guilt over the deaths I had allowed through my previous inaction, as I had been working with incomplete data, but I did feel a new sense of responsibility.

(While my current lifestyle entails very little human interaction, and I despise Socialism in any form, I am very much pro-social. The idea of saving a civilian population from an exterior threat has always appealed to me.)

To defeat an enemy, one must understand them, as ~~Earnest~~ Ernest Hemingway understood the fascists in Spain. Until now, my forays into researching the predator had been idle and amateurish, but the very night I witnessed the drunkard's death I began again, this time in ~~ernest~~ earnest.

There is much knowledge that is, for various reasons, suppressed. For example, the extinction of a grand pre-historic civilization by flooding and mudslides, and the Aryan lineage of the ancient kings of India. But even in the dark corners of second-hand bookstores and web forums, where such suppressed knowledge flowers freely, I found no documentation of the predator's existence.

It was then the feeling I had ~~bore born~~ carried since I was a child crystallized into thought: I was the only one who knew. Through genetic luck of the draw, I and I alone could perceive the predator.

For this reason, I was forced to do my research in the field.

∼

THE NOCTURNAL NATURE of the predator was obvious; each of my encounters had ~~been~~ taken place during a night journey. But for all their bulk, the organisms were clearly mobile, as I had never seen one in the same location twice. (This despite returning several times, compulsively, to the metro entrance where I had witnessed death.)

Its carnivory was clear to me also, now that I had seen the mechanisms of its spiny maw were adapted for the shearing of meat as opposed to the grinding of plant matter. But what of its bloodline? From what evolutionary branch had it descended? I required a live specimen to study, and after a fruitless, sleepless week, I found one crouching among the weather-chewed benches in St. Louis Square.

It was no doubt awaiting some unlucky ~~vagrant~~ unhoused person, unspooling its chemical tendrils through the cold dark air, but for the moment we were alone in the park. I approached it slowly with my pawn-shop camera in hand. Though I knew the quality of the photographs would be low, given the lighting, it still seemed prudent to acquire visual evidence, so I took some two dozen shots from a variety of angles.

The predator seemed undisturbed by the flash and click, even as I moved to within arm's length of its amorphous body. Here I began to wonder ~~at~~ about its sensory perception: since it had no apparent eyes, ears, or antennae, I decided it was not attuned to sights or sounds. Apart from its foul threshing mouth, the only observable opening was the orifice atop its head (though the head is not delineated from the trunk).

My knowledge of the pheromones, which I imparted to you very easily, was hard-won, and the first steps toward a hypothesis were taken that night in the park. When I moved to inspect the orifice more closely, approaching it from the back so as not to tempt the predator's jaws, a gush of warm vapour enveloped me.

The pebbly dark flesh became slats of wood, and I wanted nothing more than to sit, for a moment, and rest my legs. This was the predator's pheromone at full force, an olfactory overload deployed, perhaps, as a defence mechanism, if it had indeed perceived me (at last) to be a threat. But the illusion and the urge lasted only seconds, at which point I ~~was free to~~ proceeded with my investigations.

For what came next, I needed an immobile subject. After charting the visible pathways of tendon, those pinkish elastic creases that stretched from its midsection to the muscly pseudopods below, I determined I could achieve my goal with only a few judicious cuts. I had brought a butcher knife for just this task.

∼

NOTES ON THE VIVISECTION:

The vivisection was unpleasant. The predator attempted to flee after the first incision, and I permitted it, to gauge its speed. It moves by undulation, skating its own secretions like a snail, and is surprisingly swift. I pursued it halfway across the park before I was able to sever enough tendons to paralyze it fully.

From there, I began exploratory surgery. I am not sure ~~what~~ how it would have looked to an onlooker, whether I would have appeared to be suffering a psychotic break, vandalizing public property with inexplicable meticulousness, or if at such close proximity the predator's pheromone would have concealed me altogether. In any case, the predator squirmed and writhed but was unable to escape.

When I had finished with the exploratory surgery and the gathering of samples, I killed it (this was both an act of mercy and part of my research). Since I had no knowledge then of the predator's metabolism or digestive processes, I poured one (1) gallon of bleach down its cavernous orifice, followed by one (1) gallon of sickly sweet antifreeze, then stood back and hoped for the best.

It took several hours to die—I have since switched to gasoline, which is quicker. But when it did finally succumb, it solved a mystery that had been gnawing at me: the predator's absence from the fossil record, and the fact that its fresher corpses (which surely could not emit the pheromone) had gone undiscovered as well, despite the fact that the predator seemed to favour urban hunting grounds.

I took several photos as the predator's body dissolved, seemingly from the inside out, subject perhaps to the same powerful digestive fluids that liquefied its victims. I will attach those, along with the other photos, here.

(REMEMBER TO ATTACH THE PHOTOS.)

~

I HAD INTENDED to share my discoveries with those around me, which included the night security man with whom I smoked cigarettes, my neighbour to the left (the neighbour to the right should in fact be eaten), and my father, who was alive at that point but unwell. But even with (low quality) photographs in hand, I found I could not bring myself to tell them about the predator's existence.

Even just imagining their skepticism brought about a terrible anxiety, comparable to an LSD trip in my early teens during which the crowded metro became an endless termite mound. I realized it felt better, quite frankly, to NOT speak about the predator—and instead simply DEAL with it. If ~~noone~~ ~~no-one~~ nobody else is capable of doing a thing, that thing becomes your duty, and now this was mine.

This meant reducing my work hours at the liquor store, and adopting a more frugal lifestyle with fewer vices. I became less and less enamoured of the day. By day a city is a carcass obscured, swarming with ants. By night you see the bones picked clean, and better understand the joints and sockets, the haphazard evolution that so mirrors our own.

It was evolution's blind hand that blinded us to the predator. It seems a monstrous trick that we should be permitted to think ourselves, for eons now, the apex species, when in fact we remain feed for something that, in all my midnight studies, has shown no sign of intelligence. I wonder often what our early co-existence looked like, what forms (boulder, tree, hut) the predator used to assume in the early hominid brain.

Its maw puts me in mind of the ~~Anamolocarus~~ Anomalocaris; perhaps it is a descendant. Perhaps it followed us up from the waves. In any case, its reign has ended (at least in this city) and I will purge it from existence. Evolution permits that also.

∾

I HAVE LIVED NOCTURNALLY for three years now.

I wake up at 9:58 PM precisely, dress myself, and go out to my car. Before I get inside I sit on the hood and do a deep breathing exercise. I imagine I am inhaling a black jelly into my lungs, which will allow me to properly interface with the night, which is FUNDAMENTALLY DIFFERENT from the day, with no danger of sudden decompression (the bends). This is calming, especially when the air is cold and crispy and has just a trace of gasoline.

While I drive I listen to the antilullaby crackle of the police scanner, which is sometimes punctuated ~~with~~ by the sound of actual sirens. I listen to the dispatchers talk about all the White Male Suspects and Indigenous Male Suspects and Black Male Suspects, and I think it's so sad that it's so tough, these days, to be a Suspicious Male. Sometimes all I do for the first two hours is drive and ~~scream and drive and scream~~ ponder.

Most nights I come up empty, and that's the sad truth of it. I can crawl this city from dusk ~~til 'til till~~ until dawn and see no sign of the predator. I see its prey, of course: people wandering off alone from parties, sometimes too intoxicated to walk upright, sometimes taking a long dark alley as a shortcut. I could shout warnings to them, but it would do no good, and lately I fear to speak at all.

That is why I must compile my thoughts and findings in this manner (the dossier). I believe in neuroplasticity. I believe that if people read this dossier, and then the greats (Hemingway, Conrad, etc.) and then breathe the night air and see the city's bare skeleton, they would begin to see what I see.

As I GROW MORE attuned to the predator's habits and whereabouts, I grow more successful, and each successful hunt seems to trigger an even greater appetite for the next. My chief expense is now gasoline, which I use to fuel my car (the city's haphazard infrastructure does not lend itself to expeditions on foot) and as poison. ~~I have begun to wonder if I am driven by something other than duty.~~

Though my chief goal is to hunt the predator to extinction (by reducing the number of predators such that they no longer have a viable breeding population), I have also learned the following things:

DIURNAL HABITS: the predator feeds only at night, and so during the day it either adopts less inviting forms (jagged mounds of rubble, disused construction equipment) or hides itself fully in culverts and sewers.

ANATOMY: subsequent vivi- and dissections yielded more questions than answers, but it is clear the predator's skeleton is hydrostatic and its most complex organ is the gland (located inside the orifice) that produces and combines a wide array of chemical substrates.

REPRODUCTION: I briefly entertained a theory that the predator was larval, and its adult form was the flying creature sighted in West Virginia, but only until I found a predator sequestered beneath an overpass with several large ~~sacks~~ sacs growing off its body. I attempted to keep one embryo for research, but once separated from the parent's flesh it dissolved (like the parent's flesh post-mortem). The same was true for all subsequent "pregnancies" I discovered.

This last area of study still gives me pause. Other apex predators favour low birth rates, long gestations, in order to not outbreed their food supply—but my predator would seem to spawn like a fish, an unsustainable strategy even in a city as large as this one.

How do they avoid the bottleneck? Perhaps it is simply down to the human population exploding exponentially over the past decades. There is more prey than ever before, so they reproduce accordingly.

∾

I CANNOT TALK about the predator.

There is a concept in linguistics called "taboo variance," which you probably know about already because any slightly interesting ~~minutea~~ scientific minutiae gets recycled ad nauseum on the internet, and that is where I learned of it. "Taboo variance" is where a culture develops a new name for a creature they fear (most famously the bear) because they think saying its original name aloud might somehow attract it.

This is not that at all. I have never given the predator a name, but now I find I cannot speak of it even abstractly. I discovered this on my father's deathbed. His health has fluctuated greatly in the past years, so it was not a great surprise to see him go, but there in the hospital I felt the great urge to tell him of my secret burden. In fact, it seemed strange to me, all at once, that I hadn't already done so.

Earlier I mentioned anxiety; and it redoubled in that moment. I felt a horrible dread that he might disbelieve me. But I have always been strong-willed, and so I was able to ~~push~~ tunnel through that dread, and begin to speak. My words came out in no existing language. I would liken it to the sort of religious glossolalia in which the Baptists (my mother was a Baptist) believe so fervently.

Perhaps it was a comfort to him as he died. Personally I found it very disturbing.

～

I CANNOT SHARE THIS DOSSIER.

At first I reasoned it was because the dossier is not complete. There is more hunting yet to be done and I would see the city fully purged before I inform the public of the predator's existence, so as to limit their panic. After thinking this thought a thousand times, I realized the illogic of it. So I determined to anonymously upload the incomplete dossier online—but my hands, so nimble in the handling of knives and gasoline, will not obey me.

It is the glossolalia (which I tested again with an employee of a 24-hour convenience store) under a different guise. I cannot share knowledge of the predator's existence. That is why I never remarked on it as a child, that is why, even when I knew its deadly appetites, I never warned those around me or tried to ~~flourish~~ furnish evidence. I have my own "angle mort," somewhere deep in the structures of my brain, and there is only one possible reason.

～

I AM DRIVING. It is a damp winter, and the streetlamps wear halos of frost and fog. I have made as many copies of the dossier as I can, in as many places and formats as possible. This one is an audio recording; that is why I am not listening to the police scanner and is also why (hopefully) you can hear my voice. If you cannot hear my voice I have been insufficiently creative.

All apex predators must keep their populations in check. Humans have plagues and war, but the predator is too ~~hearty~~ hardy to succumb to microbial invaders, and not social enough to murder its kinfolk. Instead, it is culled by its own prey. Individuals selected from the herd, perhaps for a unique disposition (as I had vainly thought in my youth) or perhaps at random, and pheromonally programmed for a far more complex role than fodder.

Oh, there have been many like me. I am sure of it now. I am sure there are others, even now, other solitary hunters who cannot tell their tales at the campfire, who believe they are saviours but are more the Judas goat that keeps humanity in perfect step with its predator. Perhaps we are even an evolutionary whetstone, weeding out only the weakest specimens—for every predator I saw and killed, how many were hidden from me?

I cannot willingly share this dossier, but I am not infallible. If I continue to make copies, and continue to ~~keep moving~~ move, eventually an error must occur. There MUST BE an angle mort inside the angle mort. And if I stray to new hunting grounds, and hunt long enough, I must eventually find one of my counterparts in the same thrall, and perhaps free them. Things cannot go on as they have for millennia. It is unthinkable to me. It is anathema to me.

This is a night journey. I am driving until I see the lights of another teeming city. I must not use any phonebooths. I must not sit on benches.

WHAT IS WAITING FOR HER

SENAA AHMAD

THAT NIGHT, NISHA IS THINKING OF THE BIRDS, HER sister's jewel-toned birds, and how they throb with accusation when they see her now. How strange it would be if they died all at once, how beautiful, like stiff Ophelias tumbling into grief. The thought makes her yelp, partway between a sob and a laugh. The meanness of it. She's shivering and she tries to make herself stop, but she can't. Then she's standing before the old empty railway hotel, the Galatea, and it's drowning in light, and she's so lonely, she can't breathe. The night is cold and endless, and the Galatea beckons. Is she invited, or is she inviting herself in?

It doesn't matter. The doors swish open when she steps forward. A swell of heat and memory that's overwhelming, because she's been here before. She's almost sure of it. No doorman or concierge tonight, the lobby emptied of any life, but as she stands there, coatless, gripping her own arms, she has the prickling sense they were all here a few minutes ago, maybe even watching her silently through the glass, and it's just that everyone left in a hurry.

All the better. She's not bothering anyone. She's only a woman with a hole in her heart, and she's not making a fuss. Her sister would say, "It's no good to be alone, Nisha." But her sister isn't here now, is she.

The gentle tug of the furnace butters her tense joints. It comes to her slowly, on the tip of her tongue. Yes, she remembers the Art Deco dazzle of this lobby, with its expanse of black-and-white floor tiles. How could anyone forget? But she did. Those tufted emerald settees. Ahead, the marble slab of the front desk, white flushed with grey veins. Imported from the Apuan mountains, she'd been told once. Michelangelo's marble. Even now, after all these years, not a speck of dust to be seen.

In the distance, she can hear the Galatea's famous brass band playing somewhere, the cornet tolling brightly. How far away it is! All she wants is to crawl into that jubilant sound. Seal herself in. She used to have a crush on one of the drummers, but he kept his distance; he would smoke behind the hotel with everyone else, those extravagant eyebrows furrowed together. Once, she saw him touch a waitress by the crook of her elbow. Seeing him touch the waitress made Nisha go still with agony. He leaned forward and kissed the girl, and it was like he was reaching through her and kissing Nisha herself. She could feel it reverberate through her entire body.

They fired him shortly after. No one touched the girls, that was the unspoken rule; certainly not the staff.

Now she remembers. She worked here one summer long ago, cleaning the rooms, back when she still lived in town and the hotel was still open. That's right. Did it just slip her mind, all these years? Does that happen to other people? That night she saw the drummer, she had in fact been watching him from a window upstairs, unable to move or breathe in her unending desire, when she heard the smallest creak behind her.

It was the executive housekeeper floating towards the

window like a vengeful angel, her bun a flash of platinum, her eyes gleaming in the dark. She was watching, too.

Here and now, alone in her funeral best, Nisha walks up to the front desk of the Galatea. The steady clopping of her heels echo in the emptiness, the distant swirl and fervor of the brass band. What is she doing? Maybe this is grief, inexplicable in its impulses. If her sister were here, she'd get a good chuckle out of that. She loved a good chuckle. She'd say, "What about the birds, Nisha?"

And what about them?

Nisha's been good to them these past weeks, she's tried, but they're inconsolable. Her sister would have agreed. In their grief, they turn against Nisha, one by one, as if it's her fault, and they know somehow she is to blame. Even though she isn't. Laila, the dusky blue macaw who flexes her talons with menace whenever Nisha approaches, who says in her frail, angry voice, "Is that my sweet little girl?" Some line from a movie.

At the front desk, a key sheathed in its blush envelope. Before she picks it up, she knows it's for her. It's dizzying to hold it in her hand, the weight of the cardstock. How did she know it would be here? But she did. As if she can sense the Galatea, what it wants. Almost as if she never left.

A rustle, somewhere nearby. She swivels to see who's watching. No one's there. Nisha's aware of her own heartbeat thrumming against her collar. She laughs at her own foolishness, shakily. In the quiet, it's a huff of breath. It's almost an exhale of relief.

The hotel was so lively, back in its day. When she first interviewed for the job at the hotel, she'd sat in a long, crowded corridor with the other girls. That was more than a decade ago. No birds to look after, not then. There was an air of festivity to it all, like they were at a party, the grandest of friends. They were in their early twenties, college grads or younger. A freckled girl sitting in the next chair, Talia, leaned forward and murmured to her, "This feels like an audition, right?" Nisha laughed—what a joy to be spoken to! —and she said without meaning to, "Everyone's so pretty."

The girl nodded and said, unsmiling, "Exactly."

In the interview, she met the executive housekeeper, an older woman who stood to meet her but didn't come forward, just waited for Nisha to reach her. The housekeeper was tall, birdlike herself, angular and glittering in the sunlight that streamed through the windows behind her, her blonde hair shellacked into a bun. Like meeting an iceberg. She shook Nisha's hand, and it was a little like shaking the hand of an iceberg, too. The whole time, the executive housekeeper smiled with all her teeth.

"Fresh-faced," she said by way of greeting, "perfect." And here she reached out and pressed a frosty finger against Nisha's face, as if to confirm its supple quality, its youthful vigour. Horrible. Nisha tried not to flinch. Her smile must've been a mirror of the executive housekeeper's own, in that moment—as in, terrifying.

"No chipped nail polish," she was informed at the end of the interview. "Absolutely no bruises. You understand? Think of your skin as a work of art that you're supervising."

And Nisha wanted to ask the executive housekeeper: who am I supervising it for? Who gets to keep it, in the end?

But the housekeeper was already standing, facing the door. They were already ushering in the next girl.

In the lobby now, gripping the envelope with its key, she wants nothing more than to shed her clothes, this grim and absurd costume of sadness. Absurd because her sister always hated the colour black. "Are you goth now?" she once said to Nisha, when Nisha dropped by for a visit, her nails painted an offending midnight. "Is that what we're doing?" She thought black was cheap, depressing, not even a colour technically, but an abject bid for attention, a way to radiate gloom.

What a doleful thought—and how was Nisha supposed to answer? That day, she grinned at her sister, trying to emit happiness from the core of her being, as if it could be pushed out of her sternum and into the world. "Come on," she said. "You really think I look sad?"

Now, she's on a mission. No one in the hallways. Everyone's gone for the night, except the band. Everyone's gone forever—her sister; the birds. It's her and the hotel, just the two of them, the last ones left.

The indoor pool of the Galatea is exactly as Nisha remembers. It opens its slick mouth to her, black volcanic rock, pleasingly uneven. She strips to her underwear, she is beyond caring who can see what, and no one is here, anyway. She plunges in. The water is heated, lustrous in the swaying lantern-light. Far away and close by, the brass band is starting a new number, languid and easy. The pool seems bottomless, and she can relate.

She holds her breath and sinks, expanding in every direction but up.

When was the last time she did anything for herself?

The summer she worked here, they were only allowed in the pool if invited by the guests. One of the other girls, who worked as a room attendant last summer, told her about this particular rule.

Nisha had said, bewildered, "Why?"

They were in the locker room, putting their belongings away, doors slamming, spitting their gum into tissues before the start of work. The hot, bright smell of everyone's aerosolized perfume. The girl, Samantha, dropped her voice to match the executive housekeeper.

"Because no is a word *they* must not become acquainted with," she intoned with the housekeeper's contralto, her eyebrows lowered, and a ripple of laughter ran through the other girls. *They* meaning the guests.

"Right," Nisha said quietly, trying not to be heard by the others. "But why would the guests even ask us to come?"

Samantha didn't dignify this with an answer. She shut her locker door and smirked at Nisha, with a kind of significance that required no further explanation. The girls would make a game of it. How often could they negotiate an invitation to the pool from a guest; how little could they give up to finagle it. They were young and envious and working there made them feel inadequate and small, tucked away into the corners of the hotel, aware of how much everyone else had, and how little of it was theirs. This felt like a small, wicked power, this game they played. Nisha loved them for it. Anything could be tolerated if it was only a game.

Did the executive housekeeper know? She must have. She knew everything. Back then, Nisha suspected that she encouraged it. Like she wanted the girls to become attached to the guests, to desire what they desired; she wanted the girls to be hungry.

And the guests. They were something else. The young couple who brought their three sleek, whippy dogs everywhere, graceful Salukis. The dogs had their own room and it was foul. Nisha was responsible for cleaning it. The first time she pushed open the door, she almost vomited.

"They never leave a tip," Samantha warned her beforehand, and both girls stared at each other, furious at the idea. Samantha brushed Nisha's wrist with her fingers and said, "I know. I did their rooms last summer. Seriously, I know."

It didn't help. In the foul room that belonged to the Salukis, scrubbing the floor on her hands and knees, trying not to retch every time she inhaled, Nisha came up with a little story about the couple.

Something was wrong with them, she decided. Something awful. It was growing beneath their skin; they fed it with their joy, their abundance, not realizing it was there, that someday it would hatch. The two of them were absurdly good-looking, pore-less and sun-swept, so perfectly symmetrical it was unfair. Impossible that they could ever be out of sorts.

But one day, they passed her in the hallway and smiled at her. When they turned away, she saw it. The creamy petals of their faces began to part, unfolding to reveal the second face underneath.

She had to clench the handle of her cart so she didn't cry out. Her hands were cracked and dry by then. It hurt. She should've been afraid, maybe. In truth, she was exhilarated. This was her own wicked little power, she thought, standing with her cart. Like she'd made the story come true. The hallways of the Galatea seemed to expand around her, in sync with her own breathing. She inhaled and the walls flexed towards her, squeezing her in. It had been a thrill, the possibility of it all.

She was wrong. It didn't have anything to do with her. She hadn't known it, not then, but she'd been a fool to believe it. Like the girls and their game, it was only the illusion of control, wasn't it?

Now, years later, she surfaces from the water and there's a gilt tray waiting on the deck—it wasn't there before, she knows that with a ringing certainty—beside a plush towel and robe. Her size. And the room key in its rosy envelope, placed on top. Nisha leaves her clothes behind. She isn't sure which Nisha she's leaving behind, but there it is, a forlorn lump, a skin without flesh.

The robe hugs her, soothes her, won't let her go. Egyptian cotton. So soft it feels like the underbelly of a beautifully furred animal. In the pocket, a small moon: a billiard ball carved from ivory. She understands already, what she's meant to do with it. How does she know? All these little secrets, locked in her head. Where they've been hiding all this time, she has no idea.

She sets the ball on the ground beside her bare feet. It rolls away from her and she follows.

Away from the pool, turning back towards the hush of the first-floor hallways. The ball has a mind of its own. She knew it would. The brass band dims somewhere behind her.

These hallways, they float things to the surface. The drummer with the eyebrows, sipping a coffee behind the hotel, nodding to her as she passed. That long corridor the day of her interview, shimmering with good humour and sunlight. The freckled girl, Talia, who sat beside her, unsmiling. Much later, when they both worked there, she said to Nisha, "Why did they hire us?"

"What do you mean?" Nisha had laughed a little at the question. She was such a little turkey in those days. Talia was trying to convey something to her, she'd understood that, in the urgency of her voice, the seriousness of her face, and Nisha wasn't listening. "You think the house-keeper can do all this by herself?"

"But why did they hire *us*?"

"What's wrong with us?" Nisha asked, bewildered. But she knew what Talia was saying. It was the same thought she'd had before. Like the hotel and its guests dined on their desperation, their youth. The executive housekeeper, eyeing them as they passed by her at the start of a shift, on parade. She stopped a newer girl with one hand flat against her shoulder. "Take it off," she said, meaning the red lipstick the girl had freshly applied before her locker. Her eyes glittered.

Think of your skin as a work of art you're supervising,

that's what she said, months ago. Nisha leaned forward to Samantha and whispered, "The canvas is spoiled," and Samantha hid her laugh with a hand.

"The buyers will be most unhappy," Samantha said from behind her fingers, in the housekeeper's halting voice. This is what Nisha thought of a few days later, when she saw the young couple with the Salukis, playing tennis in the courts below. A waitress brought them a tray of refreshments, and the woman watched her go, frowning, her racket resting lightly against her shoulder. She walked over to the man, muttered something in his ear, and he glanced over at the retreating girl, too. What was wrong? Was it her hair? Her posture?

Everything must be immaculate. Otherwise, the buyers would be most unhappy. The light shifted and their faces stirred. Nisha could see what was growing underneath their skin, pulpy and excited, the thing that was about to hatch.

They weren't the only ones. There was the older man, the famous playwright. He was shameless, he collected blossom-mouthed young women from who knows where. His girlfriends, he called them. He left tips for the room attendants, of course, generous ones, each with a vivid note. The first note, Nisha showed to Talia, who said, "Ugh. Just be careful, okay?"

She saw him with one of his girlfriends in the lobby once, and when the opal light of day came through the glass, she could see something alive and moving in his mouth, glossy with saliva, wriggling with legs. He kissed the girlfriend, and it was gone.

Nisha had flicked herself away before she could be noticed.

Something happened in this hotel, back then. Something happened to her. She's so sure of it now. She wanders through the first floor, alone, full of unease at her own uncertainty, the billiard ball leading her way. If only she could remember what it was.

Or is it happening to her now?

At the end of a corridor, a flash of white. It vanishes before she can register it. There's a pulse in her ears. She could swear it was the glint of a platinum bun, like the one the executive housekeeper used to wear. But the house-keeper is long gone. She left years ago, with everyone else. Didn't she?

Familiar places always harbour these ghosts of the past. The girls she left behind. Her sister in the big house, not there anymore, but it's like she never left. Nisha thinks of the birds, fertile with suspicion, of the funeral, coming back to these locales of her youth. There's something painful about homecomings. They say, *You don't belong anywhere else.* They say, *Why did you come?*

The billiard ball takes a turn and she's suddenly in the empty restaurant. The brass band is picking up the tempo. She can almost picture their intent faces. The trombone is getting bold, flirty. When she was younger, she'd never had the chance to eat at the restaurant. Not once. And now there's a feast here, laid out for her. Fish braided in pastry, peaches poached in vinegary sauce.

The ceiling is spangled in light. Nisha thinks of all those stories: whatever you do, don't eat. Persephone devouring her fate, unknowing. But she is hungry, cavernous, and she knows what this is. She is no longer the girl from her memories, fresh-faced and willing to yield. She sits at the table. The first taste of fish is euphoric, divine.

The guests. They were everywhere, that summer of long ago. It was obscene, how glutted they were on their own good fortune; the heiress who lounged in the gardens with her friends, their limbs flashing gold, asking the staff to bring them small, absurd things—"A deck of cards, oh, but could you please take out all the hearts, they're bad luck"—

the famous playwright, playing tennis in his flapping bathrobe, not caring if anyone saw; or, more likely, wanting everyone to see.

Even with all they possessed, the guests had always wanted more.

And every day, a trick of the shadows, a dazzle of sunlight. For the briefest moment she would see below. She'd catch glimpses of the things that lived inside of them, teething, glistening, getting stronger.

One morning towards the end of the season, Samantha came to her. She said, "Guess who signed her first big-girl contract."

"You're staying?" Nisha didn't mean to sound horrified, but she was. She twisted her shirt in her hands, wrinkling it without meaning to. The kind of thing the executive housekeeper would notice, but she didn't care right then.

Samantha said, deepening her voice to be creepy— "Who knows. Maybe *I'll* be the executive housekeeper next summer."

There were seven girls chosen to stay on after the summer, presumably by the executive housekeeper herself. It seemed like so many. In those very last days of summer, they stopped coming in for their regular shifts. A new lull came over the locker room. Nisha never even got to say goodbye to Samantha. She was just gone one morning.

It was before the days of cellphones, where a person could disappear without warning, never to return. Nisha had found the executive housekeeper. She'd said, "What time does Samantha work now?"

The executive housekeeper gave her that horrible smile, all teeth, like an iceberg smiling. "She's not here this week."

The girls were sent to a training program, the house-keeper had explained. Did Nisha believe her? She can't remember anymore. She understood she wouldn't see Samantha again. And that was the end of it, wasn't it—she left with Talia after their last shift, with the others the Galatea had not chosen. The discards.

Now she has returned, and she doesn't know how. The meal is over. She wipes her hands on the hot towel, stunned at herself, at the depths of her own hunger.

At her feet, the billiard ball rocks in its place. It begins to roll away. Down the recently waxed parquet floor it goes, towards the floor-length gilt mirror that hangs near the hostess stand. It stops, waiting.

She stands and approaches. There's someone in the mirror, approaching her as she approaches them; her sister, wearing white, her face a mask. What's underneath the mask?

When she reaches the mirror, she understands. Of course it's not her sister. It's just her, Nisha. Her sister is gone. She's on her own. She watches the mirror version of herself flush in embarrassment. At her feet, the billiard ball quivers, almost like an animal, and hops up—over the gilt frame—into the mirror, with the softest plop.

Nisha takes a breath. She follows the billiard ball; she steps into the mirror herself.

Inside the mirror, wherever she is, she is someone else. She is old and full of hunger. She has hundreds of rooms, her twinkling constellations; she is glowing with herself. She needs more. She feels herself reaching and reaching, as if she is not a person or even a hotel but a pair of jaws, widening. Always, she needs so much more.

Then she is on the other side of the mirror. She is no longer the Galatea, or her sister—she is Nisha, gasping for air in the dark. She fumbles for a light. The rooms flicker to life around her. A hotel suite, one she recognizes vaguely. It has a cold elegance to it. A place that might belong to an iceberg.

This is where the executive housekeeper lived, all those years ago. She had an office that adjoined her rooms. Nisha had stood there once. She'd been handed a contract, hadn't she?

The memory of it comes upon her. Seven girls were chosen to stay after the summer—no, not seven. There were eight. Nisha was the last one. The contract was cool in her hands, but the rest of her felt too warm under the housekeeper's unrelenting gaze, as if she was overheating.

"I can't," she said, her voice so quiet it was barely there. "I'm sorry."

She was thinking of the young couple with the Salukis, not just the many hours she spent scrubbing after their dogs, but the way they watched the waitress on the tennis courts. Picking at her with their scrutiny.

She was thinking, too, of the face that lived beneath their flesh. Think of your skin as a work of art that you are supervising, she'd been told. And what else was a work of art but something to be consumed?

Did she want to be consumed by the thing that lived in the young couple, when it finally hatched? The insect in the old playwright's mouth? She was afraid, back then. She didn't want to know what had happened to Samantha or the girls. That's what she'd realized. She just didn't want to be the one it was happening to.

"Don't be sorry," the executive housekeeper said, reaching out and tugging the contract from Nisha's hands. She was obviously furious, but it didn't show on her face. Somehow, that only made it worse. She said, "I feel sorry for you."

In those days, the hotel took on a new air of peril, or yearning. Nisha would walk past the Venetian mirrors and her reflection would linger there, watching her with blistering eyes, waiting for her to return. As if the mirror knew; as if some reflection of herself knew, deep down, that she would come back, by the end.

Now she thinks of the birds, her sister's crown jewels,

and how they should've died when her sister died. It would've been the proper thing to do. They couldn't handle it, being alone. They stared at Nisha with such hate. *Where did she go?* they seemed to ask her. *What did you do?*

Was she invited back to the Galatea, or is she inviting herself? Is the hotel opening its mouth to her, or she to it? Her belly is full, but it feels as if she has only just started to eat. She is so lonely, so very lonely. Somewhere in the Galatea, the band has changed its tune again. She is coming home.

THE MI-CARÊME
MARC A. GODIN

They came at bedtime. At first, I thought it was the Blanchard children returning. Dressed as five capering *phantoms* under threadbare bedsheets, we'd guessed them right away but gave them sweets nonetheless. Marie-Claire was only three years old and kept tumbling over in the snow, making her older brothers very angry.

They'd forgotten something and come back for it, maybe. I was ready to scold them for making their mother stay up waiting. We were the furthest house from our tiny village, but our Maman made the best sweets on feast days, and children came no matter the weather to reach us every year.

But when I opened the door, it was instead three British soldiers dressed in red, snow piled up on their shoulders, beards encrusted with ice. Behind them I saw the trench they'd dug through the snow to our small cottage from the woods behind, cutting through the Blanchard's snow-shoe trail. They must have gotten separated from their regiment.

Their captain pushed by me and one by one they filed

inside our tiny cottage with stomping feet, splattering melting snow everywhere, and warmed their hands at our modest hearth. When his hands were warm enough, the captain scowled at me and my family: old Mémère, Maman, and my two younger brothers Jean-Francois and Jean-Michelin.

"We're neutral French," I said in my poor English.

"No such thing," he spat. "Where's your husband?"

"I have no husband, and our father is gone." I'd been helping Maman and Mémère with the farm ever since I could remember, and when Papa left us to fight in Le Loutre's War I did his chores my brothers were too small for. I wouldn't get married until Jean-Francois was big enough to carry an escaped hog back into its pen, at least three more years.

"Good news for us," said the short one with the upturned nose. He earned an elbow to his ribs from his tall, spindly friend and a glare from the captain.

As remote as we were, we'd still heard about the Dérangement, that mad effort by the English to empty Acadie of all the neutral French for not siding with them in their war. No one believed they would ever come here, to our tiny village far away from everything. Our great-great-grandperes raised up our fields from the marshes more than a hundred years ago, and we've been here ever since. None of us wanted anything to do with the endless European wars, except Papa.

The captain sniffed his nose and picked up one of the sweets still left, a biscuit baked in maple syrup the Mi'kmaq give us in exchange for cabbage, carrots, and pork.

"Living well, aren't you?" he said, pointing at the pot of stew simmering over our hearth. That, and the sweetbreads and tarts we'd spent all week preparing, were the bulk of our winter stores. It was the last feast-day of Lent when we use up whatever we can spare before returning to the fast. Every family contributed and everyone ate.

"It's for the children, monsieur."

"For us, now," he said and grabbed for the pot so quickly he scalded his palm on the handle. Without a word of Grace, they poured our stew into their bowls and slurped and snorted like ravenous animals. They must have been in the bush for a long time. If they'd asked, we would have given them food and shelter freely, though we are poor farmers on the edge of the world, far away from any Kings.

Brown sauce dripped from their moustaches when they at last lowered the bowls from their greedy lips. I thought the captain intended to talk, but he instead let out an enormous belch.

His long stretch that followed was interrupted by banging at the door.

"Who's that?" he asked.

"Children, monsieur. It is Mi-Carême," and without waiting for a response I opened the door.

Snow blasted in from the dark void outside, and with it danced a small, hunched figure, cloaked in layer upon layer of brown woollen shawls. Beneath a patched hood floated a yellow wooden mask carved in the likeness of an old woman with a jutted-out chin and beak of a nose, charcoal lines for crow's feet and laugh lines, clumps of bleached straw stuck out in all directions as hair. Her hands, tightly wrapped in grey rags to keep her fingers warm, clutched the top of a gnarled and crooked walking stick. Bright brown eyes of a laughing boy peered out of the mask, twinkling.

"Oh, Grandmama, do come in," I said with a playful voice, feeling the soldiers' eyes on us. I tried to get a clear look around the mask, to guess which of the children this must be. None of them were above changing costumes to get a second helping of sweets, but I suppose I already knew who it was. "Have some cider, have a tart."

The captain blocked me. "No, this is ours now. Have her take off her mask."

The figure tilted her head to the side like a curious dog and struck her walking stick against the floor with three sharp taps. She swayed right and left, but said nothing.

"We have to guess who it is," I tried to explain. "If we cannot guess, she takes a sweet. It is the game of Mi-Carême."

"I don't care. Take off your mask!" He reached for her face, but she smacked his hand away with her stick and bounced back two steps to the threshold of the still open door.

The other soldiers reached for their weapons. One, the shortest, had a rifle, the spindly one a pistol and knife. Before they approached any further, she backed out into the snow and hooked the door closed with her walking stick.

"It could have been Camilien," I said. "He lives close by. A troublemaker but he means no harm."

"Henry, go find her. If it's this child, beat him," the captain ordered the spindly one.

Henry grabbed our small lamp from the window ledge and whipped open the door to a face full of knife-sharp snowflakes. When the door closed behind him, silence crept around us but for the crackle of fire in our hearth, warming its nearly empty pot of stew.

"'E's made trouble for 'imself, if 'Enry catches 'im," said the short soldier.

But the hour stretched long, and Henry didn't come back. While we waited, the shorter soldier brought out a pipe, but he had nothing to smoke with it. I knew Papa had kept a small pouch of *tabac* tucked into his and Maman's straw bed, but no one told the soldier this. Restless, he stood up and paced our small room. He could cross it in only four or five steps. Back and forth he went a dozen times or so, then huffed a sigh and gazed out our tiny window by the door, watching for Henry.

"You're lucky we came by here," the captain said to me. He sat in Maman's rocking chair, pulled out a flask and sipped from it; the air soon reeked sweetly of rum. "Orders were to come this way in the Spring. Replace you with Scottish farmers, get proper use out of this land. But maybe, if we spend a good, safe night here, we put that visit off a few weeks, give you time to move on in your own way. Better than ending up in Boston or back in France."

"None of us have ever been to France, monsieur." My cousin had gone, for marriage, but she never came back. How excited she'd been, dreaming of life as a young countess in Paris, when we all knew she was more likely marrying some old man with ugly teeth in a mountainous backwater far away from any palace gardens. We all mocked her viciously, me most of all, because I knew all her secrets and she knew mine. I missed her so much when she left.

"Don't be smart, I have a temper. That right, Nick?"

Nick glanced back from the window in between his pacing. "Aye, sir."

"We are neutral, monsieur," I kept my voice strong, and Maman squeezed my hand. Mémère dozed in her corner with soft, snuffling snores. The boys were sitting as far from the soldiers as we could put them, quietly playing a game of knotted strings.

"None of you have signed the oath of loyalty, have you?"

"Non, monsieur. And we never will. We want no part of your wars." I felt the blazing pride in my heart as I said it. I was Acadienne, loyal only to Dieu, and that would never change.

The captain smiled the kindest smile I have ever seen. He set down the flask and drew out his pistol. Slowly, he lifted it to my head. My mouth and throat were dry as the winter wind.

"If I ask you to sign the oath now, will you?" How could he smile so kindly, I wondered, until I decided he might have a daughter at home; was this the smile he used when singing her lullabies?

"Non, monsieur. I will not sign." I carefully pronounced each syllable.

His smile dropped like a hot coal. I feared what he was capable of, and I feared Maman would beg to sign the oath, to spare our family.

"Ah!" Nick stumbled back from the window in surprise. "She's right outside!"

We all saw the sanded-smooth, pale wooden face with its holes for childlike eyes peering at us through the frost-rimed glass. She vanished in an instant, but her eyes struck me as still laughing. Ice crept along my flesh, and no shivering would warm me.

The captain threw open the door and stepped outside into the blowing snow. He stood in the feeble rectangle of light against the night, pointing his pistol in every direction.

"Hey!" he shouted, a solid officer's shout. "Henry, did you find him? Come out!"

"Come out!" His echo, if that's what it was, sounded queer tossed back out of the storm. "Out!"

"What's this?" he asked, and stepped out of our view, into the night. He came back, holding our lamp, glass broken and the flame out. "It was sitting in the snow."

Nick knocked a table to the floor, stumbling outside with his captain. "'Enry! 'Enry!" he shouted, but only his echo came back, mockingly: "Ee! Ee!"

The captain stomped back inside and grabbed me by the arm, pulling me from Maman and out into the snow where the wind tore at my clothing. My feet and hands froze right away. I cried out in pain, but the captain did not care. The storm roiled around us; my tears froze on my cheeks.

"Tell them!" he shouted, roaring his rum breath into my face. He held his gun to my temple; I knew he meant to use it. "Tell him to stop this, or I will kill you and leave them to bury you when the ground thaws."

I sobbed, he did not understand and I could not tell him. "It is the Mi-Carême! You have to guess who it is! You have to guess!"

"Captain, over there!"

"What!"

We both looked where Nick was pointing, at the masked figure wavering at the edge of the blowing snow. Buried in her woollen cloaks and bent over her stick, her head rocked back and forth. The wind made cruel laughter. The barrel of the captain's pistol burned ice against my temple.

"Did you find him?" taunted the figure, speaking with a young boy's voice, the words in English but thick with our mother tongue. "Henry?"

"Where is 'e you bastard!" Nick shouted and ran at her through the snow, hands balled into fists, boots exploding drifts every which way. He was young, not much older than me, and maybe handsome if he were not so short.

The masked figure jumped nimbly from foot to foot, light enough not to ever sink into the snow. With her stick in the air like a flag, dancing back and back and back until she disappeared into the blizzard. The blizzard swallowed up Nick, too. His shout was chopped short like the falling of an axe.

"Nick, don't—" the captain's orders died in his throat. He knew, as I did, that Nick was gone. All we could hear was a faint, boyish titter from out of the black night, the white vastness.

He let me go. Maybe he was in shock, he did not yet believe what he'd seen. I fell into the snow. My hands were so cold they did not even melt it; my fingers burned. I struggled to my feet quick as I could and ran with all my might for our cottage, fearing with every icy step he would grab me from behind and send me to Dieu forever.

I slammed the door behind me, drew down the bolt and let Maman comfort me by the hearth. She wrapped me in thick blankets and rocked me back and forth while we listened to the captain cry and bang at the door to be let back in.

We did not wait long. His cries stopped and I imagined him turning around to face it: the costumed figure who moved like a child and sounded like a boy. It dropped its disguise the way the Blanchard children must have dropped theirs when they got safely home, all in a heap at their feet. I imagined the figure stepping its talons out of the costume, and letting tumble from withered claws its old crone's mask onto the pile in the snow last of all.

Our great grandparents brought it with them from the coastal marshes near the Gulf of Gascony, along with our faith and our skill at raising farms out of the sea. No matter the number of children in our village, at Mi-Carême we always counted one child extra. When we cannot guess their name, we give her a sweet, and in return she keeps our livestock healthy, our harvests bountiful, and leaves presents hidden under toadstools for all the good children on long summer days. And the wicked children? Well, she steals them away, never to be seen again.

There was a gunshot, but only one. It made my brothers jump, but not me. I'd used up all my fear. After that, we heard nothing but the wind against our cottage.

It was dawn when we felt safe enough to leave. The storm had passed and the winter sun was bright, the sky clear. We packed together our dearest things, and told our neighbours what happened with the English, and then we all came to you.

Papa told us before he left: if we want to fight the English to come find you. He told us which river to follow, and which trails to take, and here we are. We'll join your resistance; we'll join your war. We will fight for Acadie.

THE SLOW MUSIC OF DRUMS

A.C. WISE

IT WAS EASIER THAN I IMAGINED, TRACKING DOWN THE last original member of Exquisite Corpse. My uncle left surprisingly detailed notes for a man with a disordered mind—left them, and then disappeared.

Died. Disappeared. I don't know.

Julian was the name on my uncle's birth certificate, but everyone called him Rabbit. We weren't close when I was growing up, only after my own father died and I discovered that I had a lot more in common with my father's brother than I'd ever had with him. We're both prone to obsession, insatiable curiosity. It's gotten me fired from more than one job, following my own line of interest rather than writing the story as assigned. Rabbit wasn't a journalist, but I bet he was difficult to work with too.

I've been telling myself that Rabbit died, for the sake of closure, but I'm pretty sure that's a lie. He mailed me a key, wanted me to follow him. Left a mystery for me to unravel, knowing I'd be the one to help my not-quite-aunt Jessi sort through his stuff once he was gone.

Before he vanished, Rabbit and I had been talking a lot on the phone. Late night calls—or early morning ones, depending on your perspective. The calls were mostly him rambling, me listening. I didn't follow everything he said, but a few things stood out.

He said our family is cursed.

He said maybe it was on account of some people I'd never heard of up in St. Sauveur, and that Exquisite Corpse was part of it too. He told me they're a band that doesn't really exist, a band that has only ever played one song. They're still playing it, technically. Somewhere out there, someone is rolling their fingers over the skin of a drum, and carrying on a thing that was started almost fifty years ago.

No part of the song has ever been recorded. No one person has ever heard the whole. By design.

The band got its name from the surrealist art movement, which was in turn inspired by an old parlour game called Consequences. One person draws a head, folds the paper, and passes it on. The next person draws the body and so on. The players do eventually get to see what they've created together, their beautiful monster. Not so with the band.

The contributing musicians are scattered across the world, and even if the logistics for gathering them all together weren't impossible, most of them are dead now. Suicide, mostly, from what I've heard.

Consequences, like the original name of the parlour game. Not everyone could live with what they'd done. But the song was never meant for them anyway, Rabbit told me, never meant for us at all, and by us, he meant humankind.

The key Rabbit mailed me turned out to unlock a file cabinet in his office. Jessi, my-not-quite-aunt, and I had to excavate a tunnel through piles of textbooks and journals and newspapers and architectural drawings to even get to it. Rabbit and Jessi were never married, never lived together long enough to be considered common-law, but she cared for him, and she knew he needed someone to look out for him, so she never went far.

She didn't want anything from Rabbit's apartment, but she said I was welcome to it. The only things I took were the spiral-bound notebooks I found in the locked drawer, and a carving buried under a pile of receipts and old bills.

The carving was of a rabbit, curled tight into a little ball like it was sleeping, or afraid of something bigger than itself and trying not to be seen. Warm red-brown wood, knife-marks deliberately left in place, varnished, and just the right size to fit in the palm of my hand.

The notebooks, among other things, contained a list of names. The only one not crossed off on the list was Jerry Kirkpatrick's, along with an address in St. Sauveur.

During one of our late-night calls, Rabbit told me how St. Sauveur used to be a charming little town until the local butcher and grocery were replaced by high-end farm-to-table restaurants, and multi-million-dollar rental properties replaced all the family homes. It's all skiing in the winter, water parks and hiking and various festivals in the summer now. No one really "lives" there anymore.

The Laurentians are beautiful in the fall, and I'm between jobs, so why not just go? See if Jerry Kirkpatrick is still there, the lone hold-out who didn't vacate his land to make way for a new vacation home.

The tires make a satisfying *thu-thump* as I cross over a small wooden bridge. A right turn onto a winding road, and I almost shoot past the handmade wooden sign pounded into the dirt at the end of a long, crooked drive, but luckily there are no other cars behind me.

Kirkpatrick.

Silence falls on me as I climb out of the car. It takes a moment for sound to kick back in—grosbeaks and chick-adees off among the trees. The river rushing behind the house at the far end of the drive.

Trees cluster in on all sides. Jerry Kirkpatrick's whole property strikes me as a place that doesn't want to be seen. I sling the bag with Rabbit's notebooks and his carving over my shoulder and walk down the drive. There are carvings tucked among the trees—animals and faces that aren't exactly human, but not exactly inhuman either.

I assume Kirkpatrick built the house too—a wood-shingled roof, blending into the trees, part gingerbread and part storybook castle, with an honest to goodness tower protruding on one side. I wonder if he had a kid, or kids, who grew up living in that tower room. The house looks organic, both in the crunchy granola sense, and like it was grown, pushing its way up out of the ground like a mushroom. I knock against the screen door's frame, painted deep forest green and maroon.

Jerry Kirkpatrick opens the inner door and peers out at me through the mesh.

"Huh," he says, like he was expecting me, but also surprised that I made it this far.

He looks like what I would have expected from one of the founders of an experimental band—which is to say, a stereotypical aging hippy. Grey hair surrounding a shining bald spot, worn loose down to his shoulders. A beard to match, escaping the confines of his chin, and resting neatly against his chest. He's even wearing tie-dye, cargo shorts, and sandals—a bleach-stained hoodie his only concession to it being fall.

"You're Rabbit's kin." Not a question, and he steps back, holding open the door.

I don't know if my family is cursed, like Rabbit said, but I do know certain things run strong in our blood. The family resemblance being one of them. My father and his siblings all look alike, and all my cousins and I do too. Rabbit never had kids, but if he had, I could have been one of them.

Jerry leads me down a dark, narrow hallway, to a surprisingly bright and sunny kitchen.

"I just made a pot of tea. We can take it out onto the back porch, and I can tell you some of what you came here wanting to know." Jerry lifts a tray, already holding two mugs alongside the teapot.

"Thank you." I hold open the screen door since his hands are full.

The rocking chairs look like Jerry's work, as does a low table made from a tree stump. The river sparkles, gushing and whirling through a series of eddies and miniature rapids just past the ragged edges of Jerry's land. He points to a spit, jutting out into the water.

"Used to set off fireworks out there every year on Canada Day. Kids loved it. All those families are gone now. I'm the only one who stayed."

"The money wasn't tempting?" I ask.

I can only imagine what the property developers offered to try to buy him out.

"Not so much. I prefer a simple life, and besides, I'm planted here." I don't miss his odd choice of words. "If you stay past sunset, you'll see why."

Jerry raises his mug. Steam curls over the edge. I add honey from the tray to my own mug and match his salute.

"What happens after sunset?" I ask.

"The stars come out," Jerry says, unperturbed. "I'll take you over to the hollow, then, if you want to see."

He gestures back toward the house, but I take it he's referring to something on the other side.

"The old Campbell property," he says, answering my unvoiced question.

He goes on to explain that it's technically higher ground than his property, but he calls it the hollow because it's far more cleared of trees than his own land. His property sits at the lowest point in the valley—the base of the bowl. The

Campbell land is one side of that same bowl, the only side that's not currently occupied by a multi-million-dollar home.

"Because it's cursed," Jerry tells me.

The same word my uncle used when he said maybe it was to do with some family around here, land that stained everything and everyone in the valley.

"It's all connected," Jerry says, once again answering something I haven't asked yet.

"To Exquisite Corpse?" Once again allowing me to hold back the question I'm avoiding, the questions about Rabbit whose answers I don't want to know and suspect I already do know.

"Everything. Everything is connected in the valley, and Exquisite Corpse is part of it. It was born here even if it didn't start here. It's planted in this ground too."

In Rabbit's journals, he said the song—the one, singular, drawn-out, multi-part song—that Exquisite Corpse's various members have been playing for the last fifty-odd years is a message. A very specific message meant for something that communicates much slower than we do, that lives at a different rate. The kind of something that could hold all the parts of the song together, because fifty-odd years would mean nothing to it. The message, from what I gather: we're here, we're ready, there's nothing on Earth worth preserving, come and end the fucking world.

Oh, Rabbit, what did you do?

"Why?" I say, and Jerry gives me a half smile in the light that's just starting to turn the same colour as the honey sweetening my tea.

"Is that really what you want to know?" he asks in turn.

Yes and no. Rabbit's journals described the smoky bars and cafes where Exquisite Corpse first played. Not even proper clubs really. University cafes. Small, nowhere, hole-in-the-wall venues. Places that weren't even cafes or clubs—

empty warehouses and falling down homes. Sometimes only one or two people would attend. Sometimes no one at all. Exquisite Corpse didn't care. The song wasn't for us, after all.

That wasn't the only thing in Rabbit's journals, though. They're full of bits and pieces, all jumbled together. Something about how someone maybe related to our family went looking for their former military commander in the arctic and never came home. About how there were bees who planted children—planted, that same word Jerry keeps using—or maybe the other way around, and the terrible things that grew from those seeds. About keepers, like shepherds, walking slowly and endlessly across the sky. About how signals could be amplified by particular designs to make, or open, or strengthen a gate between the stars.

So, the real question I want to ask, with the answer I'm not ready to hear is: *Rabbit, what did you do?*

Whole pages of his notebooks are darkened with ink, only the tiniest smudged spaces left blank—white stars with the faint blue page lines showing through. Rabbit sketched a building like a hive—a building, or an art installation, I'm not sure.

Rabbit told me about a city design competition, during one of our late-night conversations. He didn't specify which city, whether he'd entered a design or not. He didn't mention the hive. He changed the topic, colony collapse disorder, or how the weather was bad for apple orchards this year. The calls were like that—disjointed, fragments, not all of them leading anywhere. It was hard to know what to hold onto, and what to discard.

Jerry sets his mug down and stands, hands braced on his back, joints popping. The light through the trees is deep gold now, lowering toward the river. The sun sets early at this time of year.

"You staying for dinner?" Jerry asks.

"If you don't mind."

I should go. I shouldn't let curiosity get the better of me, because that might be the curse Rabbit was actually talking about. Nothing to do with bad land, or anything deep and weird and sinister. Just our inability to let go.

"It's nothing fancy, just leftovers," Jerry says. "I always make enough to freeze, and then add fresh vegetables alongside. You can help me chop."

Jerry sets vegetarian chili that smells delicious to re-warming on the stove. I dutifully help him chop vegetables to roast with herbs and olive oil.

"Used to be a man and his wife that took care of a lot of the properties around here," Jerry says. "Her name was Jeanette; his name was Marcel. They had a vegetable garden, and they always shared whatever they had with the other families in the valley. I remember the beans, specifically. I miss those. They're never as good when you buy them in the store."

He pours us each a glass while we cook. It's not even yet five, but I don't think I'll be going far tonight.

"The Campbell property is right across the road," Jerry says, as if once again reading my mind. "We could get smashed and walk there in the dark and be fine."

Once the vegetables are in the oven, I gather up the courage to ask another question.

"Does it bother you that so many members of Exquisite Corpse are dead?"

Jerry leans against the counter with a melancholy expression, but he doesn't seem offended.

"Part of the idea was that spreading the song out across multiple hands meant that it wouldn't weigh quite as much, no one person would be responsible for the apocalypse. I guess that didn't work out as well as we thought it would."

"Or the people who killed themselves didn't want to stick around to see the recipient of the message," I say.

"Sure," Jerry says.

He picks up the knife, runs it under water, and dries it before slipping it back into the block beside the others.

"But I decided to take the bet." He answers the part of the question only just implied by what I said. "I'm sticking around as long as I can on the chance that it will be the most beautiful thing in this or any world."

Jerry pours more as we sit down to eat, and lights candles. Full dark gathers outside. The chili is perfectly spiced, the vegetables roasted to perfection. We talk about nothing—sports, the weather, how much the valley has changed. We don't talk about Exquisite Corpse or the end of the world. I don't ask if Rabbit ever put hand to drum and made himself part of the call. After our plates are clear, we finish the wine. Jerry tells me about his son, who did indeed live in the tower room Jerry built for him, and how he died of brain cancer while he was in medical school. Far too young. He talks about his art—the custom woodwork he does for clients, and the pieces he never sells.

"Like this one." I take my uncle's carving out of my bag.

Jerry's eyes light up briefly, but the sad smile returns, the same melancholy as when he talked about his son and the dead members of the band. All that death weighing on him, all the time he's been alone. I could see that being the kind of thing that might make a man want to end the world, but for Jerry, it happened the other way around. Consequences—the name of the parlour game. Did Jerry know? Were they always necessary sacrifices he was willing to bear?

"Rabbit asked me to carve him," Jerry says. "This is what I made."

Candlelight plays across the wood, makes the rabbit's fur ripple as if it will wake in my hand and run. Jerry reaches out a finger, but stops short of touching it. He made the rabbit, but it isn't his anymore.

"You about ready to head over to the hollow?" Jerry asks.

I nod, because we've already drunk all the wine. I tuck the carving back into my bag and help Jerry clear the table. He retrieves a heavy-duty flashlight from the pantry cleverly hidden behind a set of built-in shelves, along with another bottle—not wine this time—and a box of matches.

"There's a pair of boots by the door," Jerry says. "You might want to swap out your shoes for those and borrow one of my jackets against the cold."

I do as he suggests, and follow Jerry into a night that's surprisingly still, the same silence as when I first pulled into his drive. Jerry turns the flashlight on, which I suspect is for my benefit rather than his. The beam catches on his carvings; like a strange game of freeze tag, I imagine them moving a split-second before being hit by the light. At the road, Jerry sweeps the beam in either direction, but there are no cars.

"All this used to be gravel," Jerry says. "They paved it when the big houses went in."

He swings the light back in the direction we came, off to the side of the road, where all I can see is overgrown weeds.

"Old boathouse used to be down there." Like it's a landmark I should know.

I try to picture Rabbit here as a young man, hiking up the hills, throwing himself off a dock into the river back when nobody cared that it was too dirty and dangerous to swim.

Across the road is another drive, wider than Jerry's, not set as far back among the trees. Metal posts with a single chain strung between them guard it. Jerry skirts around the pole on the left, continuing to swing the light around, narrating our journey.

"Garage is over there," he says, before turning to illuminate a flat stone; it takes my brain a moment to process it as a grave. "Campbells had a dog that went missing during a storm. Her body washed up three days later. They buried her here."

That's the least of what's buried here—my mind makes the unwelcome leap, and I push the thought away.

The drive slopes upward, gravel crunching under our boots. There aren't any overt no trespassing signs, but it feels like we shouldn't be here. Nobody should.

When Jerry first mentioned the hollow, I couldn't believe that land this valuable would sit unoccupied, but I get it now. It feels wrong. The moment we stepped past the chain, it got under my skin, made itself a home.

"Used to be a gate down there," Jerry says, letting the light sit on the wall of trees. "Or a door—a wooden frame at least, covered in weird carvings. It was here when the Campbells bought the land. They never did find out who built it, but something stepped through before they tore it down."

Jerry moves the light away, keeps walking, like what he's saying is the most natural thing in the world. I see it. The gate, the door he described, a spindly thing that makes no sense—two pieces of wood planted in the ground, one across the top to make a frame. The thing stepping through is spindly too, tall, scraping against the wood even as it ducks down. It's not there, but I can't help breaking into a trotting run to catch up to Jerry.

"The old house," Jerry points the flashlight to the right at the top of the hill.

White paint, black roof, glass boxes on either end. A glassed-in porch on one end, a dining room with barely any walls, just windows, on the other. Like the land, the house feels wrong. A building that makes no sense, a place where bad things happened. I want to lean away, and I'm grateful when Jerry steers us left along a pine-needle littered path.

"Pool there." He points to the far end of the path. "Pool house."

The light jumps between the two features, giving me a glimpse of each. The beam jerks to the right, almost as if something yanked at Jerry's arm, coming to rest on a rock, spattered with layer upon layer of paint.

"When the Campbells built this place, any time they had left over paint, they just tossed it here. Not very environmentally sound. The kids used to love climbing on Paint Rock though. Until one of them slipped and hit their head. Died on the way to the hospital."

Jerry moves the light away, takes a few steps further along the path.

"There was a rumour that the Campbells buried the kid here, like they buried the dog. They both belonged to the land. I can't imagine it's true though." Jerry's voice suggests he can imagine it, and now I can imagine it too—one kid, dozens, bones forgotten among the trees. Still birth. Accidental drowning. Suicide.

"Anyway, this is us." Jerry uses the light to indicate two stumps, cut and polished like the one on his back porch.

In between, a carefully built bonfire, just waiting for a match. Jerry gets the fire lit and settles down. I could run, but instead, I take the other stump. He pulls the unmarked bottle from his bag, holding it up to catch the light.

"Make this myself," he says, tilting it so the liquid rolls inside.

It's got a thickness to it, amber, like whisky. Jerry produces tin camp mugs, pours us each a measure. Sweet, like mead, but with a sharper bite. It burns going down.

Sparks rise. The air smells of pine sap. I'm glad Jerry lent me his jacket. Curses weren't a thing I ever believed in, until Rabbit disappeared. Now, I can't stop being aware of the land stretched around us. I don't doubt Jerry's stories, and that there's even more he hasn't told me. This place resonates. Did the land birth Exquisite Corpse, or was it the other way around? Is the mere suggestion of a curse enough for such a thing to take hold? Is there a place where it begins, or does it all just go round and round until the end?

"You want to know about Rabbit," Jerry says. "How involved he was."

"I guess so," I say.

I could keep telling myself he's dead, but I'm more and more certain it's not that simple.

"You want to know if he ever picked up a drum. If he ever contributed to the song." Neither phrased as questions.

I look at Jerry across the fire. He's holding a small drum, only about as wide across as his hand. I never saw him pack it or take it out of his bag. It's braced between his knees, his fingers resting on it contemplatively, but not playing, not yet.

The music is there—thunder behind a skin of clouds. The fire makes Jerry's eyes hollow, like he's wearing a mask, his own face stretched and dried like the head of the drum, something else looking out at me from within.

"Will it make you feel better, knowing?" Jerry asks.

"Probably not," I say.

The only person I told I was coming up here was Jessi. She looked at me sadly, kissed me on the forehead, and told me to be careful. I heard all the things she didn't say—that I was too much like Rabbit, that she'd spent all those years looking after him, and she couldn't look after me too, and that she was sorry.

The same way I feel the land around us, I feel the sky overhead—a weight leaned up against it, pressing down from the other side of the stars.

"Rabbit used to run around these parts," Jerry says.

"Not with the Campbells specifically, but on their periphery. Close enough to be part of it."

I don't have to ask what he means. I'm part of it now, too. His fingers rest on the drum, not tapping, but about to.

"He was the kind," Jerry says, "even back then, who got fascinated with things. He might take an animal apart to see how it worked. I'm not saying he did, I'm saying he could. He wanted to know everything."

A pause, a sip that I find myself mirroring.

"He wasn't there at the start of it, but in a way, we all were, just by virtue of being in the valley. Once the idea of Exquisite Corpse started up, Rabbit got caught in our orbit. After that, he was always on the edges, walking his own path."

Jerry drains his mug, grimacing, but still pours himself another, and I hold out my cup for the same.

"Understand," Jerry says, "I felt a calling, a compulsion. The song wasn't a choice for me. Rabbit, he got so wound up in whether a thing could happen, he didn't stop to think whether it should."

Nothing Jerry says surprises me; I wish it did. I pull out one of Rabbit's notebooks, flip to the page with the hive. It looks different than I remember. A thing of negative space, the rest of the page ink-scribbled in, inter-locking levels winding around each other without beginning or end.

"Have you ever seen anything like this?" I ask.

Jerry takes the notebook, squints in the firelight. When he hands it back, it occurs to me that I could drop it into the flames, but it probably wouldn't change anything.

"Yes and no," Jerry says. "It's part of it, but I don't know how."

Instead of burning the notebook, I look at the page again. Jerry doesn't have to explain—I see it, whether I want to or not. Rabbit's design, spiralling upward from some public plaza, an art display, an architectural curiosity. People climbing it and falling down again. Jumping, because they can't conceive of doing otherwise. A compulsion, like Jerry said, an overwhelming desire to fall.

The sky and the other buildings and the trees all blurring past in the gaps between those winding stairs. A new architecture superimposed on the city they know, making it strange. And when they hit, some of them won't die right away. They'll lie there, looking up at the stars framed by the hive as they breathe their last in incredible, shattering pain, and find them changed and made strange too.

It's part of it, the music, the song. The slow communication with something living differently through time. Those bodies hitting the pavement—they're the sound of drumming too. Caught by the hive, resonating and amplifying a call out among the stars.

"Rabbit didn't have to pick up a drum," Jerry says.

An answer I already know.

"Where did he go?" My throat is dry, scratching around the words.

"Far away, but not so far that you can't follow." I don't grasp Jerry's words, until I do.

Tap.

One finger dropped onto the skin of the drum, like a fat drop of rain preceding a downpour. The sound travels all the way up and down my spine. An offer. Take up the drum. Add to the song. Become a part of the same thing Rabbit was—the family curse, the insatiable curiosity. Be a part of something so much bigger.

"Look up," Jerry says.

Or maybe he doesn't say anything at all. Maybe my head is yanked back by nothing, lifting of its own accord. Maybe whatever's in Jerry's bottle—honey from bees who planted children in the ground and grew terrible things, tended by the vast keepers slowly moving across the sky—is making my head swim.

The stars waver, rearranging. Picking up the vibrations of the drum, answering the song that's been playing for half a century, maybe more.

Tap, tap, tap.

Jerry's fingers rattle across the surface of that pulled-taut skin, but the sound is so much louder. It fills the valley, echoes back from the hills. Can they hear it in all those million-dollar houses? The sky shivers, suggesting a new architecture amongst the stars, faint lines of silver traced upon on the dark, and hidden among the trees. Bones among the roots where the children were planted to make frames of their own. Doors. Doors upon doors, just waiting for something to step through.

I'm up, stumbling, nearly tripping and pitching into the fire. Running back down the hill, down the side of the bowl in the dark. I won't make it to my car. I'll fall, break my face against the gravel, or I'll turn around—compelled.

Yipping follows me. Laughter at first, maybe Jerry's, or maybe a sob. But soon enough, it's not laughter or tears, nothing human at all—that too-tall thing scraping the frame of the door that no longer exists on the corner of this land.

I pelt past the dog grave, running frantically, and not daring to look at what might be coming down the hill behind me. Laughter. Footsteps. The sound of drums. I'm going to make it. I'm going to make it. I'm not going to make it at all.

Oh, Rabbit, what have you done?

CONTRIBUTORS

Senaa Ahmad's short fiction appears in *McSweeney's*, *The Paris Review*, *Best American Science Fiction and Fantasy*, and *Best Canadian Stories*. She's received the generous support of the Canada Council for the Arts, the Ontario Arts Council, the Toronto Arts Council, and the Speculative Literature Foundation. A finalist for the National Magazine Award for Fiction, her work is the recipient of a Pushcart Prize and the Sunburst Award. She's working on a short story collection.

Originally from Vancouver, **Siobhan Carroll** now lives and gardens in Philadelphia, a city where it doesn't rain as much as she'd like. She had her first publication in *On Spec*'s fiction writing contest back in 2000, and since then, has energetically written dark, weird, and occasionally funny short stories for magazines like *Lightspeed* and Tor.com. You can read more of her fiction on her website at http://voncarr-siobhan-carroll.blogspot.com

David Demchuk is the award-winning author of *The Bone Mother*, a disturbing mosaic novel infused with Eastern European folklore, and *RED X*, a hybrid horror novel/queer memoir set in Toronto, Canada. His third novel *The Butcher's Daughter*, co-written with debut author Corinne Leigh Clark, explores the Sweeney Todd legend from the perspective of his pie-baking helpmate Mrs. Lovett, and will be published by Soho Press (US) and Titan Books (UK) in 2025. Born and raised on the Canadian prairie, David now lives by the sea with his husband in St. John's, Newfoundland.

EC Dorgan writes dark fiction and monster stories on Treaty 6 territory near Edmonton, Canada. She has recent stories published in *Augur, The Dread Machine*, and *Metaphorosis*. She is a member of the Métis Nation of Alberta.

From Alberta, **Hiron Ennes** is the British Fantasy Award-winning author of *Leech*. In their spare time, they're a rogue harpist and a mad doctor. Their areas of interest include forensics, infectious disease, and petting your dog.

Richard Gavin's work explores the bond between dread and the numinous. His short fiction has been collected in six volumes, including *grotesquerie* (Undertow Publications, 2020), and has appeared in many volumes of *Best New Horror* and *Best Horror of the Year*. Richard has also authored several works of esotericism for distinguished venues like Theion Publishing and Three Hands Press. He resides in Ontario, Canada. Online presence: www.richardgavin.net

Marc A. Godin is a gay/queer writer of weird and tender fiction who hasn't settled down in any one place for very long. Currently in Sydney, Nova Scotia, when he's not writing he can be found gardening, walking the family dog, and thinking deeply about the end of the world. This is his first published story.

Camilla Grudova was born in Canada and now lives in Edinburgh. Her critically acclaimed debut collection, *The Doll's Alphabet*, was published in 2017. Her first novel, *Chil-*

dren of Paradise, was long-listed for the Women's Prize. Her most recent book is a second collection, *The Coiled Serpent*. In 2023 she was named one of Granta's Best of Young British Novelists, a once-in-a-decade accolade.

Our cover designer **Vince Haig** is an illustrator, designer, and author. You can visit Vince at his website: barquing.com

Nayani Jensen is a writer, historian of science, and Rhodes Scholar from Kjipuktuk (Halifax, Nova Scotia). In both her academic and creative work, she is interested in interdisciplinary approaches to history, climate and fiction. Her writing has appeared in publications such as *Nature (Futures)*, *Augur Magazine*, and *The New Quarterly*.

Born in Charlottetown, Prince Edward Island, **Michael Kelly** is the former Series Editor for the *Year's Best Weird Fiction*. He's a World Fantasy Award, Shirley Jackson Award, and British Fantasy Award-winning editor. His fiction has appeared in a number of journals and anthologies, including *Best New Horror, Black Static, Nightmare Magazine, The Dark,* and *The Year's Best Dark Fantasy & Horror;* and has been previously collected in *Scratching the Surface, Undertow & Other Laments*, and *All the Things We Never See.* He is the owner and Editor-in-Chief of Undertow Publications, and editor of *Weird Horror* magazine.

Rich Larson was born in Galmi, Niger, has lived in Spain and Czech Republic, and currently writes from Montreal, Canada. He is the author of the novels *Ymir* and *Annex*, as well as the collection *Tomorrow Factory*. His fiction has been translated into over a dozen languages, including Polish, Italian, Romanian, and Japanese, and adapted into an

Emmy-winning episode of *LOVE DEATH + ROBOTS*. Find free reads and support his work at patreon.com/richlarson.

Lynn Hutchinson Lee is a multidisciplinary artist/writer from Canada. She was first place winner of the 2022 Joy Kogawa Award for Fiction, with her literary fiction short-listed for three other awards, including the Guernica Prize. Her writing appears in *Room; Fusion Fragment; Food of My People* (Exile Editions); *Weird Horror* (Undertow Publications); *Wagtail: the Roma Women's Poetry Anthology* (Butcher's Dog, U.K.), and elsewhere. She is co-editor of *Through the Portal: Stories From a Hopeful Dystopia* (Exile Editions). Her novella *Origins of Desire in Northern Orchid Fens* is published by Stelliform Press. Find her at lynnhutchinsonlee.ca and on X @LHutchinsonLee

David Neil Lee's "Midnight Games" trilogy pits H.P. Lovecraft's Cthulhu Mythos against an embattled working-class community in David's present home town of Hamilton, Ontario. Besides *The Midnight Games* and its sequels *The Medusa Deep* and *The Great Outer Dark,* he is the author of the novel *Commander Zero,* and the best-selling reference work *Chainsaws: A History.* An improvising double bassist who has performed across Canada as well as in New York City, Washington, Amsterdam, and the U.K., David has also written *The Battle of the Five Spot: Ornette Coleman and the New York Jazz Field,* and collaborated with Paul Bley on the late jazz pianist's autobiography, *Stopping Time.* He is currently working on a book adaptation of his PhD dissertation *Outside the Empire: Improvised Music in Toronto 1960-1985,* drafting a biography of the Canadian children's author Catherine Anthony Clark, and finishing up a long-deferred sci-fi novel, *Snakesland.*

Cover artist **Serena Malyon** is a Canadian illustrator who works in watercolour, acryla gouache and Photoshop. She grew up in a household of artists and spent her early days drawing the knights and maidens from her books. Since graduating from the Alberta College of Art and Design in 2012, she has built her career on her love of fantasy, adventure and storytelling. Her illustrations blend whimsical stylization with contemporary compositions and colours to create a unique look. Her work has appeared in a variety of media, from young adult and fantasy book covers and interior illustrations to magazines, maps, picture books, textbooks, graphic novels, tabletop games and video games.

Premee Mohamed is a Nebula, World Fantasy, and Aurora award-winning Indo-Caribbean scientist and speculative fiction author based in Edmonton, Alberta. She has also been a finalist for the Hugo, Ignyte, British Fantasy, and Crawford awards. She is an Assistant Editor at the short fiction audio venue *Escape Pod* and the author of the "Beneath the Rising" series of novels as well as several novellas. Her short fiction has appeared in many venues and she can be found on her website at www.premeemohamed.com.

Silvia Moreno-Garcia is the author of *Silver Nitrate*, *The Daughter of Doctor Moreau*, *Mexican Gothic*, and many other books. She has won the Locus, British Fantasy, World Fantasy, Sunburst and Aurora awards. She lives in Vancouver, BC.

David Nickle is an award-winning author of numerous short stories and novels. His most recent novel is *Volk: A Novel of Radiant Abomination*, concluding the "Book of the Juke" series begun with *Eutopia: A Novel of Terrible Optimism*. Some of his stories are collected in *Monstrous Affec-*

tions, and *Knife Fight and Other Struggles*. His home online is at davidnickle.ca.

Naben Ruthnum is the author of *Helpmeet*, *The Grimmer*, and other books. He lives in Toronto.

Rory Say is a short fiction writer from Victoria, BC, whose work tends toward the dark, strange, and speculative. Stories of his have appeared in *Weird Horror*, *Uncharted*, *On Spec*, and *The New Quarterly*. A mini-collection, entitled *Different Faces*, was recently published by Dim Shores. Read more by visiting his website: rorysay.com

K.L. Schroeder is a speculative fiction writer, PhD microbiologist, and aging goth from Treaty 6 Territory & the Métis Homeland, Saskatoon, who currently resides in Stockholm, Sweden. Their writing can be found in the *And Lately, the Sun* climate fiction anthology and as semi-finished novels lurking on hard drives.

Simon Strantzas is the author of six collections of short fiction, including *Only the Living Are Lost* (Hippocampus Press, 2023), and editor of several anthologies such as *Aickman's Heirs* (Undertow Publications, 2015). He is also co-founder and Associate Editor of the irregular non-fiction journal, *Thinking Horror*, and columnist for *Weird Horror* magazine. Collectively, he's been a finalist for four Shirley Jackson Awards, two British Fantasy Awards, and the World Fantasy Award. His stories have been reprinted in *Best New Horror*, *The Best Horror of the Year*, *The Year's Best Weird Fiction*, and *The Year's Best Dark Fantasy & Horror*, as well as published in *Nightmare*, *Cemetery Dance*, *Postscripts*, *The Dark*, and elsewhere. He lives with his wife in Toronto, Canada.

A.C. Wise is the author of the novels *Wendy, Darling* and *Hooked*, the short story collection *The Ghost Sequences,* and the novellas, *Grackle* and *Out of the Drowning Deep*, which were both released in 2024. Her work has won the Sunburst Award, and been a finalist for the Nebula, Stoker, World Fantasy, British Fantasy, Locus, Shirley Jackson, Aurora, Ignyte, and Lambda Literary Awards. In addition to her fiction, she contributes review columns to *Apex* and *Locus* magazines. Find her online at www.acwise.net.

COPYRIGHT